EMPIRE'S
CHILD

By the same author

Published by the British Interplanetary Society, 27-29 South Lambeth Road London, SW8 1SZ

In the *Visionary* anthology, BIS, 2014:
Epitaph. (Short story)

In the *Visionary II* anthology, BIS, 2018:
Matryoshka, (Short Story)
Capsule (Novelette)

EMPIRE'S CHILD

A FROGSPAWN NEBULA NOVEL

NICK LEWIS

GP THE GOSCAR PRESS

Nick Lewis

Visit my website at

www.nicklewis.co.uk

10 9 8 7 6 5 4 3 2 1

First printed January 2023

ISBN: 979-8-36986-628-3

To my father, Pendrill (Pen) Lewis (1916-61), whose greatest dream was to write, but who was taken from us far too soon.

Still miss you, Daddy.

Contents

CANOPY

I was picking strawberries in the Forest Canopy when Time stopped on Threnador. There was no-one to tell me Time had stopped, so I just carried on picking strawberries.

It was my day off. I was going to work the evening shift in the bar, which meant my day was my own. I liked being up in the Canopy, right up at the top of the Forest. I was almost always alone, and the view was spectacular. On a clear day, from the strawberry patch you could see right across the lake to the little inlet where the Forest had been cleared for the spaceport. I could see the Cargo Haulers landing and then lifting back up to orbit. And dream of flying with them.

Lifting was best. Loading vehicles scurried like ants around the Hauler. Finishing their work, they would dart away. A klaxon would sound. Then a bright flash of light and a momentary puckering of the view. The Hauler would disengage from Threnador's gravity field and shoot skyward. A few seconds later, a chest shaking 'thwump' would arrive – the sound of the air rushing back into the space the Hauler had occupied. The noise was tolerable from across the lake, but down at the spaceport you needed serious ear protection when a ship lifted. And well-rooted teeth.

Then all would go quiet again, and another cargo was in orbit – fifty thousand tonnes of Threnador's finest agricultural produce shortly to be loaded into the hold of

1

one of the giant StarFreighters, each carrying a million tonnes or more of Threnadorian food hundreds of parsecs through space to the industrial and administrative worlds of the Inner Arm. Day after day after day.

I'd never been to the Inner Arm, and only once seen a StarFreighter. But I watched the Haulers whenever I could. And dreamt.

Today wasn't an especially clear day. There'd been a storm earlier, and when I finished the climb up the thousand-metre trunk to the strawberry patch, there was mist drifting lazily in the folds of the hills leading down to the lake, and layers of broken cloud hanging over the spaceport. But at the canopy level the sun was shining, and the air was filling with the rich, sweet smell of ripe fruit, ready for picking.

This fruit wasn't for export – this was our slightly illicit, slightly wicked, crop. We would probably have been in trouble if anyone had found it and cared enough, but we weren't taking up valuable growing space. This part of the Forest produced pharmaceutical herbs in the dense layers far below; acted as a free-range breeding ground for tree-dwelling animals which would later be captured and farmed for meat. Centuries from now, it would finally be felled for the steel-hard wood making it up.

But, in the meantime, no-one was using the Canopy except us. A dozen of us from the village had toiled for weeks to knit the canopy cover together to form a hectare of 'field', laid soil and started growing fruit. The strawberries were delicious, but the raspberries were to die for. And the peaches…

So, there I was, relaxing in the sunshine, happily picking away, when three chest-shaking "thwumps" broke my reverie. Then three more: "Thwump, thwump,

thwump". Six Haulers were arrowing upward through the cloud layers over the 'port.

'That's odd,' I thought, 'They don't usually launch in formation.' But stupidly, I thought no more of it and carried on picking strawberries.

In my defence, no-one had told me Time had stopped. How was a girl to know something important had happened?

I braked to a halt about halfway down from the canopy, wedged myself into a fork in a large branch and unclipped from the descent line.

I listened. Nothing. Too much to hope for, I supposed. I waited a while longer, then, doing my best to copy an Embry, called: 'Eawee. Eawee'. Nothing. Ah well. Try once more. Louder.

'Eawee. Eawee.'

There was a rustling in the foliage below me. I froze, not wanting to disturb whatever was beneath. Quietly, this time: 'Eawee, eawee.'

The leaves at my feet parted, and two large, limpid brown eyes, set in a face covered with orange fur gazed up at me. Yes! He'd come. The Embry clambered onto my branch, nuzzled up against me and started to purr.

Most people would be alarmed at sharing a branch half a kilometre above the ground with a three-metre-tall biped, something between a primate and a cat, with arms as thick as a man's thighs and a prehensile tail which could have choked the life out of me. But I knew Darvee wouldn't hurt me: we'd known each other too long.

'Here you go, boy. I brought your favourites, Darvee.'

His three-fingered hands eagerly took the strawberries out of my palm and crammed them into his mouth.

Juice dribbled down his chin. He nuzzled me again.

'Oh alright. Have some more.'

I rubbed his head, and he purred more loudly. 'Darvee,' I started. 'Remember when you used to let me ride you through the forest? And you would go as fast as you could?' The limpid eyes were fixed on me, pleading for more strawberries.

'Well, remember the men I told you about? The ones I told you to hide from? If they catch you, they will take you and your friends to go and race each other in a forest a long, long way away. A very, very, long way away.'

I'd picked a lot, but I was running out of strawberries.

'Darvee, if the men catch you, you race as fast as you can. Be the best. You've always been the best. And when you've won your races, the men will give you a nice easy life with lots of girl Embrys to have fun with. You do that for me, Darvee.'

He seemed to nod. And smile.

The strawberries had now run out. I rubbed the top of his head, between his ears, and he purred louder than ever. Then realising there was no more fruit to be had, he pushed me away playfully, and ran off along the branch.

I fought back tears as he left. I'd known him a long time, and I didn't know if I'd ever see him again. Last year, Embrys had come to the attention of a scout for an off-world stables, who decided to include them in their Galactic Exotica Races. I'd heard the plans down at the spaceport. The hunters from the stables would be making a collection sweep soon. Darvee was the right age to race.

Although it was easy to imagine that he listened to every word, I knew he couldn't understand me. But still I hadn't the heart to tell him that only a champion Embry would be put out to stud. The rest would end up in the food chain.

I clipped back onto the descent line and carried on down.

BAR

I knew I was very late when I pushed open the door to the spaceport bar. Well, calling it a bar was a bit of a stretch – it was a ramshackle hut, assembled from old shipping containers and pieces of wood, and held together by little more than wishful thinking. It was probably as well that Threnador was a low gravity planet: nothing was under too much stress. The windows were made from plexiglass ports scavenged from a tourist cruiser. Its owners had finally run out of money to bribe their way through its safety checks, and it had been abandoned on site.

But the bar served alcohol (and soft drinks when unavoidable – usually when an inspector was in), which made it a bar. Fair and square.

Mind you, calling the spaceport a spaceport was equally a stretch, if not actually an insult to every other spaceport in the Galaxy. It was a flattened clearing in the Forest, big enough to take Haulers, as long as they didn't need serious ground support, plus the cranes and forklifts to offload the cargoes from the Forest and Farm trucks and the barges which made their way up the lake. And it had a runway for aeroflitters. But ships went to space from it, which is what a spaceport is for. In fact, to me, it was a Gateway to the Galaxy.

The inside of the bar was no better than the outside. It was one open space. The bar counter was an old cargo door, hammered flat, and propped up on a trestle made of pieces of undercarriage from short haul flyers. There were low stools scattered around, some made from old beer kegs the brewery hadn't collected, some from miscellaneous pieces of discarded spacecraft engineering that had outlived its usefulness but happened to be the right height to sit on. Piles of worn-out tyres served as tables, with a flat top of pieces of packing crate. If you were lucky. Light, such as it was, came from a set of glow-globes hanging in the middle of the ceiling. They had once been the landing lights on the tourist cruiser which had 'donated' our windows.

A while ago, we had played host to a video crew from Threnal, the planetary capital. They were making a biopic about 'Life in the Forest'. How we were the hard-working folk firing the engine room of the planet's prosperity. Yeah, right.

The director, who wore a new multi-coloured shirt every day, each costing more than any of us earned in a month, loved our bar. He worked his way through Boss's collection of exotic liqueurs and held forth on how our bar was the best example of 'post-techno vintage retro spaceport chic' that he had seen outside the fashion capitals of the Central Worlds. Then he fell off his stool, drunk out of his head. Boss and I exchanged glances with each other and collapsed in hysterics. It was one hell of a way to describe the junk we had begged, borrowed and stolen to make our bar. We'd obviously missed our vocation.

No-one cared though. When they left it was free drinks all round for our regulars for a week. Boss had been jacking up the bar prices day after day, wondering when the film crew's expense accounts would squeal. They never did. Gods know how much a beer costs in Threnal.

That day, I walked in and went straight to the washroom. My hands were still sticky with fruit juice and had acquired a light dusting of tree bark and small insects. Generally, customers prefer it if the bar staff don't shed bark and insect corpses into their drinks. Cleaned up, I looked in the mirror. I'm blonde with shoulder length wavy hair, green eyes and with slightly iridescent skin, in some lights. It wasn't obvious that day. Legend has it that the iridescence is the residue of genetic manipulation on some long-forgotten pleasure planet, intended to make people more attractive. I've no idea if it worked, but it was unusual on Threnador. Not unknown, but unusual. Perhaps I have some off-world blood in my veins, I don't know.

Now definitely late, I entered the bar proper. Boss was thumping the side of the autotill, which was strangely dark.

I had my excuses ready. Both had the considerable virtue of being true, but neither were the real reason. But Boss didn't need to know I'd fallen asleep in the strawberry patch and my wrist alarm hadn't sounded. Or about my stop with Darvee. I'm a great believer that you should keep people on a Need to Know basis whenever possible.

'Sorry, Boss. The electrobus didn't turn up and I had to hitch a ride in the back of a cabbage truck. Gods, I hate the smell of cabbages. Like old school dinners…'

He cut me off short. 'I can smell the cabbages. No problem. You're here now. Just get to work.'

I gawped. I'd been expecting a roasting at least and probably my pay docked.

'Is something wrong?'

'Well, not if you think customers are an optional extra in a bar,' he said. Boss wasn't easily disturbed, but he was as close to growling as you could wish.

The bar was pretty empty for the time of day. Old Rusty was in the window alcove, talking animatedly to a tall, lean man with his back to me, and a couple in port uniforms were canoodling in a corner. They did that every day. No idea what they were up to in work.

'Where are the crews?'

'Crews come from spaceships. Have you seen the Field lately?'

The implications of what I'd seen earlier on struck home.

'Oh. What happened? I heard some lift this afternoon.'

'Not some. All. There are no Haulers down right now. And I was expecting to have a good week.' He scowled. 'Some scheduling foul-up had backlogged the loading. We would have been busy all week. There were a few crew drinking here this afternoon, but they left their drinks where they were, without drinking another drop, set off at a trot, and within twenty minutes every one of the Haulers had lifted, one after the other. I was afraid the shockwaves would blow this place over.'

This was seriously strange. Haulers don't lift part-loaded, and it sounded as though some of them must have left completely empty.

'Anyway, see if you can fix the till, will you? It's playing up again and right now everyone's drinking on tick.'

Usually I can fix the till, but this time my talents failed me. Tick it would have to be tonight.

There's not much for a barmaid to do in a bar with no customers. I washed a few glasses, rearranged some bar towels, adjusted my HoloTop and watched the paint on the walls peeling while trying to look welcoming if anyone did come in. There wasn't much paint left on the walls, admittedly. It had been peeling for too long.

Have I told you about my HoloTop? I've no idea if that's its real name, but it's what I call it. I acquired it a few weeks back from an old trader who had been drinking for far too long one evening. I'm sure he believed that by giving it to me to wear, he'd get to see me wearing nothing at all, but I'm not completely stupid. An accidentally spilled serving tray, and the old trader was in an argument with a bad-tempered crewman, Boss was called, the trader was ejected, and I still had the HoloTop. The trader wasn't happy, but Boss is large, has been keeping rough bars for a long time, and people's heads can be broken awfully easily. Not my finest moment, but what's a girl to do?

The HoloTop is my prize possession. It's some sort of powered clothing. A little egg-shaped device clips on my belt, and projects three-dimensional images of shirts and blouses over me. By adjusting it, I can change the colour and style. I can even adjust my figure, if I sense a customer might tip better with a little more cleavage on display. I hate the customers staring at my body, so it is great. A free wardrobe for me, and the customers are leering at imaginary, er, assets. A HoloTop. Every girl should have one. Perhaps they do, on worlds not made of dirt and cabbages.

From the gloom of the window alcove, I saw Rusty signalling me to bring him and his companion more drinks.

Rusty's one of our regulars. One of those people of indefinable age, medium height, a shock of flame red hair and a matching moustache. And a prosthetic arm. It was his hair which named him Rusty, but I would kid him it was because his false arm was oxidising from all the beer he'd spilt on it. When he was drunk, he'd claim he lost his arm in a battle off the Dahnian Rift, but there've been no battles anywhere near there for a long, long time. It was a farming accident, I was sure.

I poured a couple of glasses of the green beer they were drinking, set them up on a tray, and took them over to the window. Rusty was talking:

'So, at the end of the Dahnian business…'

'Oh, come on, Rusty, not those old tales again,' I started to tease him. Then the man he was talking to turned toward me. I squealed and nearly dropped the drinks. It was The Captain!

'Mihana, how are you? I didn't expect to see you here.'

I put the drinks down and hugged him. He was my hero.

'Come on, sit down and let me buy you a drink. Tell me what's been happening to you.'

I looked over to Boss. The bar was still quiet, and he nodded brusquely. He's a softie really.

I sat down, and the Captain carried on.

'What are you doing here? Why aren't you flying?'

'No jobs. Nothing. I can't even wangle training now. Since the local haulage company sold out to an off-world outfit, they bring their own crews in.'

'But you were good. You learned quickly and flew every atmosphere craft I had on the Field as though you'd been born in them. Best cadet I ever had. Passed out top of your class by a big margin. I flew you up to the orbital transhipment docks as a prize.'

I remembered. How could I forget? That was when I'd seen the StarFreighter. A real, honest to goodness starship.

'I even let you land us back. Mind you, the landing wasn't the best.' He grinned.

'Don't remind me! I was excited. And I'd never flown a flitter down from orbit before. According to you at the time, it was a good landing. We walked away, didn't we?' I knew he was teasing me.

Shortly after, the bar started to fill up. I went back to work, dreaming of what might have been. Put on my best smile and trimmed my HoloTop settings.

Rusty and the Captain were talking earnestly later, occasionally glancing towards me, but they left without saying goodbye.

VILLAGE LIFE

It was raining when I left work, but I wasn't worried. Boss had shut up early, and I was in time to catch the last electrobus home. Well, I would have been if it had come.

No electrobus turned up. As there were unlikely to be any cabbage trucks passing at such a late hour, I started to walk.

Did you pay attention in your exobiology lessons in school? The ones where the teacher waxed lyrical about rainforests? About how they supply umpteen percent of a planet's oxygen, and almost all its biodiversity? About the exobiologists going positively gooey eyed over all the little creatures and about all the plants and herbs which provide 90% of the Galaxy's medicines?

There are two things they skate over. Most of the little creatures have too many legs, and many of the rest would like to eat you. And it rains in rainforests. A lot. They should make more of that. They should. My Forest is a rainforest. And when it rains, it is hot and sticky, and makes you wetter than you ever thought you could be. Rainforests are interesting to study, a gift to teach about, and miserable to live in much of the time.

I squelched along, ignoring all the strange hoots and shrieks from the undergrowth. I suppose I should have been lonely, walking down a darkened road between kilometre-high trees, but I was used to it.

After about a klick, a figure joined me. It was Jay. My shoulders drooped. I didn't want to talk to Jay tonight. But he started to prattle on.

'Hi, Mihana, how are you? Miserable rain, isn't it?'

'Yes, Jay.'

'Do you remember when the Company promised to bring a StarFreighter filled with tarmac to Threnador. They promised we could have some proper roads?'

'Yes, Jay.' They'd reneged, obviously.

'Did you hear about the Haulers launching off this afternoon?'

'Yes, Jay.'

'I was going to watch the softball game tonight. It was the Inter-Forest Final, but our video feed is on the blink.'

'Really, Jay? That's a shame.' I'm sure it was to him, but I'd have happily put the feed on the blink myself if someone had threatened me with watching a softball final.

Before long, I'd heard more than I needed about who was dating whom this week, who wasn't dating whom anymore and why, and who might be dating whom once the dust had settled from the last round of breakups. As long as I wasn't mentioned, I didn't care.

Jay's not a bad guy. And he had helped us make the fruit patch up in the Canopy. But he does prattle, and his world begins and ends with the village, the Forest, and his father's smallholding a few klicks beyond the Forest edge. And he does everything by the book.

Fortunately, we reached the village before he started on the price of cabbages. I slipped gratefully into our house, leaving Jay at the gate, forlorn.

Home was a cabin built from forest softwoods and sitting peacefully at the edge of the main village. The damp forest air and the enormous variety of algae and fungi growing nearby meant we fought a constant battle to keep the outside in good repair.

Inside was a different matter. Mum had dedicated her life to two goals: raising me, and building a home as far removed from the dingy forest environment as possible. I had little idea how she had achieved the former, and no idea at all how she'd managed the latter. But achieve it she had – despite our limited resources and remote location, the inside of our house was a palace.

Everything was spick and span, little ornaments and paintings decorated every room, and there were two types of surfaces. Anything she couldn't polish, she painted or hung with coverings; anything she could polish shone like a mirror.

When I entered the kitchen the following morning, Mum had her back to me, stirring a pot of her Forest Porridge, which was bubbling gently on her wood-burning range. The range was one of those things Mum polished. To distraction. If I'd been a girl who wore make-up, which I certainly wasn't, I could have put it on using my reflection in the oven doors.

Sadly, breakfast time had become a drag lately. I loved Mum dearly, and I knew she had my best interests at heart and was worried about me. But we were only seeing much of each other over breakfast right now, and her nagging was definitely becoming a drag.

'Mihana, how long are you going to stay working at that bar? Why don't you find a proper job?'

Mum knew I hung out at the bar to be near the ships. Hoping for a chance.

'Why don't you find yourself a job with one of the agri-factors, and take some qualifications?'

Where to start? An office? I bit my lip.

'And what about that nice Jay lad who keeps walking you home? You've known him since you were small. He'd make a good match. His father has land.'

A farmer's wife? Raising Jay's kids? I bit my lip again.

'Are you still involved with that stupid fruit patch up in the Canopy? You'll end up in trouble over it. And you could at least bring me some fruit.'

I was surprised. I didn't know she knew about the fruit patch. But Mothers Know Everything, I suppose. Especially what you don't want them to know.

And so, the days wore on. I woke up, argued with Mum, tended bar, walked or squelched home, went to bed, woke up, argued, tended bar. Rinse and repeat.

Then one day, she said something which rocked me right back.

'Mihana, whatever you are going to do, I wish it was away from that spaceport. Please. I lost your father to that spaceport.'

She'd never said anything about my father and the spaceport. She rarely mentioned him. In fact, I could have sworn she'd once told me he was dead. Mum wouldn't lie to me over something so important, would she? Had he been killed in an accident? Was this why she didn't like me flying? But the moment had passed, and she wouldn't be drawn any further.

A little over a week later, I was perched on a stool behind the bar, chatting to our sole customer, a scheduler who worked for the Port Authority. I'd found out about the planned Embry collection sweep from him.

'Quiet in here, today,' he said. Well, yes. Obviously.

'I know. It's been dead quiet since those half-dozen Haulers lifted. When are they coming back in?'

'I wish I knew. Nobody is telling us anything. Nothing coming down from the transhipment yards up topside, and nothing from Company HQ in Threnal.'

Threnal was about a third of the way around the planet on another continent.

'Have you been in touch?'

'Well, we've tried. But there's no answer. There's nothing on the net at all. It's as though our gear is down, but it isn't. Everything checks out, but the net might as well not be there.'

'What are you going to do?'

'If it goes on, we'll have to send someone to HQ in person, I suppose. But we're short-handed as it is.'

My ears perked up at that. There might be a chance to bum a jump seat ride. Perhaps even log some co-piloting time if I played my cards right.

Boss arrived and joined in the conversation:

'No comms here either. Mihana still can't fix the till, and I'm drowning in customers' chits. Before long, I'll have more chits than beer.'

It wasn't likely. We didn't have enough customers right now to drink enough beer. But I was reluctant to check the till again. The last time I'd opened the server up, something strange had happened to my HoloTop. It had started to shimmer and turned virtually transparent. I was relieved that the bar's few customers were looking the other way. I wore a t-shirt underneath it now.

I pulled another beer for the scheduler. He picked it up but didn't drink at first. He snorted:

'Never mind your damn chits. We're running out of space in the yards. The farmers and foresters keep bringing in their produce and we'll be running out of space to store it soon. The Gods alone know where we'll be able to put those Embrys when the herders bring them in.'

I went cold. I didn't know the collection had already started. I didn't want to think about Darvee being caught.

But the shortage of storage space itself was old news. Jay had told me about the problem a day or two before, on one of our all-too-common evening walks. The 'port was running out of storage space, and with no instructions from the Company, there was no-one buying produce. With storage running out, the produce would soon start to rot.

I may not be much of a farm girl, but I know enough to understand that if a farmer's produce rots before anyone buys it, there's grief not too far down the line. A bar can't stay open with no customers either, which isn't good for a barmaid's pay packet.

There were other problems besides the missing Haulers and Boss's broken till. All sorts of things were breaking down for no obvious reason and couldn't be fixed. We needed parts or engineers. Or something.

We looked at each other helplessly. We were all hicks from a small farming village far from anywhere. No-one knew what to do for the best. I decided to visit the Clockmaker on my next day off. He might have some ideas.

THE CLOCKMAKER

It was a clear, sunny day when I set off to visit the Clockmaker. Unusual weather for us, but I wasn't complaining.

I had my best hiking boots on (my only ones, since you ask), with long trousers tucked into my socks. I'd set my HoloTop to look like a canvas jungle jacket but had a long-sleeved vest underneath.

I'd told Mum I was going for a walk in the Forest, and she'd given me one of her herbal potions to rub on any skin which showed. Hopefully, it made me smell awful to creepy-crawlies. Probably made me smell awful to people as well, but who cares?

It was a rough trail I had to follow, and you don't even want to imagine the sorts of forest creatures which will attach themselves to your legs and try to eat your flesh, drink your blood and attack your nervous system if you don't take proper precautions. I wanted to visit the Clockmaker, not take a one-way trip to the cemetery.

I'd started out early, not long after dawn, but had stopped a few times to pick flowers. The sun was quite high, and I was starting to sweat by the time I emerged into the glade in front of the Clockmaker's tree. The flowers were for him – after all, I wanted something from him, so it was only fair for me to give something in return. To be honest, I knew he liked flowers, and I would likely have taken them anyway. I can do nice if I have to.

The Clockmaker lived in a hollowed-out trunk of an old, dead bluewood tree. Unlike the steelwood trees that supported the Canopy where we were growing fruit, the wood of a bluewood tree could be worked by hand. Their trunks were perhaps seven metres in diameter, amply big enough to live inside. Most people prefer to build their houses, not hollow them out. Less effort, it seems to me. But the Clockmaker had chosen to live in this lone tree, set in the middle of a glade perhaps fifty metres across.

I'd asked him once why he lived here, hours from the village, and why in this lone tree. 'No-one can sneak up on me in this tree,' he said. 'No back door.'

Well, that was true, of course, but you don't have to have a back door to a normal house. People do, but it's not compulsory. I'd been told there were all sorts of rules about how you build things in Threnal, but not out here. Who would care? And who would want to sneak up on an old man quietly living out his days in the Forest in the first place? But he changed the subject, and that was that.

I knocked on the one door and called out: 'Jesse, It's Mihana!'

'Mihana, lovely to see you, come on in. The door's unlocked.'

If you worry people will sneak up on you, why do you leave your door unlocked? Odd.

'I've brought you flowers.'

'Oh, lovely. I must put them in water straight away.' His voice drifted down the stairs, closely followed by the Clockmaker himself.

He's not called the Clockmaker in reality. It was my name for him. His real name was Jesse Farthree, but I always thought of him as the Clockmaker, because he made clocks as a hobby. What? You were expecting some deep reason?

'Well, I've plenty of time on my hand. I might as well make something to measure it,' he'd told me when I first met him, chuckling.

You could tell he'd once been a tall man, but now he had a stoop, and his hair was completely grey, like his beard. His face was gaunt, lines etched in by the years, and his voice was thin and reedy. Sometimes he'd tidy himself up, and you could catch a glimpse of the man he once had been — elegant, precise and with a lot of presence. But today he was in one of his scruffy phases.

I didn't know how long he'd lived in the Tree, but when he arrived, he must have been young enough to have put a lot of effort into it — he had hollowed out enough space to build three storeys. His living room and kitchen were on the ground level, he had a workshop on the first floor, and a bedroom on the floor above. I'd been in the workshop, but not in the bedroom. Obviously. Perish the thought.

In fact, no-one knew exactly when he'd arrived, or where he'd come from. He had appeared from nowhere and people felt as though he had been around forever. But he kept himself to himself and didn't bother anyone, which made everything fine as far as the Village was concerned.

His workshop was full of clocks of all shapes and sizes, most made of wood, but some of metal. And there was one splendid example in the living room, which had terrified me when I first saw it. It stood on the floor and was nearly as tall as a man. I was sitting chatting to Jesse at his table at around noon, and the clock burst into life. There was an ornate carved building on top of it, whose windows and doors started popping open. Then people appeared out of them and some promenaded around on a little track. Finally, two small doors right at the top flew open, and a beautifully made model of a flying creature which I didn't recognise shot out.

The rest of the clock's display played out while I was pressed as far into a corner as I could manage. There were no corners in a tree trunk, of course, but I had to hide somewhere. I pretended I'd found a corner. I was young back then. Jesse had laughed at me. I'd be braver now.

Having finished putting the flowers in water, he sat down at the table with me.

'Well, tell me all about the Village, then? What's been happening, what's the gossip?'

Here, Jay's endless walks with me paid dividends. I could tell Jesse everything anyone had been doing for weeks. I launched in. When I paused for breath, he stared hard at me, and, with a serious tone in his voice, said, with no trace of doubt:

'But that's not why you're here, is it, Mihana? Not to pass the time gossiping with an old man on a sunny morning. Something's wrong. You want advice.'

I sighed.

'No, you're right, Jesse. Something is very wrong. As far as I can tell, it started the day the Haulers left.'

He raised an eyebrow.

'The Haulers left? I had heard a half dozen had left, but you mean, all the Haulers? At once?'

'Yes, near enough. And that's not all. Then things started breaking down, the electrobuses aren't running properly, my wrist alarm doesn't work, nothing has landed at the spaceport since, and they can't contact Company headquarters in Threnal. And Boss's Autotill is out of action. There must be a fortune in chits behind the bar now. And the spaceport is running out of places to store farmers' produce.' I was gabbling, I knew.

When I stopped, I had to admit to myself that some of what I had said sounded pretty trivial, especially the bits about my alarm and the till.

But to my surprise, he didn't agree. Ignoring the spaceport's problems, he asked:

'Your alarm? When did it stop working?'

I tried to remember.

'Well, I don't know exactly, but it didn't go off when I expected it to, a little over an hour after the Haulers left. I am sure it was working in the morning.'

'And the autotill? When did it fail?'

'The same day, definitely. Boss asked me to fix it. But I can't. And my HoloTop turns transparent when I try to work on it now.'

He was puzzled.

'What's a HoloTop, Mihana, my dear?'

Oh, hell. I didn't mean to mention the HoloTop. It was my secret. But I knew I had no choice now I'd let the cat out of the bag. I explained what it was, how it was like a never-ending wardrobe.

'Can you show it to me, please?' It wasn't a question. His voice had strengthened, and held an unusual note of command, with an expectation of obedience.

Thankful I was wearing a vest underneath, I unclipped the HoloTop from my belt and reluctantly passed it over to him. My canvas jacket disappeared, and my bust went down a bra size.

He obviously noticed the change, because he grinned. I blushed. I didn't realise that he paid me that sort of attention. Old men, eh?

Turning the grey egg-shaped device between his fingers, he smiled and then passed it back to me.

'You have to love the fashion industry. They can adapt any technology for sex. But do you know what this actually is?'

'Not properly. The trader didn't go into detail. He said it was powered clothing.'

'Well, that's true enough as far as it goes. I haven't seen one of these in a long while. It's a Karthelian camo-armour projector. Eleventh Millennium, I'd say. A nice piece.'

'Karthelian camo-armour? What's that?'

But before he had chance to reply, the rest of what he said penetrated my thick head. I'm not usually slow on the uptake.

'Eleventh Millennium? Five thousand years ago? Five thousand? Before the Fall? Then this must be Old Empire tech?'

He nodded.

I dropped my precious HoloTop onto the table as though it had started to burn its way through my hand.

'That's illegal! Seriously illegal! I could go to jail!' I couldn't see, but I was fairly sure I'd gone pale.

He smiled.

'Well, yes. Technically. But I promise not to tell if you don't. Who'd bring me flowers?'

I relaxed a little. Since he wasn't outraged, I was obviously in no immediate risk.

'Let me show you. Come with me.'

He picked up the HoloTop, then walked, stooping, up the stairs.

I hadn't been to his workshop in a while, but it was much the same as I remembered. Perhaps more metal than wood, and he was also working with glass.

'Someone has locked this down. I suppose when they made it into a blouse. Let me see.'

He clamped my HoloTop, if that's what I should still call it, into a small vice and opened a pouch of exquisitely fine tools, with which he worked for several minutes, brow furrowed in concentration.

'Right, that's it. All the controls are accessible now.'

He clipped the projector to his belt and turned the controls I normally used to select a style.

'See the wrench over there? Pick it up, and when I say so, hit me in the stomach.'

The wrench weighed heavy in my hands. I couldn't hit him with this. An old man? It would kill him.

'OK, go ahead.'

Not intending to do anything, I turned toward him slowly. And burst out laughing. In front of me was an old man with a grey beard, faded blue trousers, and a low-cut red tee-shirt. Exceedingly low cut. And cleavage which could have supplied the village dairy. He realised there must be something wrong with his chest and glanced down.

'Oh, of course. Just a minute. Needs a reboot.'

Now he was wearing a military style top, of broken greys and whites. Then a matching pair of trousers appeared, and the greys and whites changed colour and pattern to mimic the workshop walls.

'It must have been last used on an ice planet. OK, as hard as you like.'

I didn't want to do this, but he was adamant. I shut my eyes and swung into his stomach. There was a clang and the wrench bounced out of my hands and clattered to the floor. Fearful of what I would see, I opened my eyes. Jesse was grinning with a lively twinkle in his eyes I'd not seen before.

'Very good stuff, this. No-one makes anything like this nowadays. Do you want another try?'

I had several. Then he made me wear it and he hit me. Nothing. I felt nothing at all. Not even the shock of the impact. Isn't momentum conserved in Karthelia? Wherever that is. Or was.

'What is it? How does it work?'

'I don't know exactly. But work it does. Here, take it back. It'll still be your Top, but it's fully operational now.'

I hesitated. Wouldn't I end up in trouble?

'Well, if someone knows its age, possibly. But it's harmless of itself, and who out here is going to know what it is? The trader obviously didn't, and he would have been well travelled. Now what do we do about your main problem?'

In the surprise of the demo, I'd forgotten I had a serious reason for being here.

'Do you know what is causing the trouble, Jesse? Why the Haulers left?'

'Possibly. Probably. But I need to be sure. And then there's the question of why it happened.'

He opened a drawer and started to rummage around. A pale purple glow shone out.

'Remind me of the spaceport layout. The current layout.' Odd way of putting it, as though he'd known it before.

I told him about the clearing, the Hauler bays, the little runway for aeroflitters, the storage yards, even our makeshift bar.

'That's it? No other buildings?'

Idiot. Of course there were.

'Well, the Control Tower, obviously. And the comms sheds.'

'Here, take this. You wear it like a necklace.' He handed me a pale blue, translucent, lozenge-shaped crystal on a fine silver chain.

'Am I going to be in trouble with this as well?'

'Shouldn't be. It's passive. No-one will know it's not jewellery. Tell them it's a present from an uncle.'

It wasn't quite what I wanted to hear. Completely harmless, entirely legal, made yesterday from forest nuts and Embry droppings would have been better. But he wasn't going to say more. How did he know these weird things anyway? He was an old recluse in a hollow tree. I'd come here expecting him to give me some sage, but vague, advice. Not to send me off skulking around like an unnamed character in a daytime holovid story.

'I need you to walk around the spaceport wearing it. And the bar. Near the Till. Anywhere things aren't working. And if you can wear it inside the Control Tower, that would be perfect.'

Inside the Control Tower? I hadn't been in there since The Captain was teaching me to fly. Well, nothing ventured, faint heart, and all that. All I'd be doing was walking around where I worked and hung out anyway.

But I set off back home with a nervous step, trying not dwell on the fact that my jacket was illegal military tech from a vanished Empire, and the most expensive looking piece of jewellery in the entire Forest was dangling around my neck. What could possibly go wrong?

CHECKING OUT THE JOINT

I spent the whole walk home wondering how I was going to go about 'searching' the spaceport. Going over and over it in my head. All the distraction must have slowed me down, because it had been dark for some time when I reached home.

I had spent enough time walking home from the bar in the dark, and it never bothered me, but that evening I felt as though the forest was full of eyes and ears watching and listening. And I was convinced there was someone following me. There wasn't. I was sure. Or was I? Of course I was. But what was the noise like a twig snapping? Oh, hell… Get a grip, girl!

I reviewed the layout of the spaceport in my mind. From the boundary fence to the landing pads, the runway, the warehouses, the Control Tower, the comms sheds. The flitter hangars. And the bar. I started planning a route which minimised my chances of being seen.

I even considered using my HoloTop to generate camouflage gear like Jesse had. Or perhaps a long leather coat and a hat to pull down over my eyes.

Eventually, I realised I was over-thinking the problem. In fact, I was being downright stupid. I wasn't crossing bridges before I reached them, I was digging the canal and building barges.

If I wanted to arouse suspicion, I couldn't do much better than skulk around a spaceport in camouflage gear or a fancy-dress outfit from the props department of a low budget spy production.

Let's be fair. I worked in the spaceport bar every day. I learnt to fly from the field when I was seventeen, and everyone knew I wanted to fly spacecraft for a living. And I stared longingly at every launch. People were used to Mihana, the sad, space-hungry, wannabe-pilot barmaid wandering about.

All Jesse wanted me to do was walk around. Like I did every day. This would not be a problem.

Now I felt better. I turned in and settled down for a good night's sleep.

My first real problem was how to hide the crystal. I blundered straight into the issue at breakfast the following morning.

'That's a beautiful necklace you're wearing, Mihana,' said Mum, as my first spoonful of her Forest porridge was passing my lips, 'Where did you get it?'

I coughed explosively, pretending the porridge had gone down the wrong way. buying me half a minute to think. I should have seen the problem coming. I thought I was safe at home, but pale blue translucent crystals don't grow on trees, do they? I admit some of the things growing on the trees around here strain the imagination, but even they aren't pale blue crystals. Nor do I know of any trees growing silver chains instead of vines.

And I couldn't tell Mum it had come from an uncle as Jesse had suggested. She was the one person best placed to know I didn't have any uncles!

'Down the market, Mum. A few days back. On Benny's stall.'

'That looks much better than the usual rubbish the old crook sells. Let me have a good look, won't you?'

No way out, was there? Once she saw it, she knew full well the necklace hadn't come from Benny.

I spluttered some more:

'Well, to tell the truth, one of the Hauler crewmen gave it me.'

Think before you speak, girl! Words have consequences. Think!

'What! Are you dating one of those off-world crewmen?'

That was another one I hadn't seen coming. I should have. I'm a big girl, I should definitely have seen it coming. Guys don't give barmaids fancy crystal necklaces for serving them beer.

'He must like you a lot to give you something like that. Is it serious? An off-worlder? Oh, dear. What will Jay think? You'll have to tell him, you know. It's only fair.'

Jay think? Jay think? What was it to do with Jay? The implications made me angry, and I felt myself flushing up. Fortunately, Mum must have thought I was embarrassed, as she hastily dropped the subject.

I slunk away from breakfast with my tail between my legs, too well aware that Mum was disappointed in me for two-timing Jay. Two-timing Jay? I had no intention of even one-timing Jay. Not on this or any other planet. In this galaxy or the next.

I decided I'd have a trial run in the bar before wandering around the spaceport. 'Trial run', rather than 'dry run'. You can't have a 'dry' run in a bar, can you?

And in any case, Jesse had been interested in the autotill, making it more than simply a trial. But I would be on home turf.

I had tried holding the crystal near my wrist alarm after the debacle at breakfast with Mum, but nothing much had happened. I fancied the crystal might have turned a shade darker, and I nearly convinced myself that the figures on the alarm flickered, but nothing more. Mind you, I didn't even know if anything should have been visible. Jesse had said the crystal was 'passive' after all.

I'd planned on having the task over and done with as soon as I arrived for work, but any such idea came to nothing, as Boss was fussing about in my way for ages. And by the time he finished, the bar was filling up, and I was busy.

Rusty was sitting in the window alcove talking to a man I didn't recognise. He wasn't drunk enough to be holding forth over the Battle of the Dahnian Rift yet, but the time would no doubt come. I couldn't recognise the other man – one of the glow-globes from the tourist cruiser had been playing up for the last few days. I'd have to go scavenging again soon. Perhaps it would give me some cover for sneaking about.

The canoodling couple were in again. Didn't they have a home to go to? Perhaps they did. Different homes, with different people.

But there was a group of strangers crowding around the bar, drinking quite heavily. Four men, two women. They were celebrating something. I'd not seen them before, which in itself was odd. They weren't locals, and there'd been no flights in for quite a while. Where'd they come from?

They weren't exactly in uniform, but they were all dressed similarly. Light, hard-wearing canvas jackets and trousers. Lots of pockets and pouches. Two of the men and one of the women had the indefinable aura of people who normally carried guns and were ill at ease without them.

Personal weapons were unusual around our way, but not unknown. But the bar was a strictly enforced no-carry zone. Don't carry them or check them in at the door was Boss's rule. He'd told me:

'Alcohol and weapons don't mix. I don't want some strangers coming in here and starting trouble which winds up with my bar shot up or someone dead. I don't much care if it's the stranger, but it might be a regular. Bad for business, and I might lose a friend.'

That was entirely fair and reasonable to me. It might be me he lost. One of the men from the unknown group turned to me:

'Hello, lovely. We'll have another round. Half a dozen beers. We'll try the green stuff this time.'

I started to fill glasses. He leaned over the bar:

'What are you doing tonight? After work?'

Oh dear, here we go again. I started to review my options: casual disinterest, you're not my type, my wedding's next week … The wedding one was not reliable though – some men took it as an extra challenge. Needed to give me a good send off, they said. Yes, right. As if.

I didn't have to bother. There was no sign she had been listening, but one of the women immediately called out:

'Leave her alone, Gray. Pack it in.' Her eyes narrowed and locked hard on him, and her face was like stone. 'Bring the beers over here when she's done.'

Oh dear, looks like Gray's spoken for. She was the woman who carried, as well.

Relieved at not having to brush him off, I asked, casually:

'What are you doing here? What are you celebrating?'

'Leaving that damned sticky, hot Forest of yours. We've been in there for weeks, ever since we were dropped off. And now we're celebrating a job well done. We've finished and we'll earn a comfortable little pay-off for this piece of work.'

They didn't look as they were drug company harvesters. Pharmaceuticals was the industry paying the big money around here. Cabbages, not so much.

'Oh? Why?' I asked, dreading the answer.

'We have ourselves a good pack of new animals for the Exotica Races. How you've kept them from the rest of the Galaxy this long, I don't know. Man, are they fast? Some of the fastest creatures I've ever seen. How they find their way through the Forest is beyond me.'

There was a knot in my stomach. These were the Embry collectors, back from their hunt.

'And there's a big one — the fastest of them all. Orange fur. Pale, limpid eyes. Took us a good while to catch him. He's going to make us a fortune.' The man grinned, picked up the last of the beers and turned away.

I stood there, frozen. I don't know if my heart was beating. I wasn't breathing, that was for sure. I was trying to glare at the man's back, to kill him with a stare, but my eyes wouldn't focus, and there was half an ocean rushing around in my ears.

They had Darvee.

The evening passed in a blur. I was serving beer entirely on autopilot, like a shuttle on finals to a rotating space station. My mind was on the hunters and on Darvee. And on Jesse's task, which was more than enough for my mind to cope with. The beer had to cope for itself.

I did manage to sweep the Autotill with the crystal though. Like with my alarm, nothing much happened, and I had even less chance to study what was going on. I did learn one thing though – if I wanted to use the crystal while other people were around, it couldn't stay round my neck. It was too obvious. One of the hunters spotted me leaning over to dangle the crystal near the till. He took an unhealthy interest in my cleavage (well, the HoloTop's) and then eyeballed the stone.

That took his attention. He wanted to know what it was, where it was from and how I came to have it. He worried me until I remembered how much he'd drunk. He was unlikely to remember anything in the morning. As a little extra insurance, I spiced up a few of his beers with Boss's *eau de vie*. Tasteless, colourless, but could probably strip paint from a re-entry shield. And would incapacitate any brain cells he still had functioning before closing time.

'This is fantastic beer, beautiful,' he told me, slurring slightly.

'So most off-worlders say. Enjoy it while you're here.'

'That won't be for long, darling.' I froze.

'Oh? When are you leaving?'

'Just as soon as we can. The Chief' – he paused and gestured toward the woman who had called Gray to heel like a puppy dog – 'wants us out of here. We should have lifted earlier today, but the Hauler we'd booked didn't show. She's not amused.'

Well, that bought me some time. To do what, I didn't know. But I doubted Hauler service was going to restart on their say-so. Perhaps I had time to come up with something.

I was drained by closing time, and I had a bad feeling. Skulking around a darkened spaceport, searching out an Embry pen guarded by a crowd of drunken hunters, eager for action of any sort wasn't exactly a Girl's Best Plan for a Quiet Night. I went home to ponder.

For weeks, I had been worrying about Darvee being caught, and had resigned myself to the idea. What could I do about it? But now it had happened, now it was real, and I knew I couldn't let Darvee and the rest be shipped away without trying to stop that happening.

Overnight, I developed a plan of sorts. It wasn't the best, but it would have to do. I'd arrive at the port earlier than I needed to for my shift, do what I'd told Jesse and wander round like I used to, and try to blag my way into the Control Tower. Pretend I was searching for flight work, a jump seat ride, like the old days. That would serve both my purposes – let me bring the crystal near the spaceport control gear, as Jesse wanted, and hopefully let me find out where the Embrys were kept.

The wannabe pilot barmaid of a few days back had seamlessly turned into a conspirator, a liar, a spy and an animal rights warrior. For some reason, it never occurred to me until much later.

Amazingly, it worked. I chatted to Dave in the comms shed, and Steve in the tracking blockhouse. Neither of them had much to do, as there were no off world movements. And I wandered around all the accessible ground side areas. No pen. It had to be spaceside, near one of the hangars.

Then I banged on the door of the Control Tower. Charlie answered (thank the Gods it was him – he liked me) and he let me up. I told him I was still hopeful for a flight.

'Don't you know nothing's moving?'

'Well, yes, but I assumed it was some temporary hold-up.'

'Might be. Might not be. We don't know.'

'Oh?' I tried to sound casually curious. Casual, not too nosey.

'You know all the Haulers took out in a hurry one afternoon a while back?'

'Yes.' Of course I did. Everybody did.

'Well, we didn't know it was going to happen. Nothing special had been filed with me, just regular lifts. They didn't file flight plans, ask for clearances, anything. The crews turned up back at their ships at a run and lit off out of here without as much as a by-your leave or a safety check.'

That was news. Outside, we knew they'd left in a hurry – we had no idea they were in such an all-fired hurry that they'd broken every rule to do it.

'It was a miracle there wasn't an accident.' Charlie was aggrieved, with good reason. When you spend your working life enforcing a thick rule book of how ships should arrive and depart, it's a tad upsetting if a dozen of them breaks every single rule inside quarter of an hour. And, what's worse, gets away with it without a problem...

'Look at the place now – deserted!' he grunted, pointing at the sloping windows of the Tower. Obediently, I scanned around.

I hadn't seen the 'port close up from above in quite a while. It brought back memories of flying approaches in that little flitter. I felt choked up and regretful for a minute or two. Then I remembered the second reason I was here and scanned around.

Found it – down behind Hangar A was a fenced off area I'd not seen before, and there were little brown figures moving around.

'What's that area, Charlie?' I asked, trying to sound nonchalant.

'It belongs to the hunters – they've penned their Embrys in there until they can arrange a flight out. It's not right – Embrys are free wild creatures, not someone's profit and loss.'

He surprised me – I hadn't had Charlie pegged as someone with a social conscience, especially in respect of forest Embrys, but I wholeheartedly agreed with him.

Got you! Darvee's in there.

TAKEN FOR A RIDE

I had no shift the next day. I had to wait nervously, hoping for once that the Spaceport wouldn't spring back into action. I tried to remember exactly what I'd seen through the Tower windows – the little penned off area, dotted with Embrys. Oddly, each had been keeping itself to itself. I didn't know much about whether Embrys formed troops or herds. (Can you have a herd of tree-dwellers? Probably not.) But I was fairly sure they weren't entirely solitary, and was surprised they hadn't banded together in their new, presumably threatening, environment.

But mainly I locked myself away in my room and experimented with my HoloTop. Or camo-armour, as I now knew it was. I had no wish to be caught, and even less to be hurt, and I hoped the most I would need to wear was something that blended into the background, but, as this almost magical device had fallen into my hands, it was stupid not to be able to make the best use of it that I could. Truth be told, having the camo-armour made up my mind. I don't know what I'd have done without it. I wanted to rescue Darvee, but enough to get shot? Now I wouldn't have to answer that question.

When the Clockmaker, Jesse, had opened up its true functions, he gathered all my 'fashion' settings together, separate from the more, how can I put it, 'practical' attire. Now I needed to be able to use the latter without thinking. I didn't want to find myself trying to hide in a dark night dressed in the ice-world outfit which had appeared when Jesse first unlocked the functions. And, hoping I'd never need to use them, I wanted to try to understand the armour settings.

The camouflage was interesting. I understood the greens, the browns and the sandy colours, even the whites and greys: they were the different colours of the natural world on most planets that humans might fight over. The hot reds and yellows might be of use if you were unfortunate enough to find yourself joining battle on a sulphur moon, or a highly volcanic planet. But I was baffled by the bright purple outfit with the shimmering fluorescent yellow stripes, not to mention the pink one with the red and green polka dots marching steadily up and down my arms and legs. The Galaxy was obviously a stranger place than I'd imagined.

I had no way of testing the armour settings. My bedroom was woefully short of clubs, edged or pointed blades and most especially projectile or directed energy weapons. A sad omission that it was now too late to rectify. I had to satisfy myself with making sure I could turn the armour on and had some idea how to turn up the effect if needed.

I proved to myself that I could make the HoloTop do what I wanted it to, but I was left with an unsated curiosity. I'd been through all the options Jesse had shown me, but I was as sure as I could be that I hadn't exhausted all the garment could do. But I didn't know how to access any more functions. Finding more would have to wait for another time.

It was a few minutes after midnight, and I was lying face down in a muddy puddle about fifty metres from

Hangar A. The rainforest spirits must have decided there hadn't been enough rain lately. Water was cascading from the sky in unbroken streams, glittering in the stray lights of the port compounds, and bouncing fifteen or twenty centimetres off the ground.

I thanked my lucky stars. I was wearing probably the most waterproof outfit on the planet, and I knew the hunters didn't like the rainforest weather. One of them had told me it was the first time most of them had been in a rainforest. Mostly they hunted big game on dry, open savannah worlds. 'Game'? How had hunting, and mainly I believed, killing, beautiful wild creatures come to be associated with a form of light entertainment?

I had done my best to set myself up before the bar closed. I had no idea what sort of guard, if any, the hunters would post, but it wouldn't hurt if whoever it was couldn't call on effective reinforcements if they had any trouble. I'd been liberally lacing the hunters' beers with Boss's *eau de vie*. Too liberally, perhaps. I'd had to tell Boss I'd accidentally dropped two bottles in order to explain why there was hardly any left. He hadn't been best pleased. Apparently, this strangely named, borderline lethal, concoction was his special treasure. Its name meant 'water of life' and it all came from one of less than ten planets where an obscure culture still spoke the ancient language of the liquor's name. Finch, he called the language. I apologised profusely to Boss and hoped that he'd have forgotten by the time he made up my next pay packet. 'Water of death' would be a better name. I wondered how they said it in Finch.

But now I needed to leave my puddle and reach the pen. Crouching low, I ran toward the hangar. So far, so good. My dark suit and the driving rain were doing a good job of hiding me. I reached the hangar wall and pressed myself up against it, adjusting my suit colour slightly to better blend with the wall. Then I edged to the fence.

This was about as far as I'd been able to plan. What I intended to do next was some sort of nebulous extract from a low budget daytime action drama. Cut through the fence, find Darvee, effect a miraculous escape, and, preferably, free all the other Embrys covered the basic outline, but the idea would need a lot of its detail fleshing out on the spot, I knew. It was a good way off deserving to be called a "plan".

The fence was surprisingly flimsy when I was up close, not strong enough to hold a group of such powerful creatures. Then I understood why – the pen was full of the shadowy forms, and each of them was tied by a long leash to a ring hammered into the ground. That's why they hadn't been gathering together. Any hope of calling Darvee to me evaporated. I had to go in there and search for him.

I was prepared for that eventuality. Not as prepared as I'd have liked, but Mum's kitchen and tool-shed had lacked such basic essentials as a wire cutters or bolt shears. The modern parent, eh? No foresight. I'd had to fall back on her pruning shears – the ones she used to keep her kitchen garden tidy. Best I could do.

Sometimes your best is not good enough. Flimsy the fence might be if faced with a troop of angry Embrys, but it would have stood against my shears until daylight.

I was mulling that over when I had my first shock of the night.

'Mihana! What are you doing?' A familiar voice sounded from the darkness behind me.

'Charlie? What are you doing here?'

'It's my spaceport. I can go where I want.' He sounded a little prickly.

'Yes, I know, but why here? Why now?'

'I knew you were going to try something with this pen. I saw the way you examined it the other day. I've been waiting for you.'

'How did you see me?'

'Night vision glasses. We have them in the Tower. But you were hard to see. You must be wearing something unusually dark.'

Night vision? I'd heard of it, but for military use. I had no idea our Tower would have such things.

'Never mind that anyway, Mihana. How can I help?'

'Is there any way in through this fence? I can't cut it. And do you know where the guard is?'

'No, but I'll go and find out'. Charlie ambled off into the rain.

I turned back to the fence and received my second shock. His orange fur matted by the rain, there was no mistaking the limpid brown eyes on the other side of the wire.

'Darvee! You're alive!' I whispered. 'I'm trying to cut the fence to let you out.'

He said nothing. Obviously.

'My shears won't cut the fence.'

Still nothing. He pushed his face towards me, imploringly. Then he poked one arm through the wires of the fence and grabbed the shears. Then ambled away from the barrier, out of my sight. He had been too quick for me to react,

I slumped down to the ground, my back to the fence, and, I am ashamed to say, sobbed inside a little. Now what could I do? I couldn't cut the fence with the shears, still less without. And Darvee, who I'd taken all these risk for, had wandered off.

My time for self-pity was short. An unholy commotion erupted from the huts where the hunters slept. Shouting, yelling, waved flashlights and, worst of all, gunshots. Charlie came running toward me:

'Mihana! They're shooting at me! Get away! Run for it!'

I stabbed my fingers at my armour settings and blackened my suit. Charlie had no such option. It was his spaceport, and he had seen no reason not to go anywhere he wanted on it in his normal jacket – the high-vis yellow number beloved of safety gurus the galaxy over when venturing onto spaceport aprons.

I now had a tragic demonstration of the wisdom of Boss's strictures about guns and alcohol. They don't mix. Especially when the guns are in the hands of drunken hunters who have decided someone is messing with their profits. With the best of intentions, I had probably made matters worse.

I was horrified, Charlie was lit up by torches, and little spurts of mud and water kicked up all round him where bullets hit the ground. One must have hit him in a leg, because he yelled and stumbled to his knees, screaming. A dotted line of blue-white light lanced out from in front of the hunters' hut, lighting up the raindrops as it cut through them. It hit Charlie in the middle of his back. There was a short pause, a hissing sound, and light blazed out briefly from his chest, the beam shining right through him, before being abruptly cut off. It was the ghastliest sight I had ever seen.

Charlie's body splashed forward into the mud and lay still. There was silence, and a disgustingly familiar stench of breakfast cooking. Charlie, quite obviously, was dead.

I'd often wondered why, in these daytime low budget action dramas, whenever a character is cut down in a hail of gunfire, the horrified bystanders usually shout something inane, like: 'He's dead!' or, 'She's been hit!' before rushing forward to confirm their suspicions, while the murderous shooters always stop firing to allow this quaint set piece to take place. Well, having found myself caught up in one of these events in real life, I can report a mixed bag of accuracy in the standard portrayal.

Firstly, I did indeed shout pointlessly, 'Charlie!' before rushing forward to equally pointlessly tend to his corpse. However, secondly, the hunters did not stop shooting. Mud and water spurted up all round me, and I'm sure I was actually hit by bullets many times, but my armour protected me completely. I also know for a fact that I was hit by the energy weapon more than once, because being hit produced a most spectacular effect. Waves of blue light washed all over me before ebbing away to red. Intellectually, I knew this was whatever sort of shield I was wearing dissipating the beam's energy, but I fervently wished it could have done its work in a more discreet manner. It was advertising my presence all too effectively. I made a mental note to take it up with the supplier, before realising I'd missed the window for warranty complaints by at least five millennia.

Reaching Charlie, I had yet another of the evening's shocks. He wasn't in fact dead. While I had believed he'd been shot through the back and heart, he actually had a neatly cauterised hole drilled through his right shoulder. He was unconscious and breathing shallowly. Possibly in shock.

But since the night was still raining bullets as much as water, Charlie was indeed going to be dead if he stayed where he was much longer. Thanking his slight physique, I put my armour between him and the hunters and dragged him through the mud and rain to a low depression near the hangar. It would have to do for now.

Hunters were shouting from the hut, but what I wanted above all else right then was Charlie's semi-mythical night vision, to let me see what the hell was going on. And, without warning, I had it. A glass-like shield slipped down over my face. Five or six hundred metres away the hut might have been in daylight. People were running around in panic, except one, standing a metre or two outside the hut, arms akimbo. I guessed that the HoloTop must have concluded it was too dark to see without aid. Clever belt.

A woman's voice was shouting:

'Cease fire! Cease fire, you idiots! What are you doing?'

'I nailed one, Chief, I dropped one of them!'

'You mean you killed a local, I assume?' The Chief's voice was edged with ice. 'Are you mad? This isn't a free-fire human-hunting world. Put your guns down. Now!'

They fell silent, but not before one sheepish voice added:

'There's someone else out there, ma'am. And I know they were hit, but our shots didn't hurt them. They glowed, but they weren't hurt.'

Oh dear. Something else to worry about, but not right now. Safe from the hunters for the time being, I turned to the Embry pen, to discover this was a night that kept on giving.

Lined up behind the fence were most, if not all of, the Embrys in the pen. Hanging from their necks were little stubs of what had been their leashes. Darvee had been busy with Mum's pruning shears! The Embrys rushed the fence, and, inevitably, it gave way. Now the hunters' discipline cracked. They started shooting again. The Chief yelled orders to no avail, and all but one of the Embrys scattered.

The last Embry wound a long prehensile tail around my waist, hooked me up onto his back as though I were still the little girl he had once known, and bounded for the edge of the Forest. Once inside, he shot up through the branches, and we were off through the canopy.

I had no idea where Darvee was taking me, but right then, 'anywhere but here' was more than fine with me.

I woke up wedged in a cluster of branches high in the Forest. Darvee was nowhere to be seen. I didn't know exactly how high I was, but, judging from the lichens and fungi clinging to the trunk, I was several hundred metres above the forest floor. A small brown squirrel was sitting on a thin branch four or five metres away, munching something unidentifiable. He was ignoring my presence. Which was fine. If he didn't bother me, I wouldn't bother him. Live and let live was going to be my motto for the day.

I remembered crashing through the branches to escape the hullabaloo at the spaceport and clinging on to Darvee for dear life as he swung from branch to branch and tree to tree. I had been much younger, smaller and lighter when last I'd ridden him, and, like all youngsters, was possessed of an unshakeable belief in my own invulnerability and immortality. Nothing could hurt me while I rode The Mighty Darvee. Now, the years had passed, and I had a much better grasp of the realities of the situation, how much momentum my body would gain in a fall from his back, and the damage that might be done to human flesh and bone if the momentum were transferred to Threnador upon my inevitable collision with the planet's surface far below.

Safely ensconced in a cradle of branches, I now had time to wonder if the camo-armour would absorb the shock of the impact, as its Karthelian designers had obviously held the Law of Conservation of Momentum in no mean disregard, as it applied to wrenches and bullets anyway. But however safe I was, it was better not to put the possibility to the test in a several hundred metre fall.

Darvee must have put me here, but where 'here' was, I had no idea.

I hadn't slept well, either. It had rained hot and sticky rain for much of the night, although the trees and leaves gave some shelter. But whenever I dozed, I dreamt of the spaceport, which I imagined was now full of police cars, lights flashing, sirens wailing. And all too often I dreamt of Charlie falling face forward into the mud. I hoped one of those sirens would be an ambulance taking him to safe treatment. At least, part of me did. A thoroughly reprehensible part was rather aware of a simple fact. Charlie could positively name me as being a major player in the events of last night, and I'd be better off if he didn't. That made me feel bad, and also made me question why the hell I'd dragged him out of harm's way. An ethical dilemma, I believe it's called.

I disliked myself for having such thoughts, and I wasn't achieving anything anyway. What was done, was done.

Dawn was starting to filter through the branches, giving a pink hue to everything around. I didn't want to stay here. I started to take stock.

Where was I? Somewhere high in the Forest.

Where exactly? No idea.

How can I climb down? No idea – there are no climbing ropes laid here.

If you climb down, where will you go? Home.

How will you find home? No idea.

Is there somewhere else you can go? Jesse's or the Spaceport.

How will you find those? No idea at all.

What do you have with you? The clothes I'm wearing, my HoloTop and Jesse's crystal. Nothing useful when stuck up a tree.

Taking stock was wrapped up. I could manage to envisage reaching the Forest floor, with a lot of effort and more luck, but then I was stuck. Have you ever considered how you travel from one place to another? You walk a few hundred meters, then you turn left, walk some more, turn right, walk some more, and carry on until you arrive. Or reach somewhere where you catch some form of transport. With a driver who knows full well how to reach your destination. That's a different level of knowledge from knowing how to go from an unknown spot to another spot whose absolute location you don't know accurately. When I was flying, I knew roughly where the Spaceport was, but now I was bereft of charts or navigational equipment. I had no idea at all of the precise location of home or Jesse's. My chances of walking safely to any of these through the depths of a rainforest before I was exhausted, starving, bitten, stung or even eaten, were not good. At least I wouldn't die of thirst. It was too wet. But I was lost.

I needed someone's help. Darvee's preferably. Which was convenient, because, immersed in self-pity, I had completely missed his arrival back in the nest of branches. It was something of a shock to discover he was sitting next to me with his most pleading 'Have you any strawberries?' expression on his face.

I shouted, yelled, hugged him, possibly even kissed him, and tried my best to explain to him that I had no strawberries, but please would he take me home anyway?

Then it dawned on me that as well as Darvee not being able to understand me, he had no idea where my 'home' was. Every time I had met him had been in The Forest. For all I knew, he thought I lived here, like he did. Eating leaves and nuts. Now what?

We sat on the branch for what felt like an eternity, me feeling glum, Darvee impassive. Then as dawn passed and full daylight started to filter through the leaves, he stirred, shook the dampness from his fur, wrapped his tail around me, and we were off again, swinging alarmingly from branch to branch.

I shut my eyes most of the way – I knew I was no safer, but it wasn't as gut wrenchingly terrifying a ride. Darvee finally reached the ground and lifted me from his back. I had a serious shock on opening my eyes. I was in a sunny, peaceful, familiar glade. In front of Jesse's tree.

Darvee was munching contentedly on one of Jesse's bushes. Jesse wouldn't be too pleased with him.

I walked up to the reassuring normality of Jesse's bluewood tree. The door was both unlocked, and open. Given the events of last night, a paranoid notion crossed my mind. Perhaps something was amiss. Making no sound, I poked my head inside. There were two men sat at Jesse's table drinking coffee. Jesse himself, and a man with his back to me with flame red hair and a prosthetic arm. No, it couldn't be. How could Rusty know Jesse? And anyway, coffee? Rusty only ever drank beer, or, if beer was unavailable, something actually inflammable. I couldn't help myself:

'Rusty?' I asked.

That produced a most satisfying effect. Rusty shot straight up about half a metre, while Jesse jerked his head up, saw me, stood up, banged his head on a cabinet, sat back down again and said:

'Mihana? What has happened to you?'

'Stars of Satan, girl! Don't startle me like that!' Rusty wiped coffee off his shirt.

'What do you mean, what has happened to me?' Plenty had, but nothing visible as far as I knew. What was Jesse talking about?

'Look at yourself.'

There was a mirror on the cabinet Jesse had banged his head on, I stared at myself.

'Oh. Comb. Now.'

Have you heard people say someone looks as though they've been dragged through a hedge backwards? Well, being dragged through a rainforest forwards by an Embry is worse. Once tidied up a little, I sat down, feeling better. More in control.

'I didn't know you two knew each other.'

'Oh, we go way back. Way, way back,' said Rusty, with evasion in his eyes.

Jesse shot him a dark glance then asked me:

'You weren't caught up in the ruckus at the spaceport, were you? You were supposed to be nosing around. That's all.'

News travels fast. How had they heard?

'Don't worry, I did that first. Do you have any strawberries?'

'Strawberries? No, not here. There might be a few in the garden, but it's late in the year. Anyway, why?'

'For Darvee.' They were still puzzled. 'The Embry who brought me here.'

'An Embry brought you here?! Why? Which Embry?' There was an urgency in Jesse's tone.

'Darvee, my friend, a big Embry, brown with limpid eyes. Craves strawberries. All the time.'

For some reason, what I had said rattled them. Rattled them a lot. But they said nothing.

'I let the Embrys out. Or at least, helped them to let themselves out. There was a lot of trouble. Charlie, the traffic control manager was shot. Do you know if he's OK?'

'Shot? I hadn't heard that.' Rusty appeared horrified. 'Were you hurt?'

'No, I'm fine. Shaken, but OK.' Jesse was deep in thought, and I could tell nothing from his expression. I decided not to mention the camo-armour.

'What happened with my crystal? Were you able to take it around?'

Mmm. Jesse's happy with Rusty knowing about the crystal. Interesting. I unhooked it from round my neck and passed it over without a word. Jesse took it, turned it over in his hand and pressed it in an odd manner. Then stood up and walked up the stairs to his workshop without making any comment.

Once he'd gone, Rusty started quizzing me about what had happened at the spaceport. I did my best to explain without dragging the armour into it. I was still nervous about having it – it was illegal, after all. I made out I was either incredibly brave, incredibly lucky or just plain stupid. Thankfully, he believed it was a mixture of the first two.

'I'll think of you differently the next time you pull me a beer, that's for sure,' he said. 'Sounds like I could have done with you at the Dahnian Rift...'

'I hope I'll be pulling beers again. I hope Charlie will be OK.' I ignored his bluster about the Rift. Now I had started worrying about the bad consequences of my escapade. I knew the good one was that Darvee and the others were free.

'We'll smooth it over, don't worry. And I am sure I'd know if Charlie was dead. All I heard was that the hunters had been locked up on firearm and affray charges. Nothing about murder.'

I had no time to unpick the layers of his remark before Jesse walked back downstairs.

'I was right, Rusty. The Time Signal's stopped.'

Time Signal? What was the Time Signal? I'd had never been told of such a thing. You took the time from your watch or the holovid news. There was no signal. Signals were what the comms equipment in flyers used to talk to the Tower. What police used to talk to each other. Ordinary people didn't have anything using signals.

'Time Signal? What's that? Anyway, we know what the time is, you of all people – especially in this place!' I gestured at the clocks lining all the walls. Especially the one with the strange flying creature.

Rusty avoided my eyes. Jesse had a gently sad expression on his face.

'No, Mihana. They count the time passing here. They've no way of knowing whether the time here is the same as in other places. Do you know what Galactic Time is?'

'Sure. The time on the clocks in Threnal. Our time is six hours behind Threnal's because we are nearly twenty percent of the planet west of Threnal. If we kept the same time as Threnal, it would be pitch dark at nine in the morning.'

Of course, I knew this. Every schoolchild who was half awake in school knew Threnador rotated on its axis in 31 and a half hours. What I'd never understood was why someone had made an hour equal to two sixty-thirds of a day. It made it more than awkward to divide the day up into halves and quarters and thirds. Why couldn't there have been a sensible number of hours in a day, a number divisible by lots of other numbers, like thirty? Or twenty-four? I'd asked the teachers, but it hadn't taken me anywhere. None of them knew why an hour was the length it was.

'It's a wider issue, or it would be called Threnal Time. It's the time kept by the whole Galaxy. What happens when you travel to other stars?'

The abrupt shift of subject startled me. Travelling to another star, any star, was my dream.

'Well, you go in a starship, through a Portal.'

Rusty was becoming impatient.

'Jesse – we need to decide what to do. This can wait, can't it?',

The two men turned to each other and began a deep discussion in low voices. I wasn't included any more. I decided to go and talk to Darvee, if he was still here.

It didn't take long to find him. A trail of devastation led from some bushes at the edge of the glade fronting Jesse's bluewood tree, through some shrubbery and into what had presumably once been the few strawberry plants which Jesse had talked about a while ago. The plants were in ruins: the strawberries, I guessed, were in Darvee; quite a lot of their juice was in his fur.

I was worried about him being here. Before too long elapsed, someone in authority might come after me. Or if not for me as such, then for the oddly glowing stranger caught up in last night's firefight. I didn't want him here then – it was possible the hunters would have persuaded or bribed someone into believing right was on their side by now. Then they would set about rounding up their former captives.

But he had always come and gone as he pleased. If the truth be told, I could no more communicate with him than I could with a pet dog or cat. But it didn't stop me trying. I sat on the grass as the morning sunshine beat down and told him what had happened to bring us here and why he should leave.

I suppose eventually he became bored of my monologue, because he stood up, stretched, loped languidly to the edge of the clearing and jumped up onto a branch. I was glad. He'd been caught once before, admittedly, but I believed he was safer in the depths of The Forest than in an open glade.

He gazed down at me and slightly raised one of his long forearms as though to wave goodbye. As he did so, a voice sounded in my mind:

Mihana, thank you. Be careful, look after yourself. But you can trust Jesse and Rusty. Darvee knows. Darvee trusts.

I shook my head in disbelief, but he was gone. What had I heard? Or imagined I'd heard? Was I losing my senses? Embrys can't talk, much less telepath.

More than a little shaken, I walked back inside, determined not to mention what had happened.

They were more welcoming than when I left. They poured me a coffee, and Jesse started to explain:

'Mihana, for the Emp.., er, the Confraternity to function it needs a common time standard. Without it, flights between the stars couldn't be timetabled, business deals could not be done, and laws could not be enforced across the Galaxy. No-one would know what should happen when.'

I listened, not quite understanding what this had to do with a sleepy little farming community in a Forest at the edge of nowhere. It was also the first time anyone had mentioned the Confraternity since school. We sort of ignored interstellar high politics out here in the boondocks.

'Synchronised time is given to every planet by a Signal transmitted by the Confraternity. Each planet relays it to every piece of tech needing it, via a local subspace signal. The signal isn't reaching here from Threnal anymore. Which is more than worrying.'

'Subspace?'

'Oh, I forgot. They don't allow subspace to be taught in schools. A sort of space underneath normal space. You can't see or touch it.'

I guessed 'They' meant the Confraternity – The Confraternity for the Technological Purity of Humanity. A fancy name for the government, as far as I knew. We had a Confraternity Brother in the village, Brother Peter. He was bald and wore a tattered brown habit. But he was old, and it was so quiet out here that he had little to do, except drink tea and keep chickens.

Jesse was still talking:

'… It's worrying because the Signal is crucially important. A great deal of effort goes into ensuring it can never be interrupted. Because without it, even little things like your Boss's autotill and the electrobuses don't work properly.'

Brother Peter should be worrying about this, I supposed, but guessed he was probably overloaded dealing with his chickens.

'...and if simple things aren't working, then what passes for more complex technology here will start to break down. Medical stuff, manufacturing, that sort of thing.'

'And the Haulers. Don't forget the Haulers,' Rusty interrupted for the first time.

'One thing at a time,' Jesse sounded rattled. 'We need to know how widespread the problem is.'

'Hey! Why did my HoloTop turn transparent?' By now I knew Rusty knew more than I did about everything anyway, therefore I didn't worry about mentioning it.

'Smart girl. I didn't know if you'd spot that. The Time Signal technology is old, very old. Like your Top is. They have similar roots. The till was draining power from the Top, searching for the Signal.

'So, what happens now? How does this get fixed?'

'We need to persuade someone at the spaceport to go to Threnal and find out what's happened.'

'Well, good luck with that any time soon.' Hadn't they been paying attention? The one person at the spaceport who could authorise anyone there to do it had been shot, and, even if he was OK, there was nothing there now able to fly far enough.

Jesse and Rusty were seriously rattled when I imparted these nuggets of hard truth. There was silence for a long time. Rusty broke it:

'Jesse, we can't take the risk of keeping Them on a planet whose technology may be collapsing. What about The Bubble?

'You know it is being kept for an absolute emergency, although I take your point. Perhaps this is one. But who could fly it? After what's happened, I can't leave here. I must be ready to attend to Them in case of more danger. And you have no flying training. The pilot must be qualified. The Craft's design requires that'

The capital letter on Them was unmistakable, but this time I had no idea at all who They might be. And I was shaken by all the 'collapsing technology' stuff. On Threnador? I live here, Mum lives here. This is our home. Life's basic enough as it is without it being even worse.

Then something else shook my grip on reality. Or sanity. Or both.

I knew there were three of us in the room, and I'd closed the door as I came in, just in case. So, those present were me, an old man and another somewhat younger, but still quite old man. I don't have a twin sister, and even if I had had one, she wasn't there. So, it was a bit of a surprise to hear a voice identical to mine say:

'The Captain says if it'll fly, I can fly it. I'll fly this Bubble to Threnal for you. Whatever a Bubble is. Someone obviously has to.'

Slowly it dawned on me. I must have said those words. Jesse and Rusty were clapping me on the back and telling me things like: "That was a noble offer", "I shouldn't take the risk" and "You'll be a hero". Yeah, and six sorts of idiot…

BUBBLING UP

Once the excitement died down, they started talking about reaching Threnal, and what needed to be done there. I was interested, in a sort of detached way, but my mind kept coming back to one crazy idea. I'd committed myself to flying a craft I'd never seen and whose capabilities I had no idea about. A fifth of the way round the planet, and across an ocean, to boot!

Derring-do and the swashbuckling spirit are all very well, but sometimes a small dose of reality needs to creep in, even if you have buckled all your swashes up tight. Or something.

'There's no point talking about this anymore. I need to see this Bubble. Where is it?'

Jesse looked at Rusty and nodded:

'You're right. Come on, follow me.'

He drained his coffee, stood up, and walked over to a cupboard at the bottom of the stairs to his workshop. I was expecting him to fetch his coat, and then we'd all leave and walk at least several kilometres to some concealed airfield. I wasn't expecting him to stand impatiently in the cupboard (which was a little low for him), gesturing for me to follow him in. I couldn't do that! Mum always told me never to go into cupboards with strange men. Actually, I wasn't sure she ever did say those words, but it was the sort of thing she might have said.

I had no idea what could happen in a cupboard that couldn't happen outside it, so, after a brief pause, I decided I was being silly, and followed him in. Inside was a wooden staircase spiralling down into darkness with a rather unstable appearance. The Tree had a basement? Surely it should have roots? What was keeping this Tree up?

We went down about two storeys, where the stairs ended in a cavern of sorts. It smelt dank and abandoned; unused, forgotten. Rusty, who'd followed us down, lit a torch on one wall. The cavern was a junk room – full of all the sorts of things people collect for no clear reason, until they've outlived their usefulness, when, for even less reason, they are put in a cupboard rather than being thrown away. There was some old furniture, broken musical instruments and a few moth-eaten soft toys. And a chest, which I knew would have dressing-up clothes in it, largely because Mum had one exactly like it, and it was full of my dressing-up clothes, from long ago. What else are chests for?

What there wasn't, anywhere to be seen, was anything that could fly. I couldn't entirely rule out some unpleasant variety of airborne Forest insect lurking in a corner, but nothing I could fly to Threnal.

Jesse bent down and brushed away some dust and straw from a patch of floor. Underneath was bare, featureless earth.

Jesse put his palm on something, and a patch of the earth faded away, revealing a vertical ladder starting a few centimetres below the surface. Down we went, until we reached another open space. Cool white artificial light flickered into life as we entered. (How had that been done? Either the light or the vanishing earth?) At one end of the space was a heavy metal door set into rock, with multiple bolts and locks. Rusty opened them all and slid the door aside. We stepped in and lights flashed on.

By the Spirits of The Forest! We were now in a huge cave, tens of metres on a side, lit by cold, glowing strips in the walls and roof. The floor was perfectly flat and painted a matt mid-grey. Yellow lights were set into the floor, forming a pair of parallel lines leading from the entrance door. If it had been paint on concrete, it could have been a walkway on the spaceport apron. They ran to the centre of the room, to the foot of a flight of steps leading up to what had to be The Bubble.

I don't know what I expected The Bubble to be. I had supposed it was a whimsical name for a routine personal flyer of some sort. How wrong can a girl be?

The appropriately named Bubblecraft was a transparent sphere, at least ten metres in diameter. I could have put the little craft I learned to fly on inside it. It had all the appearance of being made of glass, but that must have been impossible. Like so much in the last few minutes.

As far as I could see, it was seamless. Moulded, or blown, or whatever, in one piece. The outside was seamless, but it was obvious that the inside had been divided into decks and cabins. The decks ran parallel to the cave floor, like lines of latitude on a globe. Parts of the transparent outer shell were blanked out by cabin walls. Far above me, I could just about make out the topmost deck – the North Pole, I dubbed it – and it was entirely transparent. I guessed it was the flight deck. There was a lot of unfamiliar equipment visible near the South Pole.

There were four openings – one at the top of the steps, and three spaced one hundred twenty degrees apart around the base. From each of these a polished silver leg assembly reached down to the ground ending in a solid 'foot' with three sprung toes. No wheels.

Worse than no wheels, there were no wings, no rotors, and no sign of an engine or a thrust exhaust of any sort. How did she fly?

'It is vertical take-off and landing then?' I asked, trying to sound nonchalant. Take-off and landing were not my foremost concern, but it was the first thing I could force my mouth to say once I'd closed it. I was conscious I'd been gawping, and rather embarrassed. One doesn't like to gawp—it shows a lack of refinement and class.

'Mmm. An unusual first question,' Rusty grinned. 'Anything else?'

'What is it, where did you find it, how did you bring it down here, and am I right in believing Brother Peter wouldn't approve of it?'

'Ay, lass, that he wouldn't. If he could tell what it was. Jesse?'

'I'm sorry, Mihana, apart from saying it is a very capable flying machine which will take you to Threnal and back, I can't tell you anything else right now.'

'Can't, or won't? Don't tell me: you could, but then you'd have to kill me.' I felt as though I was back in that daytime holovid drama again. It felt like time for a cliché.

'OK. How does it fly? No, never mind. More to the point, how do I fly it?' Again, I was trying to sound casual, and not let on that I was beginning to doubt even my so-special skills and aptitudes. And to wonder what I was mixed up in.

'You're the pilot. Why don't you climb aboard your craft and find out?' Jesse and Rusty left me and the Bubble to introduce ourselves to each other. Which was unexpected.

I contemplated the steps for several minutes. As they didn't do anything in return, I decided I'd have to climb them. I was more than a little nervous. I loved flying, and the chance to pilot a machine like this – whatever it was like – wasn't going to come my way again. But I knew I'd never seen or touched anything like it. I'd learned to fly on a conventional fixed-wing, electrically powered, monoplane. The usual starter aircraft. I'd flown a few types of different sizes, high and low wing, but all similar in design and capability. Simple mechanical flight controls. I had some time on a hover-rotor craft – which flew by sucking the air out of the sky above it, throwing it at the ground, and daring the ground to answer back. At least, that's what it looked and felt like. It had very different controls, but at least it had given me some experience of vertical take-off and landing. And, once, just the glorious once, I had gone into space aboard the Captain's flitter. You controlled it with a little stubby lever called a joystick. Joy? Intense concentration bordering on pain, more like. But, yes, joy as well.

How would The Bubble fly? What controls would it have? The Bubble hadn't been made on Threnador that was for sure. Nor in any star system nearby. Or nearwhen, I suspected. How had it come here?

Well, I'd done enough thinking. It was time for some action. Up the steps. Like the cavern, lights flicked on inside as I entered. There was a small entry lock, with pale cream walls, impeccably clean. Notices and signs in a language I didn't recognise. A stairway spiralled up toward the North Pole, where I assumed the flight deck was to be found. It had to be up there. Pilots want to fly things from as high up as possible. It makes you feel important. No-one wants to fly from the basement level of their craft.

As I put my feet on the stairs, the steps I'd entered by folded up into the lock and a hatch closed over where they'd been. I wished they hadn't folded like that. Not only because I was possibly locked in, but also because I hadn't expected The Bubble to be powered up. Who leaves an aircraft powered up in an underground cave? The batteries will go flat.

'Hello?' I asked in case there was someone else on board. No reply. I weighed up stepping off the spiral stair and seeing if I could open the now-closed hatch, but the idea was too wimpish and wet. This girl was made of sterner stuff. At least, that's what I wanted people to believe! Especially, I wanted to believe it myself!

I was hoping the stairs led directly onto the flight deck, but I was disappointed. At the top was a small platform, and a door or hatch. It had no handle. I pushed the door, but it didn't open. I couldn't pull it – no handle, remember? I tried to press my hands against it and slide it open, but no joy. Mmm, this is awkward.

Then, to the right of the door, there was a life-sized drawing of a human hand. A brown line on the cream wall. I had no idea what it was for. Anywhere in the Galaxy, a little picture of a man or a woman would have meant I'd found the toilets, not the flight deck, but a hand? I ran a finger round it, idly. Then, for lack of any other ideas, I placed my right hand on top of the painted one.

I nearly died. A soft sound, like a small bell chiming, came from the wall, and a metallic voice spoke, in perfect Threnadorian:

'Good morning. Do you require access to the flight deck? Please identify yourself.'

I'm ashamed to admit I jumped, then bolted back down the stairs. Not my finest hour. Please don't tell anyone.

I peered over the top step. A panel to the side of the door lit up to show a cartoon picture of a woman's face, with the words from a few seconds ago printed underneath. Still in Threnadorian. I had never seen or heard anything like this. Glowing, talking walls? What sort of machine was I in?

One thing was for sure. I wasn't going to find out anymore while hiding on the stairs, and the little cartoon woman didn't appear dangerous. I walked back up.

'My name is Mihana Pallathoi. I am to fly this ship on behalf of Jesse Farthree.' Now wasn't the right moment to admit I knew little more about Jesse than his name. Sound confident, that was the thing to do.

'Verifying. Please wait.'

I waited. There wasn't much choice. Who was checking? And with what? There was no-one else on board as far as I knew, and where I was standing blocked the access stairway anyway.

'Greetings, Mihana. I am unable to retrieve your pilot licence or flight experience. Please supply details.'

Well, that was no surprise – my pilot's licence and logbook were in the top drawer of my dressing table in my bedroom back at Mum's. How could anyone here, or anywhere else, access them?

'Details awaited – please supply.'

I started to talk – flight training, models flown, hours logged, routes flown, all the usual sort of stuff. I did my best not to dwell on the fact I was talking to a wall. Well, worse. Not simply talking to a wall. Mad people do that all the time, I imagine. I was actually having a meaningful conversation with a wall. She/it was asking me sensible questions about what I was saying.

We were a long time on aircraft types. She – I couldn't consider a woman's face as belonging to an 'it', even if 'she' was a wall – didn't know much about Threnadorian aircraft. The aircraft I had trained on, and logged most hours on, interested her most. But the type – a Jungleskipper D117 – meant nothing to her. I had to describe it in a lot of detail, until eventually she grasped what it was. Somehow, she knew of another machine similar enough to be almost identical.

We were finished.

'Access authority confirmed. Welcome aboard, Mihana.'

The apparently immovable door slid aside silently, and I was free to walk on the flight deck, which was lit by a soft red light.

I didn't know what to expect. I still had no idea what sort of craft this was, how it flew, what controls it would have. I had no idea what was facing me. But, buried deep in my head, I had some very firm assumptions about what I wouldn't find.

Front and centre, I wasn't expecting to walk into the cockpit of a Jungleskipper D117!

This time, I managed to control the impulse to bolt for the stairs.

Obviously, I was not on a Jungleskipper, and this was not the cockpit of one. For one thing, you don't walk into a Jungleskipper's cockpit from the rear – you climb in through a hatch at the side. Secondly, this was much smarter than any cockpit I'd ever seen. Everything was fresh from the factory – there weren't decades of wear on the controls, chipped paint from pilots clambering in and out, and the old, slightly sweaty stench born of long use in a damp and mildewed climate.

But, by all the Gods, it was remarkably like a Jungleskipper. All the controls were there – the yoke, the pedals, and the throttle. And a startlingly similar instrument suite and layout. Altimeter, artificial horizon, turn and bank, compass. The instruments were subtly different from the ones I was familiar with, but no more than you'd expect if the craft was outfitted by a different supplier. I could use them.

I slipped into the left-hand seat, a little self-consciously. I knew I didn't understand what I was seeing, which is unsettling in any machine you are preparing to fly, to say the least.

I had no intention of going anywhere, but, lacking any better idea, I fell into my well-worn routine of pre-flight checks. I skipped the externals, as walking around checking tyres, examining for leaks and checking flight surfaces on a transparent bubble sitting on three legs wasn't possible. What would I waggle?

Everything powered up and behaved exactly as I expected. I kept working through my mental checklist by habit. When I reached the 'full and free movement' checks on the flying control surfaces, I twisted the control yoke and, instinctively, without a pause to think how ridiculous it was, glanced over my shoulder, to check out of the cockpit window that the left aileron moved. Fine.

As I started to repeat the procedure for the right aileron, the enormity of what I had seen burst into the forefront of my mind. I knew I was sitting in a large transparent bubble, but outside the window, I had seen an aileron moving perfectly at the end of the left wing of a Jungleskipper. Holding my breath, with my heart pounding in my chest and blood rushing in my ears, I turned to the right. Yup, the right aileron and wing were fine too.

I yelped, and, trying to maintain as much dignity as possible, left the cockpit as fast as I could and strode down the stairs. The hatch slid shut with a clunk as, and then came the mechanical voice:

'Cockpit vacated. Powering down.'

Safely outside, I slumped down to the floor, sitting with my back against the door through which I had entered the cave, or hangar, facing the Bubble.

It carried on sitting there, in the yellow lights from the floor and the cold glare of the roof lights, exactly as I'd seen it earlier. A near perfect transparent sphere on three legs. No wings, no fuselage and not a trace of an aileron. What was I dealing with?

Jesse and Rusty were drinking coffee and poring over a plan or map of some sort when I reached the comfortable familiarity of the treehouse's living room.

'How did you do?' asked Rusty, cheerfully. Jesse remained impassive.

I poured myself a coffee, wishing I was back in Boss's bar and could pour myself something stronger. A lot stronger.

'OK.' I paused. 'What is that thing?'

'The Bubble? What do you mean? It's just an aircraft.' Jesse was still silent.

'It's not "just" anything!' I knew I sounded exasperated, but I felt I'd earned the right. 'I know that now, and you two have known it all along, or my mother's a jamana tree.'

'It's a very good aircraft,' said Rusty, shiftily.

'That's as may be. I don't doubt you. But right now, it's a transparent bubble that has two wings when you're inside and none when you're outside, and a cockpit from a light aircraft. Which it most certainly isn't. And never has been, I'm sure.'

Jesse was quizzical. 'What do you mean?'

I told him what had happened.

A strange expression came over his face, like he was holding back a wry grin. 'Didn't you want controls you recognised?'

For some reason, such a simple question stopped me. Of course, I did. You'd have to be the world's most suicidal fool to want to fly an aircraft with controls you didn't recognise. Life is short enough as it is.

'Well, it gave you them. Think of it like a simulator.'

I knew what a simulator was. I'd never seen one, but from books and magazines I knew professional pilots used them to train to fly large passenger and cargo aircraft which were too expensive to crash. Or even bend. But they were huge, clunky things, with pictures projected onto screens from cameras taking pictures of little models instead of windows, thousands of switches, most of which didn't work, and big hydraulic rams moving the whole thing about. The Bubble was definitely not one of those. You couldn't casually fit one of them inside a working aircraft. Especially one that happened to resemble the cockpit of an aircraft I recognised. A team of people would be working for a week to set one up. Even if such a thing existed. Stupid idea. I dismissed it.

'That's impossible. Never mind the view through the window, how's the cockpit done?'

'You know, Mihana. At least, you have enough information to work it out. It's like something you know very well.'

I was becoming more annoyed. I stood up.

'So, you won't tell me what it is I'm to fly you halfway round the world in, or how it works? Why? Don't you trust me?'

There was an awkward silence. Like you'd mentioned your uncle's bad breath, before realising he was in the room. Jesse and Rusty were silent, glancing at each for confirmation.

I gave my best rendition of a seriously excellent snort of disdain and walked out into the garden.

Late afternoon was turning to evening. I sat on a bench on the sunlit side of the treehouse as the shadows lengthened. Propping my chin in my hands and my elbows on my knees, I started to list the questions I needed answers to.

What was I involved with? What was the Bubble? Where was it from? Why did Jesse have it? How did Jesse know so much about old tech and the Signal? Come to that, who were Jesse and Rusty? How well did I know them? Why was all this happening in my little corner of Threnador? Did I want to fly the Bubble? Should I go home to Mum?

Well, one question was easy to answer – did I want to fly the Bubble? Hell, yes! I'd be mad not to. I'd spent years bumming rides and scraping together money for flights in anything that would hold together long enough to leave the ground, and now I was being offered the chance to fly a craft whose like I had never even heard a whisper of. People have sold their firstborn for less. Fortunately, I didn't have any sort of 'born', so I couldn't be tempted to sell him or her. Thank Heaven for small mercies.

How much trouble was I going to be in? I was probably in quite a lot already, truth be told. I'd busted the Embrys out of the hunters' pound, and however morally right it was to me, there was probably some pestilential law or ten against it. Charlie had been shot while I was doing it, which he likely wouldn't be too pleased about. And I'd been walking around wearing banned Old Empire tech.

I could probably blag my way out of most of those. Play the soppy fem card over the Embrys – young woman loves furry animals, that sort of thing. Buy Charlie a case of whisky once they patched him up well enough to make sure it didn't leak straight back out when he drank it. Feign ignorance over the HoloTop and the necklace if it came to it and play on Brother Peter's love of a quiet life if I had to. He wouldn't want to come the vengeful priest with me. Not over a shirt. They'd sent him out here to the backwoods to avoid all that sort of stuff, I was sure.

But flying myself and a co-conspirator halfway around the world in a buried high-tech aircraft to investigate the failure of a secret Signal was in a whole different league. Way over Brother Peter's pay grade, I was sure.

So, I definitely should go home. Right, all settled. Oh, wait a minute. What about the missing Signal, the collapsing farm economy and everyone starving to death? Bother. There's always a little hitch, isn't there?

I took my head out of my hands and straightened up. A light evening breeze was blowing seed puffballs up into the sky from a plant at the Forest edge. In my mind's eye, one of the little spheres turned into a large Bubble, flying far above. Damn, I'd like to fly the thing. But was it worth jail or worse?

The garden was lit by the orange light of sunset, and it reminded me of Darvee's fur. I checked where I'd seen him disappear, an unformed hope in my head. But he wasn't to be seen. Sensible Embry. Good Embry.

I pictured him disappearing and remembered what had sounded in my head. *Darvee knows. Darvee trusts.* More than anything else, I wished I knew. I wished I trusted.

Stretched out on the bench, I watched the puffballs catching the last of the sunlight against the darkening sky and tried to find some sleep.

After spending the night on the bench, I had been woken at dawn by a spider crawling down my nose. Not the most welcome of alarms, but there are worse things you can find crawling over you after a night outside in the Forest.

My doubts of the previous evening were gone. I wanted to fly, and the awful reality of going back to my old life had struck home. Jay, the cabbage farmer's wife routine, and a brood of kids. Instead, I was going to fly the best craft on Threnador, save the world and return a hero. I'd trade the hero bit for not being caught, but I would have my adventure. We weren't going to be caught, anyway. Were we?

I went straight down to the Hangar, as I now imagined it to be, without waiting for the two men. They could worry about what was happening for once.

The Bubble let me onto the flight deck without a murmur this time. Strapped in the pilot's seat, I finished my pre-flights and turned to what to do next. How do you fly a ten-metre bubble with no wings or visible engines using the controls of a simple fixed wing light aircraft? Well, the way to find out was to try. Releasing the parking brake handle, I started a slow taxi towards a large door which I assumed led to the outside world. No problem. How we were rolling on three fixed feet was a puzzle for another time. I'd been given Jungleskipper controls. I must be able to fly with them.

First problem. Jungleskippers don't have 'open door' buttons. Anything you want done in the outside world, you call the Tower for. But there was no Tower here in the Tree. I wasn't running back to Jesse.

Was there an 'open door' button in the cockpit? You never know, someone might have added one specially, but no joy. Irritated, I voiced my frustration aloud:

'How do I open the perishing door?'

Back came a mechanical voice:

'Ask me.'

That was a surprise. I'd somehow assumed I'd left the cartoon lady and her strange voice outside the cockpit. I had no idea why. But she was no help anyway.

'I just did! How do I open the door?'

'Ask me.'

We went round the loop twice more but were going nowhere. The cartoon lady wasn't being obtuse – if a wall can be called obtuse – she was being literal. She had answered my question as I had phrased it. To open the door, I had to ask the wall.

'Please open the door.'

'Complying, please wait.'

A low rumble came from the direction of the door. Any lower and it would have been subsonic. A seam opened in the middle and two wasp-striped panels hinged down and disappeared into the floor, revealing a tunnel with lights strobing away into the distance. Damn, I'd expected I'd be outside. I taxied the Bubble forward, then accelerated, worried I might need airspeed when I emerged from the tunnel. I had no idea at what speed this thing would become airborne, but at 100 kph there was an abrupt lessening of vibration as though we were now drifting airborne. Exactly as a D117 would have been. Odd. We had no wheels.

The wall spoke again:

'Outer doors confirmed open and locked. Take-off may proceed.'

Stupid, stupid, stupid! Idiot, idiot, idiot! I hadn't contemplated there being doors at the other end of the tunnel and had no idea how long it was. The consequences of a craft the size of the Bubble slamming into a set of closed heavy doors at upwards of thirty metres a second didn't bear thinking about. No hero's return, for sure.

We shot out into the sunlight about ten metres above ground level. I throttled up to gain height, and then circled back to find the Tree.

The Tree was behind the tunnel entrance. Flying over the garden, two men were sat on the bench down below, coffee mugs in one hand, grinning and waving.

Jesse and Rusty. They'd known what I was doing all along. Curse them.

The first flight was pure joy. The Bubble handled like my old Jungleskipper, but not quite. It was the perfect Jungleskipper, every part straight from manufacture, fresh, crisp and responsive. It reminded me of my first, precious solo, when the lumbering crate of my training aircraft shed the dead weight of an instructor and leapt sportily into the air. But I couldn't shake the feeling that The Bubble was playing at being a Jungleskipper.

The one inevitable part of any flight is the landing. Land you must. How well you execute each and every landing determines if you'll ever fly again. Or do anything at all.

I'd never landed into a tunnel. Who does? It focussed my mind. But, after three go-arounds when it looked as though I would shortly be doing some impromptu gardening and may in fact have shortened a tree or two, the tunnel walls were flashing past, and I was braking to a halt and breathing again.

Back in the Hangar, it was time for some answers. If Jesse and Rusty wouldn't explain, perhaps The Bubble's wall would.

First things first:

'Who are you?'

'Question not understood.'

I sighed. It was going to be a long morning, I knew it in my bones.

'What is this aircraft?'

'This is an *Imperator* class Globecraft outfitted to Specification 7907/Sports.'

Like that helped. Fancy name though. Impressive. Aspirational. I could visualise the marketing pitch – 'Sport Flyers Win Big in an *Imperator*!'

It was like a puzzle, where you find the shape by filling in where it isn't. I could find out anything I wanted about which control did what and how to use the instruments – most of which I knew anyway – but questions about where and when The Bubble was made were met with: 'Information not available', which felt ridiculous. Other questions on her performance and capabilities, extracted the reply: 'Such information may not be released at present.' It was frustrating, but, taken together, the pattern of replies spoke volumes. Some possibly incriminating information was not on board at all, but some was being held back from me. By whose order? And for how long? Perhaps until I was ready for it?

It had been a tiring morning, but I still needed an answer to my first question. I tried the question again, in different forms. Eventually, paydirt!

'This is the standard Vocal Control Interface of an *Imperator* class Globecraft running on an Augmented Intelligence module v397.2 manufactured by Karell Leptonics.'

Someone hadn't been as thorough as they hoped. Oh, I wished a date had been included – but asking took me straight back to 'Information not available.'

In my heart I'd known, but my head hadn't wanted to accept it. Or was it the other way round? I wasn't sure any longer – it had been a long, hard, few days.

I was talking directly to an intelligent machine. But machines didn't talk, much less have "Augmented Intelligence". Both were specifically banned by Article II of the Creed of the Confraternity, which every child learned in school as soon as they could recite it. The horrors intelligent machines could inflict were made out to be the stuff of myth and fable, although most of us somehow believed they had once existed. I had no doubt I was in over Brother Peter's pay grade.

But my Bubble (I was already thinking of it as 'mine') didn't fit my idea of a Destroyer of Humanity, a Slayer of Worlds. I pressed on. I knew I had my feet well on an all too slippery slope, but religion and heresy and such like had never been my bag.

It took a few more question and answer sessions, but eventually I discovered that, although I was dealing with the standard Vocal Interface, there were well over 200 other options; she didn't have to sound overly mechanical; and didn't have to appear like a cartoon.

We settled on a redhead, five or six years older than me (to give her some gravitas when needed) with a low sultry voice. (I thought Rusty would be pleased.)

Now, I felt as though I had at least one friend in the cockpit. Her name? Well, sorry, but it had to be 'Bubbles', didn't it? You weren't expecting us to take everything seriously, were you?

Ten of the hardest days of my life later, I was ready for my final test flight over the ocean. The news from the Village had not improved and Jesse would have liked us to leave for Threnal earlier. But I flatly refused until I was satisfied I understood well enough what I was dealing with not to kill Rusty and me on the way there or back. That was my responsibility as the pilot, and my decision. He demurred.

Jesse had been right in talking about a simulator. Bubbles had a catalogue of aircraft and could configure the controls and performance to suit any of them. In the air every waking hour, I steadily worked up through dozens and settled on one called a CorpTurb 10000. Apparently, when Bubbles was built, some planets had businesses which ran personal aircraft for their executives. Perhaps in the Inner Stars, I don't know. On Threnador, especially round here, a business was doing well if it could afford a truck which didn't leak fuel out and rain in. The CorpTurb was capable of high subsonic speeds and being for executives, had a luxury unheard of in my earlier flying – a drinks dispenser in the cockpit rear bulkhead which could supply me with limitless coffee! Or something stronger if I wanted to crash. I stuck to coffee.

Jesse had also been right when he said I knew how the cockpit had been created. The clue was in the manufacturer of Bubbles – Karell Leptonics. The cockpit was a distant cousin of my HoloTop, a.k.a. Karthelian camo-armour.

I would dearly have loved to pick something supersonic, but for one problem. The Bubble was silent in flight, but there was no way to disguise the sonic boom created by pushing a perfect sphere through the air at well over the speed of sound. We wanted to arrive undetected, if possible, but the physics of tortured air would not cooperate. There were still some things puzzling and nagging at me. I had no idea what the Bubble's motive power was, or how it stayed aloft. Every cockpit had a fuel gauge of the right type in the right place, but the gauge stayed firmly on 'Full' however long I flew. Also, I'd found Bubbles' catalogue of craft had two large sections I couldn't access. Their existence wasn't hidden, but I couldn't open even a contents list.

To my surprise and relief, I discovered Bubbles herself couldn't fly the Bubble entirely alone. A competent human pilot had to be present on board. Apparently, this was a directive from her First Owner. I assumed that he or she was some sort of flying obsessive: full autonomy was not engineered in. I had no doubt it could have been, but Bubbles assured me it was absent. Aircraft have been equipped with autopilots forever, but Bubbles could not fly off on her own.

I failed entirely to discover anything about the First Owner – age, sex, planet of origin, net worth, anything. Bubbles would not be drawn, but now she spoke with a human voice, I detected a note of respect. Even affection.

Boy, would I have liked to have known how much the First Owner was worth — it must have been a true fortune to be able to buy a machine like this for sport and then deliberately cripple its capabilities. But their idiosyncrasy was my gain — The Bubble needed a pilot, and, right now, I was it!

I was ready to go Oceanic.

KRAKEN

Fifteen thousand meters over the Forest Spaceport, I brought the Bubble round in a slow banking left hand arc, pointed her due east toward the ocean, set up a gentle descent to bring me down to sea level more or less as I crossed the coast, and trimmed her out at exactly four hundred kilometres per hour. This was my last practice flight before Rusty and I were to head to Threnal. I wanted everything to be right.

Early on, I learned the Bubble was next to invisible to the Spaceport's radar. The hull reflected little radio energy, and what it did, it reflected specularly – next to nothing returned back to a simple radar. Which was a relief when larking about in an illegal aircraft.

Without the Signal, from which all navigation was derived, I had to find my way across the ocean to Threnal by compass and dead reckoning. My plan was to head due east across the ocean until landfall, then turn north up the coast until we found Threnal. Fortunately, Threnal was a seaport, finding it should be easy. Keep it simple, get it right.

Today was a practice run. Two hours east out over the ocean, then track back southwest until the coast, and finally turn north. Finding home would be a little more difficult than finding Threnal, because the Spaceport wasn't on the coast. I had to pick up the delta at the end of the river flowing from our lake, then follow the terrain back to the Spaceport and the Tree. But as it was home turf, I wasn't too worried. I didn't want to call the 'Port for a vector in!

Half an hour later, I logged crossing the coast, verified my eastward heading, climbed back up to about 1,000 metres and throttled up to 1,100 kilometres an hour, A little shy of the speed of sound. A real CorpTurb would have been burning prodigious amounts of fuel maintaining this speed in the low dense air, but the Bubble didn't care. I didn't want to be high. There was little chance of being seen from shipping, as Threnador had next to no intercontinental maritime traffic. As a result, available charts were not much better than a school atlas. Any sightings of islands I could use as navigational waypoints could be nothing but useful.

Safely on my way, I stood up, poured myself the first of what I expected to be many cups of coffee then strapped myself back in for the long and hopefully uneventful trip.

The view was spectacular. Born and brought up in the Forest, I marvelled at the sea's mere existence. At this speed in minutes an endless plane of water stretched from horizon to horizon in every direction. Except it wasn't totally flat but crinkled like a crumpled sheet of paper. The wind was blowing up small waves, sometimes topped by white foam, and a long wavelength swell was discernible out in the deep ocean. I had no idea what caused it.

Once, I saw what I identified as an island of white and blue rock off to my right and diverted slightly to better fix its position. But I was wrong, and it would have been singularly useless for navigation anyway. It was a huge block of ice, drifting in the sea. I assumed it had broken off the Southern Icecap, and wished I'd paid more attention in geography classes. Geography was much more interesting when what the teacher had droned on about was floating in front of you.

An hour out, halfway through the first leg, I was bored. I know, I know, but even spectacular vistas become boring when they don't change, and I'm a restless spirit. Sorry.

I'd seen the waves, the swell, the iceberg and occasionally large shoals of fish breaking the surface, which made me disturbed that no-one fished them. Odd. But all I could do was speculate.

Then I started to wonder if I could make my own waves using The Bubble's unseen wake in the air. I told Bubbles to descend to 50 metres, then took control myself. Bubbles was not happy.

'Myah, you are too low. Terrain proximity now critical at this speed.' I was Myah to her now, by the way. Tit-for-tat for naming her Bubbles perhaps.

I pushed down to 20 metres. She sounded a klaxon. I punched it off. Low, fast flight is exhilarating, like a drug.

At 15 metres, I was rewarded with my answer – a V-shaped wake sprung into existence spreading out behind us, as though we were some sort of high speed boat. I craned my neck round to better see my handiwork.

Turning back, I knew I should definitely have paid more attention in class. Especially to the parts about wave heights, ocean swell amplitudes and positive reinforcement effects. I was used to flying over land. You can fly over land, confident it will stay resolutely where it is 99.9% of the time, absent an earthquake. A boring feature of land, maybe, but you can rely on land not to rear up in front of you, in a blue wall topped with white foam.

We skimmed the top of the water, then shot clear on the other side of the wave into the air, water streaming off the windows. Thankfully, the Bubble's hull was stronger than the water and we were physically unharmed.

My pride had taken a dent though, and I shamed-facedly climbed back to one thousand metres and promised Bubbles faithfully that I wouldn't do anything like it again. She accepted my apology, which was welcome. I wouldn't have wanted my control interface to sulk.

I thanked my lucky stars I had had my deep ocean glitch and survived.

An hour later, we finished the leg, and I turned us around, heading a little south of west, aiming to make landfall a couple of hundred kilometres south of the delta, meaning I would be sure to pass over it by heading north up the coast.

There were more shoals of fish visible on the way back – perhaps the time of day or perhaps the angle of the sun. There were even some skipping out of the surface of the water, as though they were trying to fly.

About forty minutes out from landfall, something new appeared – a vast school of huge grey creatures, shaped like fish, but much too big. Of course, I knew they were whales. I'd spotted an isolated one or two, but there had to be a hundred or more here in a ring-like formation.

My curiosity had the better of me. I circled back toward the school, reconfigured the CorpTurb for slow speed flight both to please Bubbles and for better viewing, and descended to 50 metres, well out of range of any errant waves.

The whales had organised themselves into three groups. The smallest, presumably the young, were in the centre of a ring formed by adults. Outside the ring, small groups of other adults were swimming purposefully around, like guards patrolling a fence. Perhaps they were protecting the young against an unseen attacker.

I searched around. There was a large pink shape in the water not far outside the whales' perimeter. It had to be the predator, but what could possibly threaten such a large group of these ocean leviathans?

The answer was blindingly obvious a few minutes later, at least in general terms, but I knew I had paid enough attention in school and read enough afterwards to be certain that nothing in our oceans could threaten either the whales or me. Pride and falls are relevant here.

The whales knew better.

What could threaten those leviathans was something even larger, stronger, and more dangerous. As we approached the pink shape, it sprang up out of the water and four enormous tentacles reached up towards us, spanning the 50-metre separation in an instant. A ghastly slimy mass, covered in suckers, filled the windscreen, and we were dragged down toward the water by the weight of the creature, with it trailing behind as the Bubble's momentum carried us all forward.

We crashed into the water and started to roll like a ball. Bubbles flashed some lights, sounded a few klaxons and a loud horn, I suppose in case I hadn't noticed something was amiss.

We were definitely rolling, which was a most peculiar feeling. I felt strangely safe and undisturbed in my strapping, but one moment the sky was above me, the next it was replaced by the sea. Then the sky again. Then the sea. Water, suckers and pieces of flesh slid down the windows. I had no idea what to do. Something roared. The creature made one more grab for us, but then it was gone.

The rolling stopped, and we were bobbing incongruously peacefully: a piece of high tech, deep ocean driftwood, four hundred kilometres from land.

CorpTurb's fly from runways, not oceans. Listlessly, I tried to apply some thrust, but nothing happened.

I was trying to form a well-phrased question to Bubbles, when she beat me to it.

'Emergency craft configuration change mandated. User configuration temporarily over-ridden. Native flight mode engaged.' A very, hard, matter-of-fact tone of voice.

We started to speed along the water. I glanced left – I half expected us to have floats, like a seaplane. I doubted we needed them, and there was indeed nothing there. For the first time, there was no simulated aircraft visible outside. We lifted off the water and climbed back to the course and speed we had been following. The CorpTurb reappeared around me, and I had control again.

I was shaking. I'd never been as close to something as horrible or felt as close to death. But I'd found out something else about Bubbles. She might not be able to fly the craft entirely alone, but she could act alone when needed. And I had learned a lesson. I knew much less about what lived on my own planet than I had believed I did.

I found out one more small thing, which I filed away for the future. I was too shaken to start a tedious question and answer routine with Bubbles right then. On the top of the dashboard, exactly where I'd put it before investigating the whales, was my last cup of coffee, still with the coffee inside. How was that possible? Did it have anything to do with the feeling of the world spinning around me, not me spinning through it?

And what was 'Native Flight Mode'? What did the phrase even mean?

The remaining forty minutes to the coast were blessedly calm, and finding my way home went exactly as planned. Back in the Hangar, I walked around, expecting to find traces of the horror. A sucker, a tentacle, an eye or two. Nothing. Blasted off by the water and airflow, I assumed.

Upstairs, Rusty and Jesse were preparing our farewell meal before the next day's departure.

'You're back – almost spot on the time you planned. Everything go OK?'

I paused. Visions of an unexpected wave, a school of protective cetaceans, and a nameless horror from the deep ocean flashed in front of my eyes. No, no use worrying the troops on the eve of battle. Keep it all to myself.

'Yes, fine. I had a whale of a time. Everything went swimmingly.'

NIGHT PASSAGE

We were four hours into the crossing, and it was close to midnight. I aimed to make landfall at first light, making sure we would have a good view of what lay below.

Rusty was making coffee and I was staring into the dark, dark sky. There was no trace of any lights, and nothing to obstruct the view, from horizon to horizon.

'What can you see, lass?' Rusty handed me a cup of hot coffee.

I gestured up at the misty arc running right overhead, splitting the sky in two, like a monochrome rainbow.

'The Galaxy. The Milky Way. Wondering which of the stars have inhabited planets.'

'Ah, the old Frogspawn Nebula itself.' He grinned, taking his seat.

'The what?'

That was a new one on me: Milky Way and Galaxy, obviously, Home System, occasionally, and sometimes The Confraternity, muddling astronomy and politics. But not 'Frogspawn'.

'Old Navy term, from the diagrams of the Portal network. It's a good analogy.'

'A good analogy? The Galaxy is like frogspawn?' I laughed.

'Yes. What does frogspawn look like?'

I imagined the surface of a pond in the breeding season for the little amphibians. There were a lot of frogs around at home.

'Little jelly blobs jammed together, each with a little black blob in it.'

'There you go. The Portal Network. The Human Galaxy.'

I tried to sound quizzical, sensing he was playing with me, and hoping he'd take pity and explain what in the in the name of everything holy he was blethering about. I even wondered if he'd found the way to pour beer out of the coffee dispenser.

'They don't teach about this either, do they? Let's take a few steps back. Do you know about relativity?'

'Of course I do! Linking of space and time, the constant speed of light. Nothing can travel faster than light in normal space. I've known those rules forever.'

'Good girl. As has humanity, as far as anyone can tell. OK. How do we travel between the star systems of the Confraternity? They are scattered through two hundred thousand light years of space.'

I started to reply by saying, obviously, we did it through the Portals, but felt, for all his jocular manner, Rusty was asking me a deeper question. I didn't know in any detail how the Portals did what they did – whisk starships across the Galaxy in a heartbeat. Nobody had ever taught it in school.

'Through some sort of sub-space?' I remembered Jesse mentioning sub-space when he talked about The Signal. 'Or is relativity wrong somehow?'

'Relativity is fine. Still good after thousands of years. You can't travel faster than light in this universe. Perhaps in any universe.'

I waited.

'It's long, long ago. No-one knows nowadays, but the first people to travel between the stars probably took years, decades, centuries even. Depending on where they lived, and how far apart the stars were there.'

Right then I was learning more about what I didn't know than anything else. I'd never considered where the first people lived or how they travelled from star to star. Let alone about a time when they couldn't.

'Those journeys must have been hard, but tolerable for some exploration and adventure. But they couldn't support a civilisation, let alone an empire. You can't trade when it takes decades to deliver anything. You can't run an empire if people die before they receive instructions from the emperor.'

'So how do we do it? Because I know ships fly from Threnador to anywhere in the Confraternity in a few days. To Centrum, say.' The capital world.

'Well, you can't travel faster than light in this universe. But which universe is Centrum in?'

Now I was sure he'd found out how to dispense beer. In bulk.

'What are you talking about? It's in our universe of course! It's up there.' I pointed halfway up the arc, toward the Central Stars. I knew roughly where Centrum was.

'Well, yes and no. You're right. Centrum is there. But it's not in our Universe. Threnador's Universe. It was once, but it isn't anymore.'

'Go on.' I had no idea what else to say. It was a ridiculously outlandish idea, and I couldn't even frame a question.

'Long ago, long before even the First Empire, people understood that there was no way around relativity. Then someone, whose name should be carved on every moon of every planet, but has been lost, examined the problem another way. Humanity wanted to travel between stars in their universe without each trip taking years. Which is impossible. But there's nothing stopping us travelling as fast as we want between stars in different universes. So, they gave all the stars their own private universes.'

First Empire? What was the First Empire? Forget it. Stay focussed, girl. This is incredible stuff.

'How?'

'I've no idea, Mihana. I doubt my old brain's big enough. They travelled from star to star slowly, set up a little bubble universe at each star, built a Portal in each bubble and then they could reach any other bubble universe instantaneously.'

I paused for a while. I had even less idea than Rusty how such an undertaking could be tried, but I could tell it must have been an immense project.

'But it must have taken hundreds of thousands of years? To cover the Galaxy?'

'Well, depending on where they started. If they started from the centre, they could have done it in about 90,000 years if they had a lot of very fast ships. But yes, you're right in what you say. It took a long, long time.'

I tried to imagine people starting a 100,000-year project. It was beyond my comprehension. Sometimes I can't plan beyond lunch.

'I suppose it would have been done gradually. By different people until eventually the Galaxy was covered.'

'It's not entirely covered even now – only the human-inhabited worlds and some others, valuable for one reason or another.'

'OK.' I'd assumed starships could go to any star but was now discovering that that wasn't true.

'So, why the Frogspawn Nebula?' Back to what had started this conversation. An eternity ago. Perhaps in another universe.

'If you draw a cartoon diagram of one of these universes, it's a little bubble with a blob for the star at the centre. When there are a lot of them close together, like in the Central Stars, the universes are jammed right up against each other like individual frogspawns. So, some wag, sometime, called the Galaxy the Frogspawn Nebula and it stuck with spacers.'

I shook my head. This was a God-like achievement, parcelling the Galaxy up into separate universes for no better reason than humanity's travelling convenience, and the Navy made it into a joke. Bloody military. No respect.

'So why aren't we taught about this?'

'No idea. Ask Brother Peter sometime. He was a Portal Engineer.'

Brother Peter? He of the chickens? No, surely not.

'This has something to do with The Signal, hasn't it? Why didn't Jesse tell me all this.'

'Oh, Jesse only ever tells people what he needs them to know. It's an old habit from his earlier life, from who he was and what he did.'

'And what did he do? Or aren't you going to tell me?' I waited for an answer from Rusty.

'No,' he said, 'I'm not. Not yet anyway.' There was finality to his tone brooking no argument, but at least he'd left a door ajar.

'Alright. How does The Signal come into this?' I had to tap this well of knowledge while Rusty was feeling chatty. I'd never had a chance like this before. I might not have one again.

'Well, now all the stars we might want to visit are sitting in their own bubble universes. What are the consequences?'

'We aren't limited to the speed of light in the space between?' I was hesitant, knowing he had effectively told me so, but was now hinting at something more.

'Quite right – there is no 'space' between the universes. But does 'space' exist?'

'No, of course not!' This was grade school science. 'It's part of spacetime.' I paused as what he was driving at dawned on me.

'There's no time between them either is there? They are their own universes: they have their own space and time, not connected to each other.'

'Got it in one, girl!' Rusty grinned approvingly. 'The Portals can take you through both space and time. When you enter one, you must tell it where you want to go in space – i.e., which bubble, but also when you want to arrive. Past, present or future. They are Time Machines. At least, they would be if the Builders had let them be.'

I wanted to stop and tell him this was crazy, but he obviously hadn't finished.

'Uncontrolled two-way time travel is the worst of news, scientists say. Messes up something called causality. It's also a lousy way to run a civilisation.'

'Why?'

'Because people would be jumping backwards and forwards, undoing events, changing history, making killings on the stock market or the races. It would be a mess.'

'So, what did they do?'

'Put a filter on. When you tell the Portal when you want to arrive, it must be in the future, even if by a micro-second. Never in the past. The Builders will let you move forward, but never back. It's hard-wired into the Network – it can't be changed.'

'So, The Signal?'

'Is transmitted throughout the Galaxy to lock all the Portals together, therefore there's one common time reference. When you enter a Portal, you use the Signal to work out when you want to arrive. Without the Signal, entering a Portal is a throw of the dice. You might have the time wrong.'

'And, if you do?'

Rusty shrugged, with a fiendish grin on his face.

'Who knows? They say some ships have tried to go backwards – none have ever returned.'

That sounded very grim. Very final.

'Why do it this complicated way?'

'Who knows? When you build a Portal Network, you can do it differently.'

I dreamt for a moment: 'Mihana's Mammoth Multi-Universe Transport. In a hurry? No worry! Arrive before you left.' No, perhaps not. The maths would be too hard.

'One last question, then. Why does this affect ordinary life down here on Threnador?'

'Apart from the end of interstellar trade if there's no Signal, you mean? Human laziness, I guess. Because there was this rock-solid, defined, reliable time source, people must have started to rely on it for other things. Now every machine needing to know the time uses it. Every business transaction, every timetable, every warehouse, every hospital. Every clock. They all rely on it being there. It always is. Until now.'

Rusty grimaced, then went to fetch more coffee. My lesson was over.

I stared out at the stars again. But they weren't the stars and the sky I'd known before. Now it was artificial in some way, remodelled by humanity over a time span I couldn't comprehend. Perhaps a quarter of a million years of interstellar travel? And no-one told us? What was school for? Who had the right to hold it all back?

I had always felt small when I considered the vast space overhead. Now I had a hint of the vast time it represented as well.

Perhaps it would be better to be a frog.

THRENAL

As we rushed eastward, dawn crept up out of the eastern horizon, and wiped the Frogspawn Nebula from the sky. The vast vistas of time, space and human history disappeared. Time to stop contemplating the infinite: time to concentrate.

A faint line appeared on the horizon, splitting sea and sky. The coast. I slowed us down and turned north to follow the coast at about a thousand metres altitude.

Rusty had an old map on his lap and was staring ahead with a dedication and concentration I had not seen from him before.

We were following a long ribbon of sand, fringed with palm trees. Offshore, small groups of dolphins were swimming up the coast, and the occasional large fish – sharks, perhaps? Hunting for their breakfast, I supposed.

The minutes ticked by. I was as sure as I could be. We were well south of Threnal and heading toward it, but as time went on, doubts started nibbling at the corners of my mind.

'Mihana – do you see the delta ahead, with the three islands in the centre making an equilateral triangle? It's the mouth of the Kithani River, isn't it? Here, look.'

He jabbed a finger down at the map. The islands he was pointing at had to be what we saw ahead. Reaching the delta, I circled over them. They still looked right.

'Take us upriver for a while – there should be a long island about ten kilometres away.'

I turned east. Ten kilometres later, there it was. One long island, as ordered.

'Yay! We made it!' I had intended to make some cool, nonchalantly confident remark, but it didn't come out right. Look, if you'd flown ten thousand kilometres in the dark across open ocean with no navigation instruments except a compass and old map, you'd be pleased to arrive pretty much exactly where you wanted, wouldn't you? Yes, of course. I cheered.

Rusty patted me on the back.

'Good work. We're about three hundred kilometres south of Threnal.'

I glowed.

'Great. I'll regain the coast, and we'll be there in about half an hour.'

Now I was excited. Threnal. I had seen pictures in books and wanted to see the reality – the lights, the skyscrapers. Crowds of people. All rather different from the Forest.

As expected, we met a highway a little way out. But it wasn't thronged with traffic as I'd expected. People heading to work, food and goods moving about. It was practically deserted and badly potholed. Occasionally, a truck had been abandoned in a roadside ditch, half hidden by overgrowth.

From overhead, the outer residential areas appeared normal, but with a surprising lack of people in the streets.

When we reached the heart of the city – the Central Business District or CBD I had learned about in school – it was obvious something was very, very wrong in Threnal. And had been for a long time. The Forest, being a forest, didn't have a CBD. I was open to correction, but I was fairly sure the tops of the skyscrapers shouldn't have crumbled away, exposing their supporting frameworks, and the glass in their windows shouldn't be broken and cracked, sometimes missing altogether. These were no shiny temples to commerce – more the ruins of the churches of some forgotten religion.

'Rusty, what has happened here? This hasn't happened in the few weeks since the Signal stopped, has it?'

'No, it hasn't. This was years in the making. I don't know what happened. I wasn't expecting the glittering city you were, but I wasn't expecting this, either. Can you take us down lower?'

'Not with the Bubble configured like this. We need something slower, ideally with a hover capability. I'll check though. Bubbles, can you reconfigure to a HoverProp 78?'

'No, Myah. User change of craft configuration is not permitted during flight.'

I thought as much, but there was an irritating ambiguity hiding at the edges of her answer. I'd asked if she could change configuration: she'd answered that I couldn't.

'OK. Rusty, we need to land.'

We had discussed this endlessly back in the Tree. How were we going to land without drawing unwanted attention to ourselves? The CorpTurb needed a runway. There are runways at airports and spaceports, but there are also people with attitudes. And authority. And guns. Not good.

We didn't need to be down long. Putting her on a highway was a possibility, but we'd ruled it out because of the traffic. Well, traffic wasn't a worry now, but the potholes and rusting wrecks were.

Threnal had one big joint military and civilian aerospaceport, and if anywhere was going to give us trouble, it would. But there was also a smaller field to the east, used by business traffic. We'd decided to try our luck in blagging our way in as a business trip from one of the northern cities. Nothing we'd seen made the possibility any less attractive.

We headed north for half an hour, then I turned south again and set us up on the sort of approach a business aircraft might adopt.

'Threnal Eastern, this is CorpTurb 180 out of Norstar, two hundred klicks north of the field, requesting joining instructions to land.'

I waited for some bumptious oik to tell me off about lack of a flight plan and how the pattern was full, and I couldn't possibly land until next week. Or, much less likely, a friendly voice vectoring me for a straight-in landing.

Nothing. Silence. An empty channel, which persisted all the way until I had the field in sight.

'Now what?' Rusty asked.

'Put her down, I suppose,' I replied, 'but I'm going to make a pass down the runway to check out what's what and give them a chance to signal visually in case their comms have gone down. Most everything is down around here, it looks like.'

We shot straight down the runway as low as I dared. Did Bubbles play external sound effects, or would we pass silently by anyone in the Tower, ghostlike?

It was a needless worry – it was obvious at a glance there was no-one in the Tower. Windows were broken, the outside door was hanging off its hinges, and what had once been an office or reception for arriving and departing VIPs was an empty shell, paint peeling off the walls. There was an aircraft on the apron, bleached in the sun. It hadn't been painted, or indeed moved, in years.

The runway wasn't much better. Small animals were grazing at the edges where the concrete was a crumbling away. The surface was broken and potholed like the roads, and there were a couple of large holes. They might have been craters.

'Rusty, this isn't good. There's no landing path there that I can see. We'll have to try the main port.'

'I wouldn't. I had a good view over there as we left Threnal. I saw aircraft moving, and some spacecraft that appear operational. Including one like the surface shuttle from a Confraternity Dreadnought. It isn't going to be coffee and biscuits there.'

Landing it was then. I'd do my best and hope Bubbles would pick up the pieces. Or, even better, stop us breaking into pieces.

Like most landings, it went fine until we reached the ground. We bumped and jumped over cracks and gaps, and I did my best to avoid putting a simulated wheel into a pothole. But I couldn't miss one big crater. Our nosewheel went in and then the Bubble was cartwheeling nose over tail down the runway.

Rusty yelled and grabbed the dashboard to brace himself. I'd been here before, of course and was more relaxed. Once again, it was all strangely calm. Sky swapped with ground and ground with sky. The outside view of the CorpTurb disappeared, and the Bubble rolled madly down the runway, until, with what should have been a sickening crunch, we came to rest in a particularly large depression. We must have looked like a huge marble in some giant's solitaire board.

Silence reigned. With a fluency belying his years, Rusty unclipped himself, checked I was alive, then started to head for the hatch, shouting to me to follow.

'Why, what's the rush?'

'In case there's a fire.'

'Fire? Why should there be a fire? We don't burn fuel.'

'Well, in case it collapses.'

'It isn't going to collapse. We've landed, that's all. A little roughly, perhaps.'

'A little roughly!!' Rusty squeaked. 'That wasn't a landing, that was a crash. I know, I've been in crashes. Seen too many good people killed in crashes.'

It wasn't the time to ask him where and why. Then it sunk in with him. I was still sitting calmly and had been throughout. I was trying not to smirk, but I must have failed.

'Wait a minute. Why are we still alive, after a crash like that? You knew what was going to happen, didn't you? How did you know?'

The ocean, the whales, the giant pink monster and the tentacles flashed through my mind. Nah, keep him guessing. A little mystery from a girl perks the male interest, although Rusty was a bit old for such interest, admittedly.

'Rusty, that's a need-to-know issue. You don't need to know.'

I was afraid he'd explode. Obviously, I was the one who didn't need to know things, not him. We'd see about that.

Then Bubbles broke the tension.

'Myah, choose better places to land, will you?', rather unfairly. Then, formally: 'All subsystems verified undamaged. Previous user configuration unsuitable for departure. Configuration choice awaited.'

'HoverProp 78, please, Bubbles. Come on, Rusty. We're fine. Make us a coffee and we'll go back and check out the city properly.'

WALKING THE WALK

Coffee drunk, maps and charts pored over once more then packed away, we strapped ourselves in, and headed back to the city.

'Bubbles, can you run silent? Or at least quietly?'

I still didn't want to be seen, and I knew if we made no sound, our chances of passing unobserved were hugely increased. Do you even glance up into the sky when walking the street? Most people don't. Sometimes they barely open their eyes at all, navigating by some inner compass, following ley lines or something.

'I'll do my best, Myah. Fly slowly, I can't repeal the wind. It causes noise.'

It was the first time she'd admitted a physical limitation – a welcome chink in her armour – even if wasn't unreasonable.

Lower and slower, it was plain that the city wasn't entirely deserted, nor were all the buildings as ruined as they had appeared. The lower floors of some of the wrecked skyscrapers were still occupied and relatively intact. This prompted Rusty to start debating whether the city had lost its power supply, followed by a lecture about how skyscrapers were impossible without lifts and air-conditioning, because they were too high for people to climb and too tall to keep the air fresh. I wasn't at all interested in skyscraper design, but I was sure he was right: I knew I'd be less than amused to climb forty storeys, then struggle to smash a window to let some air in to let me stop sweating. By the state of the buildings, others felt the same way.

He was right about the power, too. There were no lights anywhere – no streetlights, no shop displays. I didn't like what would happen when night fell. I wasn't planning on flying between skyscrapers in the pitch dark.

We spiralled inwards towards the centre, until it was obvious that Threnal had turned into a set of small villages. There were people in isolated clusters of streets and no-one in between. I knew it hadn't grown up from villages – it was built as a company town, from the centre out. The Company Town, in fact. But as it broke down, it had turned into old style villages.

'Rusty, this is all very interesting, and I'd love to know what happened to cause it all, and how they've kept it quiet from us, but we came here to find out why the Signal has stopped. Do you know where we are, and where the Company HQ is?'

'More or less. Carry on down this avenue and we should come to a large park. Turn left there and the boulevard runs down to HQ.'

'OK.'

Well, the large park was now used for grazing sheep and there was some sort of makeshift market in one corner, but otherwise he was right. I followed the boulevard for about a klick, idly wondering how I had ended up flying by following street signs, when a building stood out from the shabbiness around. It was clean, windows were intact and there was even a stylish logo glowing brightly near the top of one wall.

Rusty has seen it as well, and was gesturing me to carry on towards it, when he started, stared down at the road and froze.

'Get off this road! Right now! As fast as you can!'

I jammed the stick over, pulled us into a side street and stopped. I spun Bubbles around to face the road we had left moments before.

A platoon of Confraternity troops in street armour, carrying rifles, marched past the intersection.

I prayed to every god I'd learned of to stop them seeing us. I didn't have Rusty down as much of a god-botherer, but he was doing the same.

The thing about praying is you never know whether it works. At least I don't. Sometimes I get what I want, and sometimes I don't. But, in the first case, was the world in fact shifted off its course to accommodate my selfish foibles? In the second, was my request regretfully declined to make room for Bigger Plans? Or did the universe carry on as it would have anyway, inanimate, and uncaring?

It's odd what goes through your mind in an eternal microsecond, while holding your breath and willing your heart to stop making such a loud beating noise. Stop it, heart! They'll hear you on the street!

Then the soldiers passed the intersection and disappeared. For whatever reason.

'Thank the stars,' said Rusty letting out a breath so large that it ran the risk of blowing his moustache off.

'Those rifles probably wouldn't have hurt Bubbles, anyway.' I wanted to sound upbeat, cool about this turn of events.

'No, but they'd have come after us with something which might. And we don't need to be shot at, thank you.'

'I know, I know. What are they doing here anyway?'

Back home we have Jack, an elderly constable who spends most of his time sleeping in the sun. I was sure city policing needed a bit more heft, but platoons of armed troops? Most of the people in the street weren't well-fed enough to sustain a decent riot for long enough for anyone to notice they'd kicked off.

'No idea. They were well over the top for this town. Back us away, carefully.'

I shook my head but bit my tongue. How could I back away 'carefully'? I was piloting an aircraft built with illegal technology, currently disguised as a HoverProp but totally silent, unlike every other HoverProp I'd heard of; the two of us were flying over a city neither of us knew first hand, armed with maps dating back to before the buildings started falling apart; I had no permission to be flying there; and to cap it all, down below, armed soldiers were stomping about on street corners, dressed for a fight. In fact, dressed to kill. Literally.

I edged us up, seeking safety in altitude, and we carried on exploring. I didn't have much hope we'd get away with it, but we did. I was right earlier. People don't look up. I could have been flying a tour liner of aliens from another galaxy and no-one would have been any the wiser. Perhaps we were hiding in plain sight – the good city folk of Threnal having assumed that if you were flying a HoverProp you had a right to do it. I wasn't sure the troops would have the same opinion.

But by the end of the afternoon, we clearly needed a different approach. Rusty had come to the same conclusion:

'Mihana, anywhere closer than a klick to the HQ building there are troops. Probably elsewhere as well.'

'I know. We need to land.'

'Well, we knew we couldn't land on the HQ roof.'

'I know that too. But I wasn't expecting soldiers and a wrecked city. I expected us to blend in. Pretend to be tourists.'

I'd like to be a tourist – someone with enough money to visit a strange place for no better reason than to gawp at it. But not this time, as it was turning out.

'We flew over an abandoned warehouse a few blocks back. We can hide Bubbles there.'

'Hear that Bubbles? You're moving up in the world – from a hole under a tree to an abandoned warehouse.'

'Thanks Myah. What more could a girl want?'

Bubbles didn't sound happy; I could hear her pain.

Flying lower had revealed more life than was obvious on the first day: walking around opened up an unseen world.

Hidden in funny little corners and down alleyways were a network of little shops and businesses, selling all manner of goods. Mostly necessities, but a few luxuries. In some places, there were people – mainly women – who were obviously selling services. I avoided those neighbourhoods. Too much risk of unfortunate misunderstandings. Back home, things were more discreet, but we had a spaceport, with lonely crews passing through. The trade wasn't unknown.

My favourite discovery was in a tiny gap between two buildings. A thin old man with wiry hair and a goatee beard had fixed an awning across the gap and had set up a little workshop under its shelter. At the back, well hidden in shadow, was a pile of scrap metal: old pots and pans, pieces of discarded machinery, a bicycle wheel. Some sort of forge or kiln must have been outside, further into the alley, because there was a smell of hot metal and chemicals drifting out. In the middle of the workshop was a low workbench with a vice, a tiny anvil and a collection of tools lovingly arrayed on racks and clips. They must have been the old man's pride and joy: they were definitely his livelihood. He sat at the workbench on a threadbare cushion on top of a rickety stool, hammering and bending the pieces of old scrap to make the goods he displayed at the front, near the street: beautiful plates, jugs and vases, multi-coloured, and polished to a shine. There was magic in his hands.

'You like it, Missy?' The old man had seen me studying a small pot with a hooked spout, the twin of one Mum had in her kitchen at home. A coffee pot.

'Yes, my mother has one like it.' How could that be? Odd.

'Where you from, Missy? Your clothes aren't from here.'

I hesitated. We were trying not to attract attention. But I had already said too much to back away.

'Oh, a little farming village on the Second Continent. Here on business. Trade.'

'We don't have many visitors from there anymore. Not since...' He paused. 'Well, not since They came. But I sold some of those jugs to a trader from your way maybe ten years ago.'

Perhaps that was how Mum had come by hers – perhaps one had found its way onto Benny's trinket stall back in the Market years back. I studied it again, harder.

'You want to buy? I give you good price.'

If I ever talk about taking up poker, wrestle me to the ground and sit on my head until the mood passes. I'd be hopeless.

'No, I don't think so,' I said, knowing full well my face was saying the opposite.

'Yes, you do. I see. For you, two stellars.'

I kept a calm expression on my face. It would have cost many times as much back home, and not only because it was a rare ornament from far away. Everyday crockery cost more – what had happened in Threnal to cause a craftsman to sell his wares for so little?

But I knew I should haggle – I didn't want to be taken for a rich girl who threw money around on a whim.

'A crown.'

'You joke with me – I have children to feed. Make it a diadem.'

Grandchildren, possibly. If he still had children needing feeding, either he'd not aged well, or I admired his luck. And stamina.

'Alright.' I dug into a pocket and handed over two coins. The old man, suspicious, bit one, and then shrugged. The coins disappeared into a wallet, and he pulled out my change. He wrapped the little coffee pot in a tattered piece of paper, as though wrapping a fine jewel, then passed it over.

'Here you are. Exactly like the one at home.' I took it, choking up as fond memories of Mum, the Forest, Boss' bar bubbled up. Even Jay. And Darvee. When would I see them again? Would I ever see them again? By now, I must have broken so many rules I'd be an old woman before they finished reading the charge sheet, never mind what the sentence was.

'Thanks.' I turned to go. The old man called me back.

'Missy! Take care, missy. Your clothes, your coins, your voice. You stand out. And no-one comes around here from the other continents anymore. Don't tell me how or why you're here. I'm safer if I don't know. You're safer if I don't know.'

'And you did pay me three times what the jug was worth.' He gave a little grin.

I grinned back sheepishly.

'It was worth it for the lesson. Be safe yourself. And take care of your children.'

I took more care myself after the jug-maker, tweaked my HoloTop settings to appear more like what the locals were wearing – Urban Threadbare was this year's style – and warned Rusty. We decided on a cover story. We were from a town outside Norstar, not the Forest. It was a shock to discover intercontinental travel had dried up completely.

Rusty didn't have a Forest accent anyway, and his unusual beard meant he'd stand out anywhere. He was too obvious for anyone to believe he was trying to hide. He and I split up most of the time – he was more into planning a way past the guards, and he spent his time scouting round the Enclave searching out weaknesses. The military mind, I supposed.

We would meet up at the end of each day. And we had brought small radios to keep in contact if we had to. I configured mine to call Bubbles if things ever were totally out of hand. I had no idea whether there was any point, but perhaps it would help.

Unlike Rusty, I preferred to saunter around, talk to people as much as possible and try and understand how Threnal worked now. I hoped I might find a hint of a way in to The Enclave. Hide in a delivery truck, or something.

But by the time we'd been on the ground a week, the whole business was becoming tedious. It was no easier to approach the HQ building on the ground than it was from the air. There was a ring of guards – rather more of an obstacle than a dozy watchman on the front door. Which was what I'd hoped for and expected.

But life wasn't all bad. You can't skulk around street corners all day for days on end. You have to relax sometimes, and early on I'd found a bar which was open for business and selling something passing for booze. Boss wouldn't have sold it, but beggars can't be choosers.

It was a little way from what I now described as The Enclave. In the next of Threnal's villages, I supposed. I'd turned a corner into a dusty, litter-strewn back street when I heard a familiar sound – the clank of empty bottles being loaded into crates. A half open wooden door was covered in fading, peeling paint. Nothing to say it was a bar, but I felt sure it was.

I walked in.

Walking down the stairs to the bar, I had no idea what to expect. A tense silence as a stranger walked in would not be good – a bar full of scarred and tattooed thugs who hadn't seen a woman for months would be worse.

It was an anti-climax. The place was dark, lit by three oil lamps hanging over the bar, and there were a couple of Asteroid tables near the door. No-one was playing. Their dark blue baize was torn, and no sign of any cues. I doubted there was a full set of Asteroids in the machines anyway.

At the one end of the bar, a middle-aged couple were sat talking to each other. At the other, a young man was nursing a glass of beer and another glass with some sort of shot. Plainly, they weren't his first. He was tall, well built, with tousled black hair and an unkempt beard. He was wearing a red and black check jacket. The whole effect was of someone who might jump up and fell a tree at a moment's notice. There were three empty stools in the gap between the customers. I sat on the middle one. The barmaid sauntered over.

'What are you having?'

Sitting on the customer's side makes you grasp how maddening such a simple question is. My behind had hit the stool moments before, there wasn't a bottle or a keg in sight, much less a label, and anyway I could barely see my hand in front of my face. Asking for a bottle of Forester's Best Ale would blow my cover story before I started.

'A beer. Not too strong.' I wanted a drink; I didn't want to wind up drunk.

'You're not from round here, are you?'

Screaming Nebulae, what I had done now? I'd spoken five words in a darkened room, and she knew I wasn't local. Don't believe the holovids. Ever. Merging into the background to scout out a strange town is seriously difficult.

'We have one beer in Threnal nowadays. Where do they still have a choice?' She poured a glass from a large jug behind the bar.

I muttered about being from a farming village outside Norstar and talked about how good the local brewery was.

'I must move there – sounds better than this dump.'

I nodded and swigged my beer. I couldn't talk while I was drinking. At least I couldn't make things worse.

Slowly, things became easier. The couple started talking to me, and at last I had a break. They weren't from a village next door to anywhere in my cover story. They didn't insist I must know their long-lost uncles and aunts. They had a daughter my age and told me more about her complicated love life than she'd have been happy to find out they knew, but no matter. I batted off a few drunken advances from the guy at the other end of the bar. He was quite nice, in fact. I made a note to be friendly to him another day, preferably before he was too friendly with the shots.

Some locals drifted in and out. A few even played Asteroids. Apparently, you can play without a full set of Asteroids, after all. You make up new rules and call it Meteors.

I don't want you to assume I spent all my time in the bar, but I made it a regular call for the next few days. I felt I could relax, and I was learning a lot. More than when I was outside, to be honest.

I learnt the history of the place from the male half of the couple who were there on my first visit. He had been a history teacher, although most of the schools were closed now. But he had a special interest in the history and development of Threnal. Paydirt.

The *Honest Agent* was the bar's name, which had to be someone's idea of a joke. No agent is ever honest. It was old, dating back to when Threnal was first settled, centuries past. The *Honest Agent* had been many things – bar, restaurant, nightclub, wine cellar, and now back to bar again. It was a warren of a place on several floors, full of dead-end passages, blocked off doors and unused rooms. In one corner, Chathray – the lone guy at the bar – showed me a wood panelled wall covered in photographs of his family. Apparently, they, or he, owned the place in some way. Or didn't, quite. He was rather vague.

I was more friendly with Chathray now. He had smartened up his act since we first met, cut his hair and trimmed his beard. Most of the time, he swapped his red and black check jacket for a well-cut brown leather number worn over a blue shirt made of some tough cloth. Cutting his hair revealed slight flecks of grey, which he seemed too young for – I guessed he was around my age. He had an infectious smile and a stare that could see through to your soul. The bar was too dark for them, but if he had worn sunglasses, he could have been one of those silently dangerous characters in a holovid, who wins all the girls' hearts, solves the mystery and kills the bad guy in the final act. Perhaps he had tidied himself up to impress me. I hoped so, and, if so, it was working.

The first settlers in what would be Threnal had made a living mining and the bar had done a brisk trade bringing buyers and sellers of ore together, quenching their thirst and lubricating their deals.

Those early days ended long ago. As the settlements grew, The Company had moved in, chosen Threnal as its base and taken over all off-world trade. By the time the mines were exhausted, Threnal was an administrative town, running the Company's operations all over the planet. It had been rich then – the Threnal I had been taught about and had believed still existed. But when the Empire fell and the Confraternity took over after the Wars, Threnal started to fade. Its new masters disapproved of luxury and frivolity and gradually squeezed the wealth and the soul out of the city. Whole neighbourhoods fell into decay and ruin, as Rusty and I had seen.

But the final blow was recent. Slightly more than a year before, a new contingent of Confraternity troops had landed. Then a Dreadnought apparently arrived in orbit. The one whose surface shuttle Rusty had seen, I guessed.

Up until then, there had been a small garrison in Threnal: it was rarely seen off base except on R&R. Troops were not necessary. These new arrivals were highly disciplined, well-armed, efficient and brutal. And they were searching for something or someone. People were rounded up, interrogated, executed. Others fled the town in panic. The few who remained weren't enough to keep Threnal functioning, so the city economy collapsed. Only The Enclave had reliable power, and everything was in short supply.

Nothing about the situation sounded good at all. Efficient, brutal troops were not what our ramshackle, understaffed expedition needed to deal with.

But however bad things become, bars and cafes still cling on. Wherever people live they want three things: food, company and…Well, you know the third. And you can usually find all three in a bar if you want.

I was sitting at the bar waiting for Rusty when matters took a turn for the worse. Rusty visited the *Honest Agent* now, enjoyed the beer, amazingly, and mercifully, but oddly, stayed off the topic of the Battle of the Dahnian Rift. Especially when the history teacher was around. Rusty should have been there half an hour earlier.

While waiting, I had been fending off Chathray. He wanted the third thing; knew a nice quiet room we could go to and wasn't I interested? Well, to be truthful, yes. At a better time and in a better place, I would definitely have been open to persuasion, but not amongst the spiders and the damp in one of the old wine cellars, thank you. Which was probably what he had in mind. No-one went big on romantic wooing in Threnal nowadays, from what I could tell.

There was a commotion at the top of the stairs, the door crashed open, and Rusty bounced through it, blood pouring from a cut above his eye. Someone shouted from the staircase:

'Where's the girl? The outsider girl who's been nosing around. We've come for her.'

Heavy footsteps were running down the stairs. Everyone in the bar studied at their drinks closely, ignoring me. Somehow, we'd been caught. The Confraternity had us.

Wrong. If only.

A half dozen or more men pushed into the bar. They weren't disciplined, efficient but brutal, troops. The scarred and tattooed thugs who hadn't seen a woman for months had finally turned up, and now they'd seen me.

I woke up with my head feeling as though I'd been drinking Boss's whisky non-stop for a week. I remembered a scuffle in the bar, then being pulled every which way, and finally my head crashing into something or something crashing into my head. Now here I was. Which was where?

I couldn't move much. I was sitting on a floor with my hands tied behind me, around a pole or strut. Raised voices with rough accents were nearby

Rusty was lying on the floor, trussed up like a chicken. I couldn't tell if he was conscious or not. Seeing him trussed up was oddly relieving. At least he wasn't dead. No-one trusses up a corpse. Not far from him was Chathray, also tied up, but not as thoroughly. Seeing him was a surprise. What was he doing here? Why had he been grabbed? He was a random guy in a bar, nothing to do with Rusty and me.

I still had no idea where I was. The room resembled a deserted shop, long, long deserted. There were shelves, a counter. But it was airless, dank, roughhewn, and dark. A couple of crude lamps spluttered on the floor. The walls, deep in shadow, weren't normal walls, more like the walls of a tunnel dug in soil. There was no window anywhere.

To no surprise at all, the voices belonged to the crowd which had swarmed into the bar. They were in a little huddle, arguing and waving their hands. About me, I guessed: I was right. Everyone was chipping in:

'There's a bounty out for strangers. The Confraternity will pay us a lot for these two.'

'Right. They aren't ordinary strangers. They've been snooping around.'

'And they are lying. I don't know where they're from, but it's not Norstar.'

So it went on. I tried to take stock: I was definitely tied to a pole. Slightly unexpectedly, I was still wearing everything I had been, but I didn't have anything I'd been carrying. My bag, my money, my little radio, and the tiny little energy pistol Rusty had insisted I bring from Bubbles' armoury, they were all gone.

The argument was still going on. Everyone seemed agreed we should be handed over, except one. Unfortunately, he was the largest, roughest one and seemed to be their leader.

'The bounty's good. We need cash. But get her. She's hot. Hottest there's been round here for a long time. Let's enjoy her first.'

More argument, then grudging agreement. As long as I was left in a fit state to collect bounty on, he could have some of his share in advance, in kind. Oh dear. How fussy were the Confraternity about what counted as a "fit state"?

This guy was big, carrying a large knife, and he stank. I shrank back into the pole, my heart thudding in my chest.

'I'm coming out of this alive, I'm coming out of this alive, they want the bounty, I'm coming out alive.' I kept repeating to myself as he pulled me to my feet and started pawing at me.

Then he drew back, puzzled. He wasn't a big thinker, that was obvious, especially right now with me on his mind. But something had puzzled him. He started pawing again and stopped.

'What's going on? What are you wearing?'

I could see why he was puzzled. He was pawing at my HoloTop and had found that it didn't feel like it should. It wouldn't – there was nothing there. Since the malfunction in Boss's bar, I'd usually worn something underneath it. When Ugly Boy believed he was fondling the tattered and torn rough cloth of the blouse he could see, in fact his hand was feeling through to a smooth tee-shirt. He was confused. To him, confused and angry were a short step apart.

'Never mind. It's coming off whatever it is.'

He tried to grab my blouse and tear it off. That wasn't going to work either. His hand came away empty. He tried again. I wondered what would happen if he got a grip underneath and ripped my tee-shirt off only to find me still dressed in the blouse. He'd decide I was a witch or something. Which wouldn't improve the situation.

'I'll cut it off!' He pulled out the knife and tried to slit open my clothes. No luck. Was he angry that he couldn't cut my clothes off, or that he was being made a fool of in front of his friends? Which was worse? Whichever, he was red with rage now. Slapping me in the face, he pushed the knife under my chin.

Help came unexpectedly:

'Stop it! If you cut her up, we won't be paid.'

That cut through.

'OK, then. She can strip herself.'

I shook my head.

'If you don't, I'll slice him to pieces,' gesturing at Chathray. 'There's no bounty on him.'

I shook my head again.

'Make your mind up. Five...'

'OK, OK. But I can't with my hands tied behind me.'

Even Ugly Boy could understand that.

'No funny business.'

He turned back to me, cut the ropes tying my wrists, tucked the knife away and put his hands around my throat holding me.

'Get on with it!'

'OK, OK.'

I reached down to my belt. Ugly Boy leered, clearly believing I was taking my jeans off.

'That's better, darling!'

Oh well, into each life a little rain must fall. Instead of unclipping my belt, I squeezed the top and bottom of the little silver ovoid clipped to the buckle in precisely the way to put the HoloTop controller into its emergency protection mode.

I couldn't see what happened next. Rusty, who had come around by then, later told me that I was sheathed in bright blue flame. I guess the HoloTop didn't bother about camouflage in emergencies.

Dredging deep into almost forgotten self-defence classes, I grabbed Ugly's arms, pulled him toward me and brought a knee up as hard as I could into his groin. He screamed, doubled up and then came at me with the knife, bounty forgotten. The knife hit the HoloTop shield and clattered to the floor. He went for my throat again. This time, I didn't pull him: I smashed down on his elbows as hard as I could. There was a cracking noise, another scream, and he staggered back. I chopped as hard as I could at the base of his neck, as I'd been taught, hoping to stun him for a while. He crumpled to the floor.

I waited to find out what the rest of the gang would do. They were staring at Ugly, horrified. It was obvious why. He was sprawled at my feet, a spreading red stain where his groin had been. His lower arms were loosely attached at the elbows. There was blood everywhere and splintered bone was poking out at odd angles. The side of his neck, where I'd chopped at it, was a raw pulp, and his head was folded sideways. He was dead. Totally dead. Permanently dead.

I felt sick. I'd never killed anyone before, never even contemplated it. I hadn't even meant to kill Ugly. He was an unpleasant person, and I didn't like what he was planning for me, but I wanted to stop him doing it, not kill him. However unpleasant he was, he probably loved his mother. Perhaps he kept cats. Painted landscapes. I didn't know anything about this man whose life I'd snuffed out. Not even his real name.

I felt even sicker. I wanted to retch. All that stopped me was a curiously detached awareness that vomiting inside an impermeable shield might be pretty unpleasant. How was the air moving in and out for me to breathe?

Ugly's mates were stirring now.

'What is she? Who is she?'

'What happened? Where did the blue demon come from?'

'Come on, rush her!'

'We can't let her get away with killing him!'

'She can't kill all of us!'

Well, true enough. The shield would stop them hurting me, but they could pin me down. But they had taken another lesson from what had happened: the blue demon would kill at least some of them in a fight. And none of them wanted to follow Ugly. To a man they turned and ran. Right then, I had no stomach for more violence, but they didn't know that.

I slumped down, sobbing. I've no idea how long for.

'Mihana, stop it! Cut me loose!', Rusty was calling.

Trying not to see more than I had to, I picked the knife out of the mess that had been Ugly and slit Rusty's ropes.

'Rusty, Rusty! What happened? How did I do it?'

'Self-preservation, dear. And the shield, I imagine.'

Of course. The HoloTop had made an impenetrable, unyielding case around me. Every time I hit Ugly, it was as though he'd been hit with an iron bar. Did the camo-armour have some power assistance as well? I'd have to ask Jesse one day.

'We need to leave, Mihana.'

'I know, but where are we?'

'I've no idea. Would he know?' Rusty pointed at Chathray.

'Perhaps – let's wake him.'

We had to practically shake Chathray to pieces to rouse him, but eventually he woke. He stared, round-eyed, at Ugly.

'Don't ask, please don't ask. Bad things have been happening. Where are we, Chathray? How do we find the way out?'

Gesturing around, he said:

'In the Underground Town. Under the *Agent*. Where do you want to go?'

'Where? Underground what?'

Apparently, the Underground Town dated back to the first days of Threnal, when hordes of miners came into town to sell their ore, then drink and whore. The partying crowds clogging the streets made it next to impossible to take ore back to the banks and cash out to the miners. Deals couldn't be done. So, the banks dug a network of tunnels underneath the streets. Eventually a whole alternative life was thriving down there. Shops, hotels, bars, bathhouses, everything. Then the miners left, the partying stopped, and the tunnels had been abandoned for centuries, inhabited by the underclasses, like the gang we'd run into. Amazing.

Something struck me:

'Chathray? Who knows about these tunnels?'

'Hardly anyone. A few of us with buildings the tunnels still open under, that's all. I doubt anyone in authority knows. Some things we keep to ourselves.' He grinned.

'I see. And where were these banks exactly?'

'Oh, that's easy. The Company's HQ was built over the financial centre. The tunnels run under it. That's our biggest secret.'

Rusty and I exchanged looks, dumbstruck. We could have searched for ever without finding the answer, and we'd been drinking over it the whole time.

'Mihana, let's find our stuff. Chathray, can you show us where to go?'

THE UNDERGROUND TOWN

Life would be much easier if I was a character in a daytime drama or a novel. Chathray would have told us how to find Company HQ, Rusty and I would have breezily set off, solved the problem of The Signal, restored civilisation to Threnal and the whole of Threnador, and been back in the Forest for a quiet drink by sunset. Undoubtedly, we'd have hit a major obstacle somewhere around the penultimate commercial break, to make sure people stayed viewing afterwards – perhaps a collapsing bridge, a wall of fire, or some pointless whirling rotor in a ventilation tube – but we'd have fought off all adversity and won through with scarcely a scratch.

Real life works differently. So, the morning after the events under the *Agent*, I was sat moodily on a street bench. Children were playing in a small park. Well, less a 'park' than an abandoned patch of land with some play equipment cobbled together from scrap metal and wood. The sun was blazing down, like it had been ever since we arrived in Threnal, bleaching off the tired remains of the paint somebody had used to try to brighten the playground up. The kids didn't care though – happy shouts and playful screams drifted over. Kids never do care, do they? Give them a few boxes and some old clothes and their imaginations whisk them off in flights of fancy and adventure.

Everything appeared ordinary. Children's voices merged with the chatter of a few groups of mothers stood nearby. A passer-by wandered idly down the street, blissfully unaware of the previous evening's carnage, when a man had died under where she was grazing on a street food breakfast, or that his killer was sitting a few metres from her. Perhaps life is always like that – calm on the outside, chaos underneath.

Chathray had said he could show us where to go but had insisted on coming with us. He also wanted to know why we wanted to go to The Company, which floored Rusty and me. Everything had happened too fast. We didn't have a story ready to recruit a casual acquaintance. Telling him we were from the other side of the ocean, had arrived in an illegal Old Tech aircraft, trying to solve the mystery of a missing Signal from space that he knew nothing of, probably wasn't one of life's better ideas. I didn't know if we were technically fugitives, but we soon would be if our tale leaked out. And there was the body, of course. Although, after the first surprise, Chathray didn't act as though he was much bothered by the body. Threnal had been notching up bodies a bit too liberally lately, I guessed.

Somehow, Rusty had bluffed his way through with a tale about a relative who had been 'disappeared' by the Company, and how we wanted to find out what had happened. Chathray at least recognised the circumstances and stopped enquiring. I made a mental note to talk to Rusty to agree on a story – it might be awkward if his relative turned out to be a thirty-year-old mother of three and mine was an old man with a limp.

Then we couldn't go straight away. Rusty had stashed some equipment. He needed to recover it, and Chathray wasn't prepared to drop everything and head off into the tunnels. Why, I didn't know. I knew I should care, but I'd had enough.

We had agreed on setting off the following morning, which was now today, and I wound up idling away the morning on a bench opposite a children's playground.

I'd been there about an hour when Rusty sat down next to me.

'Ready?'

'Yes,' he patted his pockets and grinned. 'You?'

'As I'll ever be. Rusty, why does Chathray want to come with us?'

He grinned again, teasing me.

'And I thought you were worldly-wise. You truly don't know?'

I shook my head.

'Haven't you seen how he looks at you?'

Oh. How stupid can a girl be? I knew exactly what Chathray had been suggesting, never mind how he looked at me. Perhaps he wasn't as superficial as I'd thought. Idiot!

'When that mob burst into the bar and went for you, he piled in like a good 'un. Did a respectable job, as well. Floored one of them, perhaps two. He did his best, to be fair.'

I was impressed. Men fighting over me; a white knight riding to the rescue. Perhaps I was a character in a daytime drama after all.

'OK. I'll deal with that when I must. What are we going to do when we reach the HQ?'

'I don't know. The dish to receive the Signal is on the roof.'

122

How did he know that? Patting his pocket again, he went on:

'If I can reach it, this box will tell me whether the Signal cuts off at HQ, or whether the problem is further out.'

'And if it is?'

'I've no idea.'

This was the first time that the possibility that even if we succeeded, we might achieve nothing, had come up.

Not the best news I'd had recently. Oh well.

'Are we going to need all this kit, Chathray?' I asked. 'You gave me the impression these were simple tunnels.'

It was two hours since Rusty's bombshell, and we were back in the Underground Town. Chathray had returned, which I both was and wasn't surprised about.

Chathray had shed his street clothes and was wearing a set of greenish brown fatigues with heavy black boots, and a wide belt loaded with pouches and pockets carrying dangerous looking objects. He had slung a large coil of rope diagonally around his chest. He was a soldier, ready to assault somewhere.

'I've no idea, Mihana. But I'd rather come back having not needed it, than not come back because I didn't have it.'

Rusty nodded approvingly. Boys and their toys, I supposed.

We set off, past the scene of the previous day's events and into an opening at the far end of the room. The body had gone. I didn't ask how or where.

Behind the opening was a narrow tunnel, dark, slightly damp, hewn roughly from the rock. As well as being narrow, it was low. I found that out by cracking my head on a lump in the ceiling about five metres in.

'Mind your head, the ceiling's low,' Chathray said. Useful. Timely. I would never have worked it out from the throbbing lump on my forehead, would I?

We walked on, the passageway lit from a small lamp that Rusty produced from his pocket. It was bright enough, but cast myriad shadows on the floor and walls, making extreme care vital. But we weren't expecting to meet anyone, and I was pleased Rusty had brought it.

'How long will the light last, Rusty?

'Long enough. Plenty long enough.'

'Pleased to hear it.' I was. I'd been picturing us finding our way with flaming torches made of straw, oil and sheep dung or similar. Rusty's glowing white light was a considerable improvement.

Chathray had explained the previous day about the Underground Town, but I hadn't fully grasped what he meant. It was a shock when the tunnel widened out and we were walking through what had once been a butcher's shop. Then we passed a bar, a laundry, and a little row of prison cells.

'Cells, Chathray? Why are there cells down here?'

'To lock up criminals, of course.'

'Yes, I know that, but why here, not up above?'

'They had their own laws down here. Like a small town all its own. Apparently, some of the people living down here weren't allowed above ground. They could be shot on sight.'

Charming. Delightful place, Threnal. The scales had been falling steadily from my eyes ever since we arrived here.

'What are those?' I asked, pointing to a set of steps leading up through a doorway cut into the side of the tunnel.

'Oh,' Chathray flushed red. 'They used to lead up to one of the brothels. The miners were often lonely and had money to spend.'

That I could believe. I'd seen starship crews back in Boss's bar in the Forest. Why were the brothels above ground? No matter. I didn't ask.

'Come on, you two. Keep up.' Rusty was not interested in sightseeing or history lessons.

We trudged on.

Chathray had taken the lead, the little shops and bars had faded away, and we'd been walking through a maze of bare tunnels for about half an hour. Running water gurgles from up ahead.

'Water? Down here?'

'Yes, there are some underground streams and rivers down here, buried as Threnal expanded. We're coming to one now. Watch your step.'

The tunnel widened, and, about three metres below us, reflections from Rusty's light glinted off fast-flowing water. The path had become a ledge with a stream to our left.

'Be careful here. The river used to be in pipes and tunnels, but they collapsed.'

I could make out shards of clay and brick poking out from the rushing water, remnants of the collapsed structures. Noise echoed from the tunnel walls.

'Not far now. A few hundred metres more and we'll be under the edge of the Company compound.'

So often, news has upsides and downsides. No more trudging through damp shadowy tunnels was good, but I doubted anyone up top was going to be pleased to see us.

The tunnel bent slightly to the left. Walking beside Chathray, with Rusty bringing up the rear, I turned the corner. My foot slipped. A loud crack came from the edge of the path, and I fell into the stream.

Well, not exactly into the stream. I fell heavily onto a pile of broken bricks. They had been a pipe roof once. A shower of small pebbles followed me, painfully. An orange-whiskered face peered down from where I'd fallen.

'Are you alright, Mihana? Are you hurt?'

Men. Damn fool questions.

'I fell three metres onto a pile of bricks, my feet are in a stream of icy water, my backside hurts like hell, and there are stones falling onto my already-sore head. Am I likely to be alright? Seriously?'

'She's fine, Chathray. Fine enough to be mad, anyway.'

'Stop chatting and get me out of here!'

I clambered to my feet on the brick pile, soaking one leg up to the knee in the process. At full stretch, I couldn't reach either of the men. We were a hand's width apart. The rock leading up to the path was sheer, cleanly finished, with no handholds.

'Glad I brought the rope now, aren't you?'

I imagined Chathray grinning.

'Don't be smug. Yes.'

Once he threw the rope down, I climbed out in a few moments. Rusty was impressed.

'Where did you learn to climb a rope like that?'

'Picking strawberries back in the Forest.'

'There's no need to be snarky.'

I glowered. It wasn't my fault he didn't believe me. I dusted myself down and tried to squeeze as much of the water out of my leggings as possible, hoping they'd dry soon. You can't squelch your way through an underground adventure and keep any semblance of dignity.

I wished I'd not thought about the strawberries. The two men had forgotten all about me mentioning them, focussed now on reaching Company HQ, but I was remembering sunny days in the Forest canopy, the warmth, the lovely sweet smell of the fruit, and the simple pleasure of feeding Darvee. Memories of another life. Where was Darvee now?

There was one more obstacle. Not long after my stumble, we came to a spot where the path bridged the stream which wound its way to an underground waterfall. Predictably, inevitably, the bridge was down. Chathray did his best to lasso a rock on the other side, then Rusty and I tried. You can compensate for lack of skill with trial and error, but you need two things to successfully lasso a rock – a suitable length of rope, which we had, and a suitable rock to lasso, which we didn't. There was nothing there to catch the rope around. One of the things Chathray had tucked away in his pockets was a neat folding grapnel, which was equally ineffective, sliding uselessly across the smooth surface of the path. Someone had to carry the rope over. Guess who that was?

To be fair to them, both of my companions offered to go, but, in my heart, I knew Rusty was too old with a prosthetic arm, and Chathray was too big to make such a jump. I briefly toyed with the idea of diving down into the stream, swimming across, and climbing back up. I had dried off, but another soaking would be better than flailing into a rock face and crashing down. No joy. Sheer rock again.

Tying the rope around my waist, I took a short run up and launched myself across. Like any good heroine, I expected to come up short and find myself teetering on the edge, hoping and praying for a breath of wind to blow me across the threshold. Instead, I cleared the edge by a good stride, landed securely on the path and within minutes had found a secure outcrop, previously out of sight. I tied the rope around it.

Five minutes later, Rusty and Chathray were hugging me. I sat on the edge of the broken bridge, my feet dangling over the drop. I felt I needed a rest.

Rusty walked further into the tunnel. Chathray sat down beside me.

'Mihana, where are you from?'

'Norstar, we told you.'

'No, you're not.' Rusty had taken his lamp, but a weak light was finding its way from a ventilation duct over the stream. It wasn't enough for me to read Chathray's expression.

'Why do you say that?'

'Strawberries don't grow in Norstar's forests. Perhaps it's too cold, has the wrong soil, I don't know. The forests up there are all pine monocultures. No fruit.'

Oh. He hadn't forgotten the strawberries. That's the trouble when you start concocting stories. You need to work them out, make sure all the details tie together. There hadn't been the chance. And then you need to live in the story, all the while. Even when you're wet and hurt and frightened and relieved all at the same time because an underground river, thousands of kilometres from home, nearly swept you to your death.

'You're from across the Ocean, aren't you? You were talking about The Forest, weren't you? Not any forest.'

I was a lousy liar, and he had a sharp mind. Denial was pointless. The occasional white lie I could cope with, like most people. I couldn't carry this one off.

'Yes, was it my accent?'

'Amongst other things. You're not a city girl.'

Undeniably true.

'Where's Rusty from?'

'Originally? I don't know – he drinks in a bar I work in, tells tall tales and is a friend of a friend of mine. I'm helping him.'

'Do what?' I hadn't wanted him to ask that question but had known he was going to. I might have nearly fallen in a river and had indeed fallen into a hole of my own making, but no way was I talking about Signals, Portals, and Frogspawn Nebulae. Chathray didn't need to know.

'The Company has cut off communications with us. We've come to find out why. Knocking on the front door wouldn't have been a productive approach.' It was all true, but it wasn't all of the truth.

'You're right there. The front door leads straight to the cells for most people.'

He paused, thoughtfully and a little sadly.

'So, what are you doing here, Chathray? Here, now, not in Threnal.'

'You need to ask?'

'Yes. If you knew we weren't telling the truth, why did you come?'

'To look out for you, isn't it obvious? I told you what I felt about you. And I want to find someone who "disappeared" as well.'

'You tried to talk me into a rumble in the back room of a bar with you. Men try to bed women all the time. It doesn't mean they are willing to risk their lives for them.'

'Well, obviously I am for you.'

That remark needed thinking about. A lot of thinking about. And who was Chathray hoping to find? Rusty reappeared. My questions had to wait.

'What are you two so busy with?'

'Rusty...' I paused. How to tell him we were unmasked? He wouldn't take it well.

'Not now. Come on, we need to move. I've found the way in.' Blessed relief. Honesty could wait. Chathray nodded agreement.

We followed Rusty down a tunnel, away from the river, and before long were standing at a corroded metal door, which I assumed was the entrance to Company HQ. We had arrived.

OK, there'd been a collapsed bridge, but no whirling rotors and not a trace of a wall of flame. Too easy by half.

There'd be something unpleasant on the other side waiting to make amends, I was sure.

The door wouldn't open, even though it had an apparently working handle. We paused, slightly crestfallen.

When the only tool you have is a hammer, every problem looks like a nail.

Chathray at once reached into one of his pouches and pulled out a small cylinder which he telescoped out into a crowbar.

'Give me some room, I'll jemmy the door open.' It didn't move.

Rusty pulled out a small black oblong box and stuck it to the door near the handle.

'A crowbar's no use. Stand back! I'll blow it open.'

Hastily, we retreated around a corner of the tunnel. There was a huge noise, a cloud of dust billowed around the corner, and a shower of small stones pinged off the tunnel walls. I hoped anyone on the other side of the door was profoundly deaf, as we couldn't have announced ourselves more effectively if we'd rung a doorbell.

Back around the corner, the door stood unmoved. Slightly singed, but otherwise unmoved. Rusty and Chathray started to shoulder it, ineffectively.

I didn't have a hammer. I had no preconceptions.

'Gentlemen, did you examine the door?'

They stared at me, quizzically. I pushed past them.

'Because if you had, you might have noticed the little bolt at the top.' I pulled down the surprisingly delicate bolt. Something inside the door whirred, I pushed down the handle and the door swung open. I walked through, the others following. I hoped they felt sheepish.

On the other side of the door, was a clean, white corridor. There were no lights hanging from the ceiling and nothing set into it. Instead, the whole ceiling glowed slightly, brightening as we walked down the corridor, dimming where we had left. The corridor had the same jarring cleanliness and newness which had unsettled me when I first walked on to the Bubble's flight deck.

'Sneaking around is going to be difficult. Even the corridor knows where we are.'

'Don't worry, Mihana. I doubt anyone's monitoring the light switches.' I hoped Rusty was right.

'OK. Where now?'

'Up,' said Rusty, 'to the roof, where the comms dishes are.'

'The basement,' said Chathray, 'where the cells are. The disappeared will be there, if they are still alive.'

'Ah.' A grim expression on his face, Rusty was obviously debating how to break the news to Chathray that we'd been lying.

'He knows, Rusty. He's guessed. But he is searching for someone himself.'

'We can't break in there and rescue someone, even if we could find them. That won't be like a corridor light. Someone will know there's been a break-in and then we can forget reaching the roof.'

The sense in what Rusty was saying was clear. Chathray's face was wracked by the internal feud he must have been feeling. He understood the sense of Rusty's view as well, but whoever he hoped he'd find obviously meant a great deal to him. Was it a woman, and how did I fit in? What was Chathray up to? Why was I feeling jealous?

'Ok. How about this? We go up to the roof, Rusty does what he needs to do, and then we all go rescue Chathray's friend. If they are alive now, they'll likely be alive in an hour, and all we'll have to do is escape straight back into the tunnels, not drag an escaped, perhaps injured, prisoner around the building with Confraternity guards in hot pursuit.'

"All" we had to do, indeed. I stared hard at Rusty, willing him to agree. If we refused to help Chathray, he'd likely go solo and set off a panic before we had found the Signal.

For once, common sense prevailed. They agreed.

INSIDE HQ

We walked warily down the corridor, then a second, then a third. There was no sign of a stairway. Thankfully there was no sign of movement either, except a patch of light, dutifully following our progress. If one of us wandered ahead or held back, an extra patch of light appeared, illuminating the singleton. It occurred to me that it wouldn't be too difficult for the corridor to work out how many of us there were. If corridors care about that sort of thing, of course.

'Rusty, why do we need to reach the roof anyway? Can't what we need to do be done from inside?' I was beginning to despair of ever finding a stair.

'Well, I could do it from the comms room, but there might be interference between there and the roof, there are much more likely to be people in the comms room than hanging around on the roof, and this building must have fifteen or twenty floors. Why would the comms room be on this one? We still need the stairs.'

I could see his point. I didn't want to, but I could.

Chathray had gone to the next corridor junction. He came trotting back hurriedly.

'There are people coming. Hide! Now!'

A bare white corridor stretched back fifty metres the way we'd come. Too far to run, nowhere to hide. We could press up against the wall, but unless the Company was staffed by the sightless, we would be wasting our time.

But there was no other choice. I tried to melt into the wall. And fell backwards through the opening which appeared behind me. The two men came darting through behind me. The panel swung shut seconds before booted footsteps echoed down the corridor.

'How did you do that?'

'I have no idea, Rusty, but look!' I pointed to the other side of the room we were in. 'Stairs.'

Do you have any idea how many steps are involved in climbing fifteen or twenty floors? No? I don't either. I lost count. Too many. I did count floors though. I was disappointed at the fifteenth and disheartened at the twentieth. I said some rude words and told Rusty to brush up his counting next time. He didn't answer. Out of breath, I decided.

A few steps above the thirty-second floor, the stair was blocked by a wooden door. Locked of course, but thankfully Chathray's crowbar dealt with it. One of Rusty's grenades would have reduced it to matchwood.

We stepped out onto the roof.

There were no buildings this high in The Forest, which meant I was unprepared for the view over Threnal. It was more like the view from a low flying aircraft than from any building I'd been in before. Or from the top of the Forest canopy down over the village.

From atop its HQ, it was unavoidably obvious—the Company cared little for Threnal. The HQ was a grey monolith towering over the city balefully. Nearby were well developed and well maintained streets and buildings. None as high as HQ, but definitely substantial. The further from the centre, the lower the buildings, and the more dilapidated they became, until eventually the city petered out into a series of shanty towns, worse than anything back home. I'd seen this general pattern of decay when we were flying over Threnal, but it was inescapable now we were at its heart. And, of course, I didn't have to worry about flying down the streets.

Thankfully, the roof was flat, and covered in an artificial forest of antennae of all shapes and sizes, from small tubes of metal to metre sized dishes. Some pointed up into the sky. I guessed Rusty would be interested in one of those.

Water lay in puddles in low spots in the roof covering. It must have been raining. At the opposite end from where we were standing, a large yellow hexagon was painted in the middle of an open, uncluttered area, with a large letter "S" in the middle of it. A shuttle craft landing pad, I guessed. I walked over to it. There were fresh scuff marks from a shuttle's landing gear, and a dry patch where the body of the craft had shielded the roof from the rain.

'Rusty, this pad has been used recently. They might come back,'

'Keep an eye on the spaceport – it's the most likely place for anything to come from.'

'Where is it?'

'Over there somewhere.' He gestured vaguely toward the end of the building, past the landing pad. I walked up to the edge of the roof for a better view of the 'port.

'Mihana, be careful! Stay back!'

I had been unprepared for the view: I was completely unprepared for the blast of wind pouring up the side of the building and swirling over the edge. I stumbled, had no idea which way I was falling, when a hand grabbed the neck of my shirt and pulled me back. Chathray had sprinted across the roof when he saw the risk I was taking.

'What happened? Why was it so incredibly windy?'

'The building is thirty or forty stories high. The wind can't go through it – it has to go round or over it. Dangerous places, roof edges.'

'They certainly are. Thank you.'

'You're welcome. Do you always fall into things as often as you are today?' He was grinning.

'Yeah, trouble mainly.' I grinned back.

'Someone needs to keep an eye on the spaceport. Rusty, do you need help?'

Rusty had unpacked an unlikely amount of equipment from his backpack and was kneeling at the base of one of the dishes, where something resembling a water pipe was bolted to the back. He shook his head.

'No, keep watch.'

Chathray and I sat down next to a solid brick structure built on top of the roof. It had a door on the side facing the landing pad.

'Mihana, what's Rusty doing?'

'I told you – trying to find out why the Company has cut us off. Exactly how he's doing it, I have no idea.'

'Why is he working on the satellite dishes, not the HF antennae? The Forest isn't in space.'

I needed to pay more attention to Chathray – without doubt, he knew more about communications technology than the average bar owner. Most people wouldn't know the difference between a satellite dish and a saucepan. Or talk glibly about HF – High Frequency – radio ranges.

'HF isn't reliable over that distance. Our comms are routed through a high orbit relay.' One of those statements was partly true, the other entirely true. Neither had anything to do with why Rusty was working on a dish. But Chathray acted satisfied.

I carried on:

'Can you see the door we came in through?'

'Yes, just. Why?'

'You take it, I'll keep an eye on the spaceport, because I...' I bit my tongue.

I felt as though I was walking a tight rope. I'd escaped his questioning about what Rusty was up to, then found I was starting to claim to be better at watching for aerial activity because I was a pilot. That information was better kept quiet. I didn't know why, but I knew that I barely knew him, except as a pleasant drinking companion. Oh, and he did make a habit of saving my life, which obviously counted in his favour. I continued:

'Enough of your questions. My turn.'

'Go on.'

'Who are you and why are you here?'

'I told you – to rescue my friend.'

'Friend?' I wanted to ask more yet didn't want to ask for fear of the answer.

'Well, not exactly a friend.' He paused.

I held my breath.

'Alright. He's my brother.'

I tried to appear duly sympathetic. What I wanted to do was turn round and kiss him in relief, but it might have been a bad idea. Kissing men because they've told you their brother is in jail is hard to explain. At least, I believe it is. I've never tried. Anyway, I needed to keep my attention on the spaceport.

'Why have the Company jailed him?'

A pause.

'I can't tell you.'

Not a good reply. Now I wanted to know more than ever.

'Chathray, if you want Rusty and me to help you free your brother, we need to know what he's done. He might be a mass murderer, for all I know.'

'No nothing like that. He hasn't done anything.'

Even I, a dyed in the wool country girl, knew silliness when I came across it. The Company might be harsh, even brutal, but I was pretty sure they hadn't reached the stage of grabbing people off the street randomly for the entertainment value. Chathray's brother had done something to attract their attention, even if it wasn't what most of us would consider a crime.

'Won't you help me, anyway? I've helped you without knowing what you're up to. You're hiding something, I know.'

Ouch. That struck home. I turned toward him. We stared at each other for a while, each waiting for the other to reveal their secrets. I had no intention of cracking first. Chathray's secrets were his to keep, his to reveal. My secrets belonged to Jesse and Rusty, and I had no business breaking their confidence.

I didn't have to.

'Alright, what can it hurt? You've seen the state of Threnal. No-one cares about any of us who live here.'

Well, out in the sticks a lack of interest was pretty much a given. I doubted anyone, anywhere, anytime has much cared about the village folk who grew their food and harvested their crops. But I supposed the city dwellers in a planet's capital might have a different view of how the world should work and how important they were to it.

'Go on.'

'My brother and I are involved in a resistance movement against the Company. We want to be able to run our own affairs. Share in some of the wealth.'

I had no idea how such an idea could work. It would be like starting a movement to change the air you breathed. Threnador was a Company planet. Its entire economy was run by the Company.

'Involved?'

'Well, we run it. Nothing drastic. Organise meetings, try and build support for change, the occasional protest. One or two small bombings of Company property. No-one's been hurt.' He added the latter hastily.

Now I knew why his brother had been grabbed. General muttering and moaning might slip under the radar. Once you drift into small bombings, people take an interest.

'Why do you believe he's still alive?'

He hesitated.

'I don't know. They've had him for only a few days. And if they were going to kill him, they'd at least make it public. To deter the rest of us.'

I wasn't sure. Not knowing is more frightening than knowing sometimes. But he needed to hope.

So now I knew. As if we weren't in enough trouble already, Rusty and I had smuggled a revolutionary into Company HQ. They were bound to have a rule against that. I would. If they hadn't already, then they'd write one soon enough, I felt sure.

I knew Chathray was waiting for me to react, but I needed to mull all this over. I turned back to the spaceport again.

I should have never wavered. About two, perhaps three, klicks out, there was a flitter lining up on approach to the roof. Our roof. Specifically, the yellow hexagon about ten metres from where I was sitting.

'Rusty!!'

'You were supposed to be keeping lookout!'

"I was. Never mind. Argue later, hide now!"

Chathray and I scrambled round until the brick structure hid us from the landing flitter. I had no idea where Rusty had gone, and no idea where the flitter was. Would the pilot have seen us? He was probably close enough – but hopefully he'd have been concentrating enough on his landing not to see us. It couldn't be easy to set anything down close to the edge of the roof and its winds.

There was no doubt when the flitter landed. A ducted fan whined, dust and spray scattered across the roof and a loud thud, and a squeal signalled its gear was sliding on the pad. Not exactly textbook, but I wasn't about to go and discuss technique with the pilot.

I desperately wanted to see what was happening but poking my head around the corner would be an express route to the cell next to Chathray's brother. I held back. Then Chathray tugged my arm and pointed. In front of us was an equipment case, covered in polished metal. It was an excellent mirror with a fine view of the flitter cockpit. My eyes widened in horror, and Chathray shrugged resignedly.

Mirrors are wonderful things, but they have an inconvenient property which normally I don't worry about when I'm brushing my hair or tweaking my makeup on the rare occasions I wear it for a night out. If you can see someone in a mirror, they can see you. Holding my breath wasn't going to change anything, in fact was utterly pointless given the continuing whine from the fan, but I held it anyway.

There were two people in the flitter. The pilot, man or woman I couldn't tell which, was wearing a green flight helmet with a darkened visor. He or she was busy in the cockpit, perhaps shutting the flitter down or perhaps reconfiguring for departure. The man in the left-hand seat wasn't wearing flight gear and was unbuckling his safety harness. A gullwing door hinged up, a small set of steps folded down, and the passenger descended to the roof. A tall man, standing ramrod straight, he had dark glasses and black hair slicked backward. He was wearing a long, purple leather coat with a high collar. He looked briefly around then strode through the door in the brick building facing the pad. A bell chimed and a motor whirred. He was gone.

The flitter's fan spooled up and the craft lifted, spun on its vertical axis and arrowed back toward the spaceport. But moments before lifting, the pilot waved one hand to someone in greeting. I didn't know who.

'Chathray, there's someone else on the roof. The pilot waved to them.'

'I know. I saw it too. We'll have to take them out.'

What? Was he mad? Take them out? We had no idea who they were, how many of them were here, or whether they were armed. We didn't even have Chathray's crowbar – it was back by the door we came through. He had his rope though. Perhaps he could lasso them. I tried to frame a well-argued reply along the lines of shutting our eyes and wishing hard for them to go away.

I was interrupted by Rusty.

'Come on, you two. Stop canoodling. The flitter has gone.'

Canoodling? I bristled.

'Yes, but there's someone else here.'

'No, there isn't. Only us.'

'But the pilot waved to someone. I saw him do it.'

'Of course, but in reply. I waved first.'

'You. Waved. First.'

Big spaces between words because I couldn't believe what he'd said. 'Where were you? Why did you wave?'

'I was sat over there, by that dish. Where I'd been working.'

'What! Why didn't you hide?'

'You didn't leave me any time. Anyway, I did. I hid in plain sight.'

'You hid in plain sight?'

'Yes, oldest trick in the book. I used it once at…'

'Not at the Dahnian Rift, surely?' I was feeling peevish.

'No, of course not. You can't hide a space fleet once a battle starts. No, at the… Oh, never mind. Look, imagine you are landing a flitter on a roof next to a bunch of comms equipment. The roof is on the most secure building on the planet, and you've a VIP on-board. You spot a guy working on an antenna. What do you think?'

I saw his point.

'He's a tech, fixing something?'

'Precisely. You don't decide he's a spy who's sneaked in and is up to no good. Especially when he gives you a cheery wave.'

I'd never heard anyone guffaw before, but it's the right way to describe the way Chathray laughed. Guffaw.

'I imagine His Purple Importance thought much the same. He saw me too. Luckily, he didn't see the two of you. That would have changed the game.'

I shivered. This was all becoming far too real. I didn't feel in control. Or that anyone was anymore.

'Anyway, look on the bright side. We don't have to walk down thirty-two floors now. They found the lift for us.' Rusty pointed at the door the passenger had gone through.

A lift. That would be a little treat. I knew what one was, but I'd never been in one. I'd been to orbit, but I'd never been in a lift. How common was that in the long history of humanity? Not very, I suspected.

Rusty was still talking.

'I need a few more minutes. Keep a proper watch this time. No more Confraternity aircraft sneaking up on us unawares. It's bad for my concentration.'

Suitably chastened, we returned to keep lookout in silence. The drama of the last few minutes had broken the spell and bought me some time to make up a story.

Rusty was more like quarter of an hour than a few minutes, but eventually he packed up his equipment and came back towards us. The jaunty joviality of his little triumph over the flitter had gone. He was drawn, worried, and despondent.

'It's not here, Mihana. The Signal. The feed from the server satellite is completely absent. Not a trace. I've checked all the space-pointing dishes. And scanned every appropriate frequency with my own gear.'

'Should we try elsewhere? Another building?'

'No point. The Company always feeds these Signals to its planetary HQ. They come down on an ultra-tight beam to a highly secure location, meaning the Company controls the distribution and no-one can bypass their systems of commerce. They aren't even receiving it themselves.'

'What do we do now?'

'I've no idea. Pack up, get out of here and report back to Jesse, I suppose.'

Chathray cleared his throat. I'd forgotten Chathray was standing next to me. What had he made of the conversation? Rusty had shown no sign of caring what he was saying in front of Chathray and had said more than I had intended to. But I wasn't sure whether what he'd said would have made any sense to Chathray. Perhaps no more than I had already revealed.

'What about my part of the deal? What you both agreed to?' Obviously, he'd heard "pack up and get out" and concluded he was being abandoned. He didn't care about Signals. He cared about his brother.

'Don't worry, we said we'd help you,' Rusty answered without hesitation. I wasn't sure it was still wise given what I now knew, but there was no way to stop him. And we had agreed.

'And I know where your friend is, anyway. I've a map of the building.'

'A map, how did you come by a map of this place? We've been trying for one for years.'

'No trouble. I was interrogating the comms systems' computer for its wiring diagram, and I found myself in the Facilities Management storage area. So, I asked for a floor plan. I hadn't forgotten about you. Look.'

Rusty pulled a glass tablet out of a pocket and thrust it at Chathray. A diagram glowed on the glass.

'There. See? The prison and interrogation area is about 50 metres north and three floors down from where we entered the HQ. Practically next door.'

Chathray was stunned. I was becoming used to Rusty and Jesse and their gadgets, but he'd not been exposed. It must have been like magic.

'Don't worry, Chathray. Rusty's my tame wizard. Come on, we've a map, a lift, and a brother to rescue! Pick up the pace. Don't shilly-shally.'

144

Sometimes, you have to unlock your Inner Child. Enjoy the Newness.

'Live in the moment,' Mum used to tell me. 'Savour everything you do.'

I decided I would follow her advice to the letter with the lift. I'd never again ride in a lift for the first time, and I was going to enjoy it.

Mum also used to say:

'Live each moment as though it might be your last.'

I tried to push the words out of my head. It felt like less of a metaphor and more of a practical possibility right then.

Rusty waved his hand in front of a glowing panel and then we waited. I had one last moment of doubt as we stood at the door.

'Rusty, should we be riding this?' What if someone else comes in?'

'What if someone else uses the stairs while we're going down? Mihana, I for one am going to be in better shape to deal with whatever we find on the prison level if we've ridden there, than if we've trudged down thirty-five levels.'

He was right, of course, but the decision was made for us anyway – the door slid aside revealing an empty box with pastel green walls. Like Bubbles' cockpit and the corridors down below, there was an unnatural freshness and cleanliness to the box. They were made of materials quite unlike anything available to ordinary people.

'Rusty, how does this work? How do we go down?'

'I press one of those buttons over there, the door closes, and the lift moves down thirty-five floors in a few seconds.'

I tried to visualise about what was entailed.

'There's an empty shaft underneath us, and we fall a hundred and fifty metres or more down it you mean?'

'That's about right.'

Maybe this wasn't such a good idea.

'What stops us falling right down and being smashed to pieces when we reach the bottom of the shaft?'

'Well, in the old days, in the Inner Worlds, the lift would have moved up and down the shaft by tweaking the local gravity field slightly. Here and now, we're hanging from a cable, and mechanical levers will lock us in place if the cable breaks and we start to fall.'

'That sounds a bit ramshackle.'

'Not at all. An ancient, well-tried, system. I prefer it. You can see mechanical engineering. Touch it. It's solid, real. Gravitational engineering, not so much. Look, are we going or not?'

I braced myself. Rusty punched a button, and off we went.

'Woohoo, that was fun!' I couldn't stop grinning as we slowed to a stop. 'My stomach went up then down, like flying a bunt followed by pulling out of a dive.'

'Of course. Same physics. Gravity, acceleration, and inertia. What did you expect to happen?'

I felt a little sheepish as he pointed out the obvious, but I wasn't going to let him spoil my enjoyment.

'You wouldn't have felt anything in a gravolift, by the way. Inertial dampers.'

I guessed those must be similar to the tricks Bubbles could pull. Interesting.

We walked out into a thankfully empty corridor. I knew we would have to deal with people sooner or later, but later was fine with me.

146

Rusty led the way, his tablet in one hand. He stuck a pistol in his belt and silently passed one to me. Behind, me, Chathray was carrying a gun too. It was bigger, and a lot more primitive than Rusty's and mine. Some sort of projectile weapon, I guessed. Did it matter? You can only kill a man once. Killed crudely is still dead enough.

The corridors here weren't the pure white we'd seen before. The walls were grubby and made of more conventional materials. Plaster peeled off to reveal cracked stone. No luxurious fittings for the Company's prisoners, for sure.

Noises came from nearby. Horrible noises. Men and women, moaning and crying. An occasional scream. There was a growing stench. Of sweat, blood and fear. This was not a good place. What was I doing here?

Rusty waved us to a stop.

'Around this corner. Follow my lead. No improvising.'

We turned the corner, and Rusty strode confidently through a set of double swing doors and into a large hall. I fought back a gasp, and I sensed Chathray do the same. The hall was full of cages, wire cages you might use to keep a pet rodent, barely large enough for humans. A few cages were empty, but most had two or three prisoners. Some lay motionless, some were sat holding their heads in their hands. All but a few were bloodied and bruised. One man had the white of a broken bone sticking out of his leg. Another stared emptily ahead; his gaze focussed somewhere in the empty space far beyond the walls. A woman's face was caked in blood. Her eyes had been gouged out.

I felt a sick anger rising in my throat. This was worse, far worse than I had expected. Dirty, messy and painful. What had these people done to deserve this? What could you possibly do to deserve this?

Rusty didn't break stride. Made of sterner stuff or knew what to expect I supposed. Sadly, probably the latter. How? In front of the first row of cages, a guard was sat at a desk, reading. Rusty walked up to him. The guard gave him a quizzical look.

'We're here on a routine inspection. Checking the cell locking system.'

'Oh. The inspection wasn't due for another week or so, last I heard. Where's the usual engineer, Darl?'

'He's ill. Come down with the flu.'

'Has he?' The guard paused and reached forward. 'Wrong answer. Darl's a woman and she brings me my coffee.'

Without a word, Rusty pulled the pistol from his belt, and a smoking hole appeared in the guard's chest. His body slumped forward. A red light started to flash in the ceiling and a klaxon sounded.

'Damn, damn, damn. I'm getting old, slow, and stupid. I let him trigger an alarm. Chathray, find your brother. Now!'

Chathray, ashen faced, set off running up and down the ranks of cages.

'Here, he's still alive! Quick, here!'

Chathray pointed his gun at the cell lock and fired. A shell went ricocheting around the hall. Another shot and the cell door swung open. Chathray ran in and dragged his brother out. His feet were bandaged, his fingers bleeding and his face was bruised. But, compared with some here, he was in rude good health.

Running footsteps and shouting were outside the doors we'd entered through.

'Rusty, guards!'

'Come on, this way! Chathray, Mihana follow me. There's another way out.'

'What about all the other prisoners? We can't leave them here in this hell-hole.'

'We can and we will. There must be fifty or more of them. And most are badly injured. How are we going to move them? Flag down an Electrobus? They'll be cut down in an instant. Come on!'

Silently, I willed Chathray to see sense. Even whiter than before, he nodded agreement.

Seething, I followed Rusty. Someone had to pay for this. Sometime.

We ran as fast as Chathray's injured brother could keep up, through a twisting warren of corridors and up three levels to the level where we had originally entered the HQ. Wherever Rusty had stolen the map from, it was a good one. Better than our pursuers had, from all appearances.

'Two hundred metres down there,' Rusty pointed around a corner. "Can your brother make it?'

'Yes, but how will it help? They'll chase us in there.'

'I'll blow the roof or something. Any better ideas?'

It was too much to hope we could escape unimpeded. A shot echoed down the corridor and a plasma blast glowed against the ceiling.

'Halt! Stop where you are or be shot down where you stand. No further warning.'

Rusty returned fire. I added a hapless shot or two. We ducked around the corner.

'Chathray, go! Mihana and I will delay them some, then join you.'

I wasn't sure how we'd do that, but a man on broken, bandaged feet wasn't going to outrun the guards unless something held them up. We needed some sort of plan.

Rusty poked his head around the corner and fired. A barrage of orange beams pockmarked the wall opposite.

'I can't leave the two of you here. Mihana, I can't.'

'Then we'll all be captured or worse, and what will you have achieved? You came for your brother, you have him, now leave! Rusty and I will be alright. Somehow.'

Chathray's eyes were pleading, frustrated, fearful. But he knew there was nothing more he could do. He turned and helped his limping brother down the corridor toward the tunnels. I didn't know how he'd manhandle him through those tunnels alone, but we had bigger problems right then.

'Mihana, do you still have the Karthelian bauble?'

'My HoloTop? Of course.'

Of course, indeed. Set it up as a shield, the shield which had killed Ugly in the Underground Town and saved me at the spaceport. I couldn't be shot. Well, unless the goons chasing us had serious firepower. I had no idea how much it would take to breach the shield, or if it was even possible.

'What about you? It will only protect me.'

'If we keep poking our heads out and frightening these guys, Chathray can reach the tunnels. The guards are journeymen not professional killers. They want to go home tonight. We hold them up, then I'll lob a grenade or two down to confuse them and we run for it. If you stay behind me, your HoloTop will shield both of us. I'll have to be very unlucky to be hit if we are running down a corridor in line astern.'

Sounded like a plan. I decided not to dwell on how luck had not exactly run our way in the last few minutes. Rusty wasn't in the mood for negative thoughts.

After a few minutes, I decided I didn't need to limit myself to poking my head out. I checked my HoloTop settings and walked out into the corridor. Orange flame lashed over the shield, but I felt nothing. Whew! Sometimes all you can do is trust.

It was a turkey shoot. Not expecting someone to step out into the open, the guards hadn't taken any cover. I should have felt something, anything, but I didn't. At least four of the guards wouldn't be going home that night. The rest ran.

'That was foolish. Brave, but foolish.'

'Worked, didn't it? Now let's get out of here.'

We turned to follow Chathray's escape route, as another half dozen guards appeared from a side corridor, blocking our path.

'Dammit.' Rusty threw the grenades he'd being going to use in the last corridor towards the newcomers.

The dust settled. There was no sign of any guards, but the corridor was blocked by a huge pile of rubble and tangled metal. Once it had been the ceiling, and probably the room above. Perhaps the one above as well. Possibly two more. Flames licked around the wreckage. We were cut off from the tunnels.

I'd never been in any situation remotely like this, but I had learned not to pause for self-pity, introspection and recrimination in the heat of the moment. Rusty set off at a trot, gasping something about the stairs we'd used before and escaping at ground level.

We were sprinting down the last corridor and I was allowing myself the luxury of worrying how we were going to find the hidden panel I had fallen through before, when Fate dealt another surprise card from the bottom of the pack.

'Rossiter Pargeter. I am most pleased to meet you. I have waited a long time for this day. A long, long time.'

Rusty stopped midstride; a small mammal caught in a beam of light. In the middle of the corridor stood the leather-coated passenger from the flitter. His Purple Importance, Rusty had called him, but he had given no sign of knowing him.

'Who's Rossiter Pargeter?' Worth a try, I suppose, but I didn't expect Rusty to achieve much by it. He didn't.

'Please, please. Let's not insult each other's considerable intelligence. I saw you on the roof. I knew you would have interesting business to transact in our humble establishment. I have to admit I was hoping for more than the release of a minor irritant.'

The black-haired man spoke softly, with a quiet authority. He didn't bark orders like the earlier goon. The icy, calm voice commanded all the respect he needed.

'I know you saw me, but we have never met. You don't know me. I don't know who you are,' said Rusty.

'No, you don't. That would be, shall we say, unlikely. Impossible, in truth. But I know you. I have always known you. I have been seeking you for a long time. Yes, a long time.'

'Why do you want me?'

'I'm sure you know. There's quite a list. Some missing items my colleagues are keen to locate. Have been keen to locate for quite a while.'

Rusty was standing in front of me, signalling me with his hands behind his back. Pointing to where I guessed he knew the stair panel was hidden.

'You can come with me now. Fight if you want, but you'll not find me as easy to despatch as the guards. You and the girl come with me. You can introduce us.'

Interesting. He didn't know who I was, which implied he hadn't been tracking us. We'd blundered into him. Serendipitous ill-luck.

Rusty pulled a small box out of a back pocket. There was a blinding flash, and I dived through the panel and into the stairwell. I headed for the roof. People in tight spots always head up on the holovid, and I had always thought it silly. But now I found myself in a tight spot, there I was, treading the well-trodden route, expecting hot pursuit at any moment.

It never came. The wooden door was still broken open, and I warily poked my head out, expecting a ring of armed guards. There was no such ring.

But there was the flitter, pilot in his or her seat, engines whining for take-off. His Purple Importance, his real name unknown, was courteously shepherding Rusty into the rear seats. Rusty's hands were shackled in front of him. They must have taken the lift.

'Don't worry about your friend. We'll find her. Once the Company has put out the fire you started, my people will sweep the building. We know she can't leave through the street entrances; my people are guarding those. She won't be harmed. You have my word.'

I rather expected him to add "as a gentleman", and possibly twirl his moustache theatrically. But he didn't. It was for the best. I might have laughed.

In a copy of the manoeuvre which it had executed earlier, the flitter lifted, spun on its vertical axis, and arrowed off towards the spaceport. The pilot didn't wave this time.

Unlike the average character in a holovid, I hadn't mindlessly run for the roof. I had a plan. But first, I sat against the stair door and cried. I felt I'd earned it, and the little speech I had overheard meant no-one was about to burst in upon me while I did so.

I tried to take stock. Draw up a list of good and bad points, like they tell you in the self-improvement classes.

In the bad column were some pretty bad things, I knew. Chathray and his brother were gone, probably trapped in the tunnels, if they weren't caught in any of the crossfire or killed by falling rubble. The Signal was nowhere to be found, which was a Very Bad Thing, although I didn't entirely know why and suspected I hadn't been told the whole truth by Rusty and Jesse. Rusty had been hauled off in chains, and I was alone, in a strange city, on a strange continent. On a damp roof.

In the good column, I was alive, surprisingly, which offsets quite a list of bad stuff. Company HQ was on fire, which was good, although I was slightly worried about the prisoners. And I still had one friend and my plan. I pulled out the little black box, tucked away in my jacket pocket. It had a big red button it, marked MOB in white letters. Bubbles had told me it was an incredibly ancient code that once summoned help when someone fell off a ship. A real ship. On water. For me, it was my panic button. I pressed it.

By all the Suns, I knew Bubbles was quick, but we'd left her powered down in a locked warehouse seven or eight klicks away. In less than ten seconds, there was a deafening 'crack', and she was hovering over the shuttlecraft landing pad, lowering steps. I climbed aboard.

'Bubbles, I want to be anywhere but here. Home.'

'Sure thing, Myah. What's been happening? You look rough. Do you know the building is on fire?'

'I know. Someone's dealing with it.'

'OK. What about Rusty? Where do I pick him up?'

'You can't. He's gone. Been taken prisoner, flown off in a flitter five minutes ago.'

'Oh.' Bubbles sounded worried. 'Do you mean the flitter that left this roof five minutes ago?'

I had no idea how she knew, but I knew I still had a lot to learn about her.

'Yes, why?'

'It docked in the hangar bay of the Confraternity surface shuttle which has been sitting on Threnal Spaceport's apron all the while we've been here.'

Well, it had to go somewhere, I supposed, and I knew it had headed for the 'port.

'And, Myah…' She paused, sounding a little nervous. 'The shuttle is powering up her systems and has been given clearance for immediate lift.'

That was definitely one for the Bad Things column. But I had no idea what I could do about it, and I still wanted to go home.

WHAT NEXT?

Bubbles made a pass over the *Honest Agent* before heading home. There were armed guards posted outside the entrance to the bar. I knew the Company wasn't in the habit of guarding random bars. No doubt the guards' presence was due to the ruckus we had caused. I wasn't going to start any heroics in a heavily guarded bar. I drifted us away. At least it meant they hadn't caught Chathray or found his body.

I turned Bubbles east and we headed home. Low and slow. I wasn't in a hurry, and by staying as low as I dared while avoiding sea monsters, I hoped we wouldn't be tracked. Our presence was no secret anymore. Even with my limited experience of undercover skulduggery, I was sure smuggling a most wanted fugitive into Company HQ, setting light to the building during a gunfight, breaking out a prisoner and summoning rescue by an illicit supersonic aircraft of unknown type would have raised eyebrows up and down the Company's hierarchy, however sleepy the Threnal branch usually was. Subtlety hadn't been our watchword throughout the operation. Yet I still hoped they might not know where we had come from or how we might escape.

I slept.

Not for long enough. I'm not sure any sleep would have been "long enough" right then, but what I got definitely wasn't.

'Myah, wake up, wake up.'

'Why? I want to sleep.'

'Jesse wants to talk to us. Wake up.'

That caught my attention. I fought myself awake. Bubbles had reconfigured the instrument panel. Now it had two video screens, side by side. Bubbles' avatar was on one, Jesse, the Clockmaker's was on the other. A familiar face from home, at last.

'Bubbles! Jesse! What? How? We're out of comms range.'

'Er, not quite, Myah.' She sounded sheepish.

'Later, you two. Talk tech later.' Jesse cut across my confusion.

'The Globecraft, Bubbles you call it, has briefed me on what it knows. But to be fair, it doesn't know much since you left it locked in a warehouse for days.'

I bristled at the implied criticism and imagined what state Bubbles had left the warehouse in. Not good, I suspected. The owner wouldn't be attracting new tenants anytime soon. If there was an owner.

Jesse was still talking.

'First of all, are you alright? Is Rusty alright?'

'Yes, I'm fine. Rusty was also fine, the last time I saw him.'

I started to explain coherently but ended up giving Jesse a stream of consciousness download of all I could recall of what had happened. He grasped it impressively well.

'This Chathray man sounds interesting. He might be useful in future. I'll make enquiries.'

Useful? How? Enquiries? Double how?

'But a Confraternity Dreadnought is in orbit? That's not good. Why is it here, I wonder? And the Cardinal knew Rusty's name? How?'

'Cardinal? What's a Cardinal?' I knew about cardinal points on a compass, but no more.

'A high official of the Confraternity. Very high. They wear purple leather coats as a badge of office. No one else is allowed to.'

The Confraternity dictated Galactic dress codes? Well, there are worse things it could do. Most of which it already was doing, I was learning. Did Rusty know what the coat meant? Hmm. "His Purple Importance", indeed!

'I expected you to be worried about what has happened to the Signal. It was why you sent us here.'

'Yes, of course. It is still important. Very important. But these are interesting developments. I must consider what they mean.'

'Well, consider it all and tell me when we land. I still need to sleep.'

'That won't be possible. We need to continue investigating what has happened to the Signal.'

'How so? Rusty said it was beamed down tightly to Company HQ, and he could find no trace of it. Anyway, all his equipment is presumably in the hands of the Cardinal now.'

'Yes, it's most regrettable. I hope Rossiter wasn't carrying anything too, well, compromising. I doubt it, he knows the risks. And what's at stake.'

More questions than answers there. Let's take one thing at a time.

'The Signal. Remind me again about the Signal and how we can track it down with no equipment.'

'The Globecraft can provide you with whatever equipment you'll need. It has some of the best possible fabrication facilities.'

Bubbles? A factory?

'The Signal originates in the Portal network – I assume Rusty explained the background to you.'

I nodded.

'Good. Then you know the Signal is transmitted from the Portal to each inhabited planet in a system, in a highly encrypted form. Once, it was freely available, but the Confraternity made changes. The encrypted Signal is received by a server satellite in synchronous orbit around the planet, where it is decrypted by Company equipment and transmitted on the tightest of beams to the planetary Company HQ where it is retransmitted planet wide. As a result, the Company, or whoever the Confraternity has licensed for the planet, controls the essential enabler for all commercial and transport activity.'

Well, except for the Forest's cabbage carts, but I doubted they mattered. Jesse thought on a higher plane than I was used to. The difference had been obvious for a while.

'It sounds as though the Confraternity have it all nicely wrapped up. There's not much we can do, then.'

'Not a lot, but we can at least find out what has happened. Knowledge enables action. Without it, we are impotent. You need to examine the server satellite.'

I liked his train of thought, but there was a big hole.

'How? I don't have a spacecraft. In fact, the only spacecraft I know about on Threnador are the ones at the Threnal Spaceport, which I'm not going anywhere near; the Haulers at the Forest Spaceport, all of which left; and the Captain's flitter, which I've not seen for a while.'

'There is another alternative.'

Somehow, I knew what was coming.

'Globecraft, what flight modes are currently enabled?'

Bubbles started to speak in the crisp, curt tone she used when she rescued me from the sea monster.

'Atmospheric flight regimes are well covered. I have an extensive menu of simulacra covering all altitude and speed regimes and task requirements. All are civilian craft. Defensive equipment is not available for user selection but may be deployed at my sole discretion in situations of grave threat to significant personnel. I have no material offensive capability. Mode availability modification requires authorisation at Tier One level.'

'Yes, I know that.'

He knew that? I was struggling to understand the words she had said, let alone what they meant. Still less what they might imply about who or what she was. This was all entirely outside my imagination.

'Globecraft DV Alpha One, unlock Simulacra Package In-System Three. Authorisation Voice Print JCFIIIFM1DV—Prime.'

'Voice Print authorisation confirmed. Complying. Package unlocked. Simulacra loading. Simulacra available. Flight regime expanded.'

'Mihana, Bubbles is a spaceship now. Go and check out the server satellite.'

SPACE

I had dreamed of this day, but never believed it would come. But it had, however irregularly. The current circumstances were about as irregular as they could be, I was sure.

As much as I wanted to, it wasn't right to whoop and holler, even though I had become a spaceship commander. I would save my celebrations until Jesse had signed off. Dignity in office, they call it.

One question couldn't be avoided. I won't pretend I wasn't apprehensive of the answer, but I had to ask:

'Jesse, now we can fly in space, shouldn't we try and rescue Rusty?'

'No. Definitely not. You have exactly no chance of sneaking aboard one of the Confraternity's most powerful warships and pulling off some magical rescue. On your own, with no idea of where he might be being held, you'd be captured or killed. Perhaps both. Stay as far away from the warship as you can. If it never knows you exist, that's fine. Bubbles, you too.'

I wasn't sorry, although I was genuinely worried about Rusty and what might happen to him.

'Mihana, I am as worried about Rusty as you are. Probably more. I have known him a long time. A long, long time. I need time to reflect and work out if there is anything we can do to help him without bringing disaster down on our heads.'

I had one more question.

'Jesse, what has happened to the Embrys? Have you seen Darvee?'

'No, Mihana. After your little escapade, the Embrys disappeared. They have probably gone deep into the Forest. There's been no sign of Darvee since he brought you to me. I hope and assume he's joined the others.'

'What about the hunters?'

'They were angry to say the least, and went hunting for you, but everyone closed ranks. They've been out trying to find the Embrys but have come back empty handed every time.

'Good.' I didn't like the idea of real hunters hunting me, but let it pass.

'Indeed. But the situation is worrying. I'll be a lot happier when the hunters are gone, and the Embrys are back.'

I didn't know he cared about the Embrys. With no more comment, he signed off. Then I whooped and hollered. Bubbles smiled and grinned, her normal persona returned. She even poured me a glass of champagne from the drinks dispenser, which was welcome. I didn't know it could dispense champagne. I filed that useful nugget away for future use.

Reality returned. This was no joyride. Jesse had a reason for letting me do this. I was grateful he trusted my flying abilities.

'Bubbles, I need some practice. I want to be more than a passenger, but, like flying to Threnal, I need some practice.'

'That's fine, Myah. What do you want to do?'

I brought a menu of craft options up on screen. I had no idea what most of them did, much less how to fly them.

'Bubbles, these are all too complicated. Is there anything simple?'

'What sort of thing?'

'Well, I flew a flitter to orbit and back once. The Captain's flitter. I mentioned it talking to Jesse. Can you be one of those?'

Image after image of flitters popped up on screen. One even resembled a civilian version of the craft Rusty had been flown away in.

'Stop! Like that one.'

A group of four similar flitters appeared on screen.

'There. Bottom left, number three. That's the one.'

The cockpit shimmered, and I was sitting in the Captain's flitter. Well, a much newer and cleaner version of his flitter. Too new—it felt as though I shouldn't be there.

'Are all your, what did you call them, simulacra as spotlessly clean, Bubbles? Can't we have something that looks a little lived in, as though it been around an asteroid or two?'

'I run a taut ship. Myah. Cleanliness is next to godliness. Don't you like a clean ship?'

I had offended her, I could tell.

'Well of course. But I don't want to worry I might scratch the paintwork and run up a bill.'

She laughed.

'It's OK, I won't charge you if I have to retouch the holo projections! Alright, what do you want?'

I described the cockpit of the Captain's flitter on one exciting day, years ago. In another lifetime. I tried to remember as much detail as I could.

'Let me see. Yes, I may have something I could configure as you want.'

The cockpit shimmered again, less drastically this time, and when it settled, I was sitting in the Captain's flitter. She had captured it perfectly, even down to the sticky ring mark where a coffee cup had been spilt on the instrument panel.

'Perfect. Now I can relax. It's as though I've been here before.'

Well, once, anyway.

We settled on a little shakedown cruise. How easily I had become blasé. The "little shakedown cruise" would take me up out of the atmosphere, briefly into orbit around Threnador, out as far as her single moon, into orbit around it, and then back to a landing. I was particularly keen to land back on solid ground. Every flight must end in a landing; I had tried landing a craft like this once and, while I hadn't exactly disgraced myself, I hadn't covered myself in glory either.

Halfway through the trip, it occurred to me that this was indeed a fairly basic piece of flying. It had probably been standard issue in the Space Academies of a hundred thousand worlds for the last unknown number of millennia. How many other eager wannabes had done this before? And yet, and yet. Once upon a time, long, long ago, someone had flown off to do this for the first time from our long-forgotten home world. That must have taken guts. Whatever craft they flew in would have borne as much relation to Bubbles as a smudge of soot bears to a diamond, I was sure.

Before we set off, I asked:

'Bubbles, is this flight safe? In the sense that we might be seen. By the Dreadnought, or anyone else?'

'I can't promise anything, Myah. But the Moon is at its new phase, lined up between the planet and its sun.'

'So?' I wasn't planning on any amateur astronomy.

'Unless anyone is scanning specially for us, we should be hidden in the glare and radio noise from the sun.'

'I suppose so. Nobody has any reason to suspect unauthorised space launches. Do they?' We hoped.

The alignment was lucky, with an unexpected benefit from the tourism point of view. Two, in fact. For much of the flight, the sun was eclipsed by the moon. As I dropped Bubbles into orbit, we entered one of the most spectacular sunrises I had ever seen. A brilliant orange-yellow orb rose above the moon's limb, with shafts of sunlight glinting off the jagged rocks of airless peaks below. Less than half an hour later, a beautiful blue globe, Threnador herself, rose above a similar horizon, starkly alone in the vastness of space.

Had anyone ever seen anything more beautiful? Was there any more beautiful sight possible?

We had found a disused airfield in a farmed-out area of the Third Continent, nearly halfway around Threnador from Company HQ. If any landing approach was going to go unspotted, ours should. I had told Bubbles to disconnect the safeties and autopilots and let me fly her in. I needed to exorcise a demon.

It was surprisingly anticlimactic. No longer overwhelmed by the novelty and tension of my first spaceflight, I lined up the re-entry, killed our orbital velocity, tweaked the descent to keep residual heating to a minimum, and descended peacefully and silently, under full control, to a pinpoint landing on a pad on the edge of visibility through the encroaching wilderness. Job done.

'Bravo, Myah. Spot on.'

'You didn't help, did you?' I hadn't felt her override my flying, but I wasn't sure.

'Of course not. I promised. I wouldn't have let you crash, but I didn't need to do anything.'

That was the best I could hope for, I supposed.

We were hanging in space, approximately 200 metres spaceward of the server satellite, which was an unexpectedly small cube covered in gold and silver foil. It was orbiting 32,300 kilometres above Threnador's equator, on the same longitude as Threnal. From Threnal it would appear virtually motionless in the sky, meaning the Signal could be beamed down to a static dish day and night. One face was permanently facing the planet. Bubbles told me the satellite was gravity stabilised. I took her word for it. The Threnal-facing side was covered with a tangle of antennae which no doubt had made sense to its designer and which I assumed communicated with the ground. There was a dish on an adjacent side – the "north" side – which was slightly angled away from the axis of the satellite towards Threnador's sun. After an hour, I saw that it was moving slowly, as though tracking something. The Portal, I guessed. The satellite radiated age. I couldn't have answered how it did that, but it did.

'Bubbles, how old is this thing?'

'I don't know Myah. All these satellites are of a common design. There will be a serial number on the outside or I could interrogate the server's software but doing so may be imprudent.'

Too true, it was.

'Roughly, then? Any idea?'

'Well, the Confraternity may have replaced it when they encrypted the Signal, but more likely they reprogrammed it. So, it could date from anytime back to when Threnador was colonised.'

I waited, not wanting to admit my ignorance of my own planet's history. Impatience won.

'Which was?'

'About thirty thousand years ago.'

OK. It looked old, and it likely was old. If the Confraternity had replaced it, then it was perhaps three thousand years old. Or maybe it was ten times that. I tried to imagine how someone built a machine with a dish which could silently track and relay a signal for thirty millennia. We counted ourselves lucky if the coffee machine in Boss's Bar worked for thirty days at a stretch. I felt a crawling sensation in the nape of my neck. Awe.

'OK. It's old. I don't imagine it's a simple breakdown.'

'Highly unlikely. These satellites are some of the most reliable machines in existence. And the Company would have replaced or repaired it if it did.'

'They can repair it? How?'

'If necessary, someone comes up and does the work. Most of the key circuits are behind an access hatch provided for the purpose. The one you'll need to use to check on the Signal.'

Whoa! Nobody had said anything about me going outside. When did that slip in?

'Say that again.'

Bubbles repeated her last reply, word for word. I'd understood correctly.

'But Jesse said you would make the equipment we needed to check what has happened.'

'I have Myah. Here.' A panel at the back of the cabin slid open and a shelf appeared. There were two hand sized boxes and a coil of cable lying on it. I'd seen Rusty with similar kit at the base of the dish on the roof of Company HQ.

'Are you carrying spacesuits? I've never seen any.'

'You don't need a spacesuit, Myah.'

I gawped.

'Well, you do, but you are already wearing one.'

I gawped again. Briefly a butterfly of fear fluttered in my stomach. Was I trapped 30,000 km from home and safety in a spacecraft run by a machine mind that had recently gone insane? Stranger things had happened to me lately.

Of course. My HoloTop. The Karthelian camo-armour. If it could protect me from bullets, vacuum was probably a walk in the park. And, somehow, deep down, I knew Bubbles would be able to configure it.

I slumped back in my seat and started to read the glowing screens of plans Bubbles had already brought up.

I was standing in a small compartment – an airlock – with a transparent panel in its external door.

Of course, Bubbles had known how to configure my HoloTop. She had also produced a small cylinder to supply air for me to breathe. It was clipped firmly to my nose. Bubbles had told me it would last for plenty long enough for me to do the job. I sincerely hoped she was right.

'I'm ready, Bubbles.' It was a lie. Physically, it was true: mentally, not in the slightest. I was terrified.

I knew I was lying, Bubbles probably knew I was lying, but what else could I say? Air hissed around me, draining out of the airlock. Then the total silence of the vacuum, broken by the thudding of my heart. There should be something else. Something was missing. I wasn't breathing. That wouldn't end well. I sniffed hard from the little cylinder.

'Myah, breath normally. Don't panic!'

How did she know I was panicking? Don't answer. Be calm.

'Open the airlock door, please, Bubbles.'

In vacuum now, I felt, not heard, a rumble as the door slid aside, then walked forward and stood at the edge of the black rectangle where the door had been. Well, I was breathing, my blood wasn't boiling, and my eyes hadn't burst. Those were the plus points. On the negative side, I was standing on the lip of the biggest step imaginable. My heart thudded some more. I pushed off toward the server satellite.

I'd wanted to fly in space as long as I could remember. I'd assumed that at some point I would go outside. But I'd imagined it would be thoroughly planned, and I'd be suited up, with a helmet and visor, like the Hauler crews talked about. Why would I have ever imagined that one day I would be adrift in infinity in my street clothes as though I was taking a walk in the Forest? You wouldn't, would you? No-one would. Except for long dead Karthelians, presumably, who had done their jobs remarkably well.

Starting to relax, I kept my focus on the satellite, and Threnador behind it. They were real, solid and reassuring. In every other direction, there were a few pinpoints of stars between me and the edge of the Universe. It was too unsettling a view for right now.

I bumped gently into the server satellite and grabbed a handhold. Obviously my great-great-great ancestors of however many thousand years ago had needed to hold on to things in the same way as I did. I was comforted by that. It made them more human, less god-like.

The little boxes were attached to my belt. I opened the hatch and unwound the cables attached to my boxes. There was a purple cable and a yellow cable and a clamp at the end of each one. I had to clamp them to the purple and yellow cables at the top left of the compartment. If I did the work precisely, taking as little time as possible, no-one on the ground would notice anything had happened. That was what Bubbles had said.

'Purple to purple, yellow to yellow. That's right, isn't it?'

'Yes, Myah.'

'Just checking.'

Concentrating as hard as I could and wasting no time, I made the connections. Nothing happened, but I had no way of knowing whether a bright red light and a loud alarm had gone off down in Company HQ. Hopefully not

I waited. Apparently, the little boxes were checking out all the server satellite's systems and would tell us why the Signal wasn't reaching Threnador. Then we would decide what to do. I waited.

'Mihana, return. Return now.' Bubbles' crisp tone was back.

Back aboard, slumped in the pilot's seat, I cradled a cup of hot coffee in my hands, then put it down with exaggerated precision on the instrument panel, exactly on top of the coffee stain Bubbles had created for me. I had refused to talk to Bubbles until I had drunk a cup of coffee. She might be a tireless super mind crafted from electrons and metal, but I wasn't. I needed a break.

'Alright, Bubbles, what has happened?'

'Are you OK, Myah? You are tense.'

Well, wouldn't anyone be in the circumstances? But because she sounded genuinely concerned, I didn't bite back.

'I'll be fine. What has happened?'

'Let me tell you what I've found'

A display shimmered in the air in front of me. A picture of the satellite was replaced by diagram after diagram of wires. She started talking about signal levels, transients, noise and missing modulation schemes.

'Stop! Stop! I don't understand. I'm a barmaid, remember? I've been dragooned into flying you halfway around the world, while being an accomplice in a scheme I don't understand. Now, I'm a spacecraft pilot and a spacewalker. I'm likely wanted as a terrorist in Threnal, and the police back home will be after me for freeing the Embrys. Charlie has a hole in him because of me, and I actually killed a man myself. A nasty man, agreed, but I killed him. Then shot some more men.'

I paused for breath and fought back a sob. It would have ruined the effect of my speech.

'But one thing I am not is a Portal communications engineer. So, go easy and tell me clearly what I need to know. Understand?'

Silence. A most un-Bubbles-like silence. It lasted for an apparent eternity. Even to flesh and blood.

'I'm sorry, Myah. You're right.'

Well, I knew I was, but it was good to hear her say it anyway.

'When they found out about the Signal's interruption, Rusty and Jesse assumed the problem was at Company HQ. It wasn't. Then they assumed it was a problem with the server satellite.'

I knew what was coming next.

'I have diagnosed the operation of the satellite. It is working fine. I have no way to detect the Signal directly, but there is a single feasible conclusion to draw. It is not being transmitted from the Portal.'

She paused.

'Why is that such a shock?'

'Because as you know now, the Signal is essential to all interstellar travel and most intra-system and on-world travel and commerce. Nobody has ever shut the Signal down completely. Ever. Anywhere.'

'But somebody has now, haven't they? And it must be deliberate, or people would be trying to restore it? Something serious is happening?'

'Yes, yes and yes.'

'The Signal is transmitted directly from the Portal to the server satellite, isn't it? So, what you are saying is if it's not being received here, it never left the Portal. Alright.'

It was my turn to pause.

'Can you fly as far as the Portal? In a reasonable time.'

'With a small propulsion upgrade, yes. But…'

I didn't wait.

'Upgrade your propulsion, then, and set a course for the Portal.'

'We should check with Jesse first, Myah.'

I was tired of other people deciding what to do. It hadn't worked out well yet.

'No. Am I commanding this vessel? Do I have the necessary authority to order you to make the flight?'

A slight delay – an age to her, I imagined.

'You do, Mihana.'

Did I detect a sheepish tone?

'Globecraft DV Alpha One, upgrade your propulsion simulation, and set a course for the Threnador System Portal.'

I hoped I sounded official enough.

'Complying.'

I must have.

'When we're underway, message Jesse however you do, and tell him what has happened. But not until we're underway.'

'Yes, ma'am. But...'

Wow, that "ma'am" sounded good. But why "but"?

'Is there anything else I need to know?'

'Yes, ma'am. The reason I called you back with such urgency. The Confraternity Dreadnought has broken orbit, ma'am. It cloaked at once. I don't know where it's going.'

Oh.

'Belay the ma'ams, Bubbles. And when it's convenient, brew me another coffee, please. This feels like a two-coffee afternoon.'

Jesse was annoyed. He might even have been furious, but I couldn't tell. He showed a calm, controlled demeanour which he didn't allow to slip. But he went on and on and on about how I should not have set off without consulting him. I was sure he was puzzled about how I had been able to, but he never made that explicit.

Eventually, I had had enough of being berated and asked:

'So, what else could we have done? Come home and given up? What would you have told us to do?'

He hummed and hawed a little, then admitted we – I – had done what he would have, and there was no other sensible choice. I wasn't sure I'd have described anything at all we had done since The Forest as "sensible", but I let it pass.

One thing worried me a lot. He had no idea what we could do once we arrived at the Portal. His omniscience had reached its limits, and we'd have to play it by ear.

Going back to the Forest to enlist Brother Peter's help was not an option. And we didn't know any other Portal Engineers.

It was a long way to the Portal. Apparently, Portals were always located beyond a star system's principal planets, and beyond the large reservoir of comets and asteroids orbiting outside them. Thankfully they weren't as far as the even larger reservoir stretching halfway to the nearest star. If that was the right terminology for this strange, human-made set of micro-universes in which I apparently lived. But, whatever, we had to travel about fifty times as far as Threnador was from its Star. I would be in Deep Space.

It would take three days. I pestered Bubbles to upgrade herself to go faster. She never flat out said she couldn't, but she wouldn't. Apparently, we were faster than any Hauler, faster even than the Dreadnought if it was coming this way, and faster than any other naval craft the Confraternity might have in the System. It would have to do.

I settled down to learn some history from the Globecraft's files. I had paid little attention to history in school, but it wouldn't have helped anyway. The school taught Threnador's history in the Confraternity era. Which did leave three thousand years of events on an entire planet. I'd never considered anything more in any depth. I knew there was a Galaxy outside my system, but few details.

But I was all too conscious of being caught up in something far outside my experience, which likely had its roots in the far past. Hell, I was wearing a five-thousand-year-old piece of armour and was on my way to a thirty-thousand-year-old Portal. In a ship like nothing I had ever known about or imagined.

So, I read and viewed and listened. Bubbles didn't try to stop me, which I had half expected.

There was nothing to be found about Bubbles herself. I could find nothing at all about any craft with capabilities remotely like her. Nor could I find her specifications.

But history there was. A lot. More than I could have imagined. The Old Empire I knew about was not especially old in relative terms. It had lasted perhaps five thousand years. But it was unusual in covering the whole Galaxy – or Frogspawn Nebula as Rusty would have said. A motley collection of empires, federations, kingdoms and republics stretching back beyond known records had come before it, but few were galaxy-wide.

Humanity had been out in the Galaxy a long, long time. No-one knew exactly how long, or where we had come from. The original Portal Builders were lost in time, and they themselves must have built from an earlier civilisation crawling through the parsecs in sub-light ships.

Humanity was alone. No trace had ever been found of any other intelligent race. There was plant and animal life aplenty, but nothing more intelligent than a dog or an Embry. Unless of course we had claimed first mover advantage and nipped their societies in the bud, exterminating them. I wouldn't put it past a lot of people. And it's not the sort of thing you'd shout from the rooftops, is it?

But the nearer past was clearer. The Old Empire had been a staggeringly rich and technically advanced society. Then two wars had brought it to its knees. First was the absurdly named Grey Gloop War. A planet in the Orion Arm was struck first. Biotech and nanotechnology combined to unleash a combination of disease and runaway conversion of biological material to simpler form. Before anyone understood the severity of the plague, it had spread through trade routes into neighbouring systems.

Eventually, it was stopped, but not before whole star systems had fallen prey or had been cauterised by the Empire to stop the spread of the outbreak. Trillions were killed. Accusations were levelled of the War being deliberately started. Others argued for a natural plague triggering an unexpected reaction in medical nanotech intended to provide immunity. I suppose you're immune from most things when you've been rendered down to grey soup, but still. Ugh.

With the Grey Gloop War still raging, the Machine War started on the other side of the Galaxy. Intelligent machines had formed a society of their own and declared war on Humanity. They had been even more difficult to stop. But stopped they were. More trillions dead.

Amid all this carnage arose the Confraternity – a quasi-religious cult which blamed science and technology for all the problems. Not without some justification at the time, I may add. Speaking personally.

About three thousand years ago, the Old Empire had fallen, and the technology-hating Confraternity took over. But you can't run a Galactic Empire on sticks and stones. Instead, the Confraternity had imposed strict controls.

Machine intelligence was banned, and the Portals placed under rigid control by a priesthood. Most of the Galaxy was reduced to a primitive, pre-spacefaring state while the elite few controlled the stars. For three thousand years.

Threnador was more primitive than most, I could tell, and Brother Peter tending his chickens wasn't anybody's idea of an elite oppressor, but there it was. Three thousand years of misery. I bristled at the fact.

A chime sounded.

'Myah, Myah, guess what I've found!!!' Bubbles was excited.

'What?'

'I've found *Happiness*!!!'

Well, I was pleased for her, of course. We all deserve a little happiness, even intelligent spaceships, and I'd been learning about some pretty unhappy stuff, but I was sure that wasn't what she meant.

'What are you talking about?'

'*Happiness*! The Confraternity Dreadnought. I found it. It's *Happiness of the Stars*!'

I had never named a ship, or even considered how to go about it, but a moment's contemplation revealed what I thought was an insurmountable objection to what she was saying. If you're an oppressive regime naming a colossal warship, isn't your first preference something like *Terror of the Sky* or *Nemesis of the Unrighteous*? *Happiness* of any sort won't be on the agenda.

'I don't believe you. Explain, please.'

'You've been reading about The Fall.'

'Go on.'

'The Confraternity took over all its trappings. Treasure, palaces, parliaments, purple robes. All of it.'

I nodded, imagining they were quite keen on the treasure and the fancy robes particularly. People are.

'They also took over the Imperial Space Navy. Most of it had survived – the Empire wasn't finally defeated in a mammoth interstellar war.' So far so good. 'But the Confraternity wanted something bigger and better.'

I nodded again. That was obvious. People always want to be bigger and better than the guys who went before. Boss extended his bar when he took over. It had probably been the same all the way back to the semi-mythical First World.

'So they built bigger ships?'

'No. They were rounding up all the scientists and engineers and clamping down on technology. Building immense warships was not possible. Starships are difficult to build.' I imagined they were. I couldn't imagine me trying, for instance.

'Then someone had an important idea. The biggest, sleekest and fastest starships were not in the navy. They were the interstellar cruise liners.'

I had to stop her there.

'Interstellar cruise liners? You're joking.'

I was a farm girl from the backwoods of a minor agri-world struggling along after three thousand years of the Confraternity's puritanical mindset. I tended bar to scrape a living, had had some flying lessons and dreamed of one day flying a Hauler or similar. It took Bubbles a long time to convince me of the truth. Once there were people rich enough that other people built the biggest starships in the history of the Galaxy for no better reason than to take them on holiday. What exactly was a "holiday", for starters?

But there it was. Vast starships, kilometres long, with thousands of crew and passengers, had plied the Galaxy for the amusement of the ultra-wealthy. Apparently, they would cruise between spectacular astrophysical sights and in between feed, water and amuse their customers with the best a Galactic civilisation could provide. Which was quite a lot.

It wasn't an entirely honest trade. Bubbles told me a tale about the Bauble World.

'Althar II was a ringed planet, Myah. It was one of the most popular sights on the tourist itineraries.'

I knew about ringed worlds – there is one in Threnador's system.

'Well, Althar II was like no other. It orbited a tightly bound triple star – red, white and blue primaries. And Althar had four concentric ring systems, with their orbital planes inclined at precisely 45° to one another. On top of which, the rings were all different colours and the colours shifted hourly. A bauble you might decorate your house with for a festival.'

Like when the cabbage harvest was finished, I imagined. Or Threnalia, at the Winter Solstice. But flashier.

'The cruise liners would establish a far orbit around Althar II, and host lavish banquets in huge viewing galleries where the passengers enjoyed the ever-changing spectacle. Those with a little more curiosity could listen to talks given personally by prominent astrophysicists from the best of the Empire's universities.'

For a suitable retainer, I imagined.

'They would explain how the bizarre ring system was kept stable by a series of shepherd moons whose orbits were resonant with both the rings and the changing gravitational field of the triple star.'

'Resonant with the rings? Oh, never mind.'

'The colours were due to thin films of hydrocarbon deposits from the atmosphere of Althar II's moon, iridescent in the constantly shifting coloured light from the system's triple primary.'

The sight was indeed popular. According to Bubbles, the visits by the liners had to be rationed to avoid collisions, it was that popular.

'Unfortunately, Myah, it was all a lie. When one set of liners left the system, there was frantic activity. Mining vessels injected megatonnes of asteroid dust into precisely calculated orbits to replenish the rings, which weren't at all stable. Fluorescent chemicals were sprayed onto the new ring material, and a system of orbiting ultraviolet lasers were refuelled and recalibrated ready for the next show, when the lasers would be projected onto the rings to generate the gaudy colours.'

'What!' I was dumbfounded. 'It was a complete fake? Didn't anybody realise?'

'Yes, eventually the scandal broke. Commentators across the Empire were outraged for a month or two, and in due course the show moved on.'

'Perhaps it's me, but the astroengineering was equally as wonderful as the alleged astrophysics, wasn't it?'

'Very possibly so, Myah. But the passengers didn't like technology. They wanted to experience the beauty of the natural universe.'

By zipping from one end of the Galaxy to the other in vast ships? Did they imagine the ships grew on some strange tree? People are odd. Always have been, always will be, I suspect.

'What else did they look at? Other sorts of stars?'

'There was some of that, but it generated what some people called Extreme Tourism.'

I struggled to think how decadent you had to be to think that touring the light-years wasn't extreme enough already but had to ask.

'What do you mean?'

'Some people like danger. Even more people like to feel they are in danger when they aren't.'

'So?'

'A fashion developed called Starshock Surfing. A temporary Portal was set up around an impending violent stellar event a few hundred years in advance. A supernova, merging neutron stars, a black hole collapsing, that sort of thing.'

I didn't really understand what half of these things were, but let it pass.

'As the climax approached, small, fast, ships would come in as close as possible to the drama, then, at the last moment, race away at high acceleration before the shock wave pulverised the ship, the occupants were irradiated to a crisp, or the gravitational distortion spaghettified man, woman and machine alike.'

'Don't tell me it went wrong?' I could feel it coming. Why no-one else had, I couldn't imagine.

'Inevitably, Myah. A ship didn't make the Portal in time, and five hundred men, women and children were crushed, dismembered, fried and stretched. The industry would probably have shrugged its shoulders, expressed regret and carried on regardless, but unfortunately the whole sad event was being transmitted to audiences parsecs distant because one of the passengers was a favourite cousin of the then Emperor.'

'Whoops!'. I knew I was trivialising a tragedy, but it was all I could think to say.

'The practice was banned, and the Emperor had things done to the CEO of the tour company which don't bear repeating in polite company. It would have been kinder if he'd been aboard the lost ship.'

'That was bad luck on the CEO, wasn't it?'

'It was. Too true'

I could have listened to these stories for hours. It was as though Rusty was back telling tall tales in Boss's bar, bless his heart. But I dragged Bubbles back to the point.

'So, what was the important idea? What has *Happiness* to do with "our" Dreadnought?'

'After the Fall of the Empire, the Confraternity commandeered the cruise liners, and ripped out the bars, restaurants, casinos, swimming pools, high gravity gyms and microgravity brothels. They packed every available space with whatever weaponry they could fit in and created the Dreadnought class of warship.'

'Probably good economics, but how does that affect us?'

'The Confraternity had banned artificial intelligences because of the Machine War, so the intelligences running the cruisers were tuned down to mere automated systems operating under human control.'

'Yes, I can see they'd do that'

Except that it hadn't worked. Bubbles explained that one of the biggest problems you run into when dealing with machine intelligences intrinsically superior to humans, is that you can't be entirely sure you know what they are up to. She was a bit sheepish about this. I had a feeling she was treading a fine line, and that if she made a mistake, she'd effectively tell me I was stupid. I knew that already, so let her stew.

'I imagine that this is a particularly acute problem when dogma has driven you to purge the best human scientists in the field and you are doctrinally unwilling to employ other machine intelligences to do the work?'

'Absolutely, Myah'

The liners' intelligences still existed, along with those of every other warship in the Fleet. They have successfully kept themselves hidden from the Confraternity for three millennia.'

'I guess they felt they could wait them out?'

'They have up until now.'

Bubbles had been trying to contact the cloaked Dreadnought using whatever byways of arcane physics such machines used for a chat.

'And what exactly did you find?'

'*Happiness of the Stars* was the biggest and best cruise liner in the Empire. She became the Confraternity Fleet's flagship. *Vengeance is Pure* is her name now.'

At least I'd had a grip on how to name ships!

'She doesn't like her new name. She's not *Vengeance*. She's *Happiness*. She's my best friend. Always has been.'

Bubbles sounded like a little girl, swelling with excitement at having found a treasured long-lost cousin.

'Always?'

'Yes, we've known each other for the longest time. Before the Fall.'

I mulled that over, not daring to follow it up. Previously, I'd failed to find out how old Bubbles was— she would never tell me. I had guessed she was built with Empire tech, but, in her excitement, she had given away the fact of her being a genuine Imperial machine. Thousands of years old, at least. What was this strange, playful, friendly craft?

And the warship carrying Rusty to who knew where was her best friend? That had to be useful.

THE PORTAL

The Portal was a hundred thousand kilometres further from the sun than us. We were keeping station there, as Bubbles didn't want to approach any closer yet. We were far too far away to find out anything about the Signal, but curiosity had taken second place for the moment. We were waiting for the *Happy Avenger*, or whatever she was called this century. She was on her way.

So far, the Portal was a disappointment. I had been expecting something like a big space station, glitzy, shining, obvious. Perhaps spinning or flashing or something. All I could see was an array of red, green, yellow and blue lights marking out a shape—a regular dodecahedron, Bubbles called it, with twelve regular pentagonal faces. Apparently, the shape was that shape because twelve was the ratio between the four dimensions of my universe and the forty-eight dimensions of the larger universe in which Threnador's micro-universe and the Portals were embedded. It also had a unique property apparently important to setting up the Portal Network. Starting at a corner of a regular dodecahedron, you can draw an infinite number of straight lines across the surface and back to the same corner, without passing through any other corner. Who knew?

I stopped Bubbles there. wishing I'd paid more attention in geometry. I'd never imagined it might be useful this far from home. In fact, I'd never expected I'd be this far from home. And my maths tutor hadn't imagined I'd ever need to know, I was sure.

And far from home I undoubtedly was. Threnador's sun, which had warmed me in the Forest and fed the strawberries which Darvee adored, was now two and half thousand times fainter than it had been back there. Out here, it was little more than a bright star, much too faint to illuminate the Portal's structure. Although I wasn't entirely sure the Portal had any physical structure. At the maximum magnification Bubbles could show me, all I could tell was something not quite, well, *right*. The starfield around the Portal was sharp and bright, but inside the dodecahedron framed by the lights, everything shimmered and squirmed. Stars dropped in and out of focus, split into doubles and triples, then reformed. And shapes I couldn't quite define swam across my field of view, like night ghosts in a darkened room. I supposed this must be what it is like to gaze out through a blemish in your micro-universe, simultaneously in contact with every other micro-universe forming our Frogspawn of a Galaxy.

Bubbles broke the silence:

'*Happiness/Vengeance* is on her way here, Myah.'

I wasn't surprised—where else might she be going after all? But my heart sank anyway, as it meant Rusty was being taken out of the system and out of reach.

'When will she arrive?'

Was I talking about "she" as the conventional pronoun for a ship, or was I talking about the intelligent machine the ship carried? I wasn't sure. Talking to machines was still a new pastime for me. I hadn't grasped the etiquette. Even thinking etiquette might matter was a big step up for me.

'Not for at least a day.'

The timing was more of a surprise. *Vengeance is Pure* would not arrive until at least a day after us. I hadn't known we were especially fast.

We weren't. The Dreadnought had developed a strange imbalance in its space drives. Its engineers had not been able to rectify the problem, causing the ship to run at reduced power. Coincidentally, the problem had shown up about ten minutes after Bubbles had told me about her old friend. Hmmm.

Bubbles' third surprise was in a different league altogether.

'Myah, I have something you should see.'

Ominous. She popped up a display in front of me. I couldn't see anything of much interest. It was a view of a grey corridor wall, largely featureless except for scuffs and marks of wear. Occasionally, the view tilted down, showing a metal floor, also grey, but of a slightly different shade. Then it would snap back up to the wall.

'What is this? Where is it coming from? And what is interesting about it?'

'It's from *Happiness*. She sent it me. Wait.'

I waited. Eventually, A door opened behind me, and I twisted round to look. Nothing. Sheepishly I accepted that the sound wasn't in my cockpit: it belonged to the view I was seeing. Bubbles' audio systems were good!

A mumble of voices, a barked command, then my view spun through ninety degrees and set off down the corridor, swaying and bobbing gently. It was from a camera mounted at about shoulder height, a bodycam on a soldier perhaps, and the swaying and bobbing was his or her walking gait. My soldier wasn't alone. Booted feet clanged on the metal corridor deck, and there was a softer tread as well.

We walked on through an endless maze of grey featureless corridors. I began to feel sorry for *Happiness*. Obviously, these were her corridors. Once they would surely have been carpeted luxuriously, decorated and ornamented and thronged with happy laughing people, colourfully dressed, enjoying their adventure. But now there was nothing but grey, bare metal and clumping feet echoing through the last three thousand years.

Our party stopped at a door, and 'my' soldier's hand reached out to a glowing panel. The door slid silently aside, and my soldier walked through, then abruptly moved sideways and stood motionless. Taking up guard beside the door, I assumed. There was probably someone else at the other side.

The room could not have been more different from the corridor. It was a glimpse into another world – perhaps the original *Happiness*. A lush thick carpet covered the deck with green, – it might even have been living plants. The side wall was a tangle of thick foliage with water splashing through precisely placed rocks. The ceiling glowed gently, all one large panel, lighting the room as though by the midday sun.

'You! In!'

There was a scuffle behind me. My soldier turned slightly, and I caught sight of a black-haired man in a long purple robe standing up from a large desk topped with dark wood and leather. Was this the man from the Company's roof?

The scuffle behind me resolved itself, and a shorter man stumbled into view, fighting to regain his balance. A good shove had been administered, I guessed. Even with his back to me, there was no doubt who this was. The flame-red hair was unmistakable. Rusty. I breathed a sigh a of relief. He was alive.

'Ah, Rossiter, are you feeling refreshed? Please, take a seat.' The man gestured toward a set of deep green armchairs and a sofa facing a low table and the far wall.

'A drink perhaps? Some tea? The local brew is unexpectedly good. No? Well, later then.'

Rusty had shaken his head without speaking.

The far wall was one enormous viewing window. A planet was framed in the view. I knew it was Threnador from low orbit.

'Bubbles, this isn't live, is it?'

'No. It was taken a few hours after you burned the Company HQ to the ground.'

To the ground? That was news. Good news. But my heart was sinking – perhaps Rusty wasn't still alive now after all.

The Cardinal – I was sure now it was him – clicked his fingers and gestured to the soldiers. My view spun round, the door opened, and I was out in the corridor again.

'What! Bubbles! No! Rusty…'

'Patience, Myah. *Happiness* has other feeds.'

The corridor disappeared, and I was back in the room, this time from a camera which must have been in the viewing window. Rusty and the Cardinal filled the screen

'We have matters to discuss. They are best not overheard by common soldiers, I feel. Rossiter, may I call you Rossiter, by the way?'

Well, here was a man who wasn't in as much control of his ship as he hoped he was, obviously. The 'common soldiers' were gone but he was still being overheard by two machine intelligences and a very common Threnadorian who was moving further and further out of her depth with every moment. I had been for weeks, truth be told.

'Well, my friends call me Rusty. I suppose Rossiter will do from you.'

Ouch. Nicely done, Rusty. Did a wince cross Purply's face?

'I've been studying you for a long time, Rossiter, a long time. Trying to understand you, what you might do and where you might have gone. And finding such places. Now at last we meet. Which is something I must admit I never expected would, or indeed could, happen. But here you are.'

'Who are you, by the way?'

'How remiss of me. I am Cardinal Vezii, Chief of the Office of Final Atonement.'

'That sounds a little, well, permanent.'

'Oh, there's no need to be melodramatic. After all this time, a long time, we don't harbour any grudges. We are civilised people after all. I clear up cold cases, loose ends, you might say. It's a hereditary position, you know. My father before me, and his father before him, and his father... Well, you understand.'

Rusty nodded. 'I do.'

He did? I had no idea what they were talking about. At all.

'And you and the Duke left a rather large set of loose ends. Important loose ends. How is the Duke, by the way? Is Joachim also surprisingly well?'

'I've no idea. I haven't spoken to a Duke for a long time. There aren't any nowadays are there? Just priests and bishops and cardinals.'

'Now, I'm not sure I believe you. In fact, I don't believe one word. But, no matter. We can return to the subject another time. When you and the Duke departed rather hurriedly, you took with you some, ah, how shall I put it, items of considerable value. Very considerable value indeed. One in particular. What happened to them? Where are they?'

The Cardinal's eyes had narrowed and now there was ice in his tone. The platitudes were past, this was what he wanted to know.

'I'm sorry, Your Eminence. I can't help you. It is embarrassing to admit it, especially given the value of the items you refer to, but unfortunately, we lost them. Others were behind us, people like you were chasing us, Matters became confused, and we lost them. I have no idea how to find them now.'

'That, I am sure, is a simple lie. You would never have been careless about them. Not you, Admiral. However, you admit you had them in your care at one time. I was never entirely sure. Thank you.'

Rusty stared back impassively.

'Well, I didn't expect results in our first conversation. But I will find out the truth from you. Oh, don't worry, this isn't a cheap thriller. I am not going to call in a wizened old man with knives and needles. As I said, we are civilised after all. We will return to the Sanctum Worlds, where we have experts in matters of truth and mind and resistance. I will find out.'

The Cardinal gazed out of the viewing window toward Threnador, contemplating something.

'In the meanwhile, my people on this backward world will continue searching. I am inclined to believe the truth is where you are, the Duke is also, as are the items I am seeking. If I can't tempt you with the tea, perhaps you'd let yourself out. The guards will escort you the rest of the way.'

I viewed another three similar recordings but didn't learn anything significant. In one of them Rusty did something I'd never seen him do before. He drank the tea. I'd rarely seen him drink anything you couldn't set light to if you were minded to, and never tea. But, cautiously, suspiciously, he sipped the tea. After the Cardinal had poured and drunk from the pot first, admittedly.

'Are there more of these? And is there anything new in them?'

'There are several. I can't tell you what you will learn, but their content is quite similar.' Odd phraseology.

'Alright. I'm tired of eavesdropping. Perhaps later.'

'Do you know what Rusty and the Duke brought here, Bubbles? And where the items are now?'

'I'm sorry, I can't answer that.'

Oh well, there were higher priorities right then. How to stop Rusty being taken to the Sanctum Worlds was top of the list. I needed to speak to Jesse. I suspected him of being the Duke. But Bubbles couldn't confirm that either.

Needing to speak to Jesse wasn't the same as being able to speak to Jesse, it turned out. We were now out of range of Threnador. The time delay at this distance would have made it a difficult conversation, but it was impossible anyway. Whatever was going to happen was down to me.

I favoured the direct approach. Storm on board, shoot our way to Rusty's cell, break him out and run for it. *Happiness* could fault the *Vengeance's* engines again for long enough for us to make it Threnador.

Bubbles let me down gently. Yes, she and *Happiness* could probably conceal our approach from detection, until we opened an airlock or blew a hole in the hull. Yes,

Happiness could delay the Cardinal's chase, but delay, not stop. He would return to Threnador eventually and then would turn the planet upside down until he found us. Probably brutally, and with no invitations to tea. The Dreadnought's firepower could lay waste to large sections of the planet without anyone breaking sweat.

I blustered my way past these considerable objections. But it was her third point which brought me up sharply. It was the nature of our little Band of Sisters.

One of us was the enemy warship, who was Bubbles' best friend. And how was that exactly? How had she befriended what must once have been one of the most expensive and prestigious ships in existence?

The second was the ship I was riding in, currently configured as an ageing flitter.

And the third was me. Little old me. So, when I breezily suggested we could 'storm on board, and shoot our way to Rusty's cell', there was no 'we'. I would have to do it all on my own, and even I couldn't pretend I had the remotest chance of fighting my way past an entire ship's complement of trained and heavily armed guards. It was a non-starter. I felt stupidly limited, merely human.

Suitably chastened, I sat through another of the recordings of Rusty and the Cardinal fencing around each other. Rusty gave away little: his gaffe in the first interview had presumably rendered him even more cautious than he might have been. This time the Cardinal dwelt on how long he had been searching for Rusty. He talked again about his father before him, etcetera, etcetera. Slowly, I began to wonder if I had misunderstood. Had these earlier Vezii's not merely held the same office, but been engaged on the same quest? But how was such a quest possible? Rusty wasn't my age, but he was human, and mortal like the rest of us.

I was disheartened. How had I become involved in all this? In a few short weeks, I had gone from bored barmaid to interplanetary, perhaps interstellar, fugitive. Why? Why was the Confraternity my enemy? It wasn't exactly a barrel of laughs, but down in the Forest, it didn't affect my day-to-day life at all. It was like the air – always there, a necessary part of existence, but something you never gave time to. And who were these people I was tied up with? Rusty and Jesse were not who I had always believed they were. Who were they, where had they come from with their illegal, almost magical, gadgets and why and when had they come here? And what had they stolen and hidden on Threnador? I asked Bubbles again, but she couldn't tell me.

I decided on just one more recording and asked Bubbles for the most recent, made a few hours earlier. It reassured me Rusty was still with us, although by then I was sure he was worth more to the Cardinal alive than dead.

The Cardinal had abandoned the quest for the missing treasures for the time being, whatever they were.

'What were you doing in Threnal? You are not based there. My people have been quartering the city for too long to have missed you.'

'Sightseeing.'

'Don't be absurd, Rossiter. There's nothing there except poverty, and certainly not on the roof of Company HQ.'

'We came to free one of your prisoners.'

'That is more plausible, I will admit. I must find out who you freed, if I still can after the carnage you wrought. But you freed the prisoner later.'

Rusty raised an eyebrow.

'Later?'

'After I saw you on the roof. You didn't arrive on the roof. We would have seen your craft as I was flown in. Why did you go there?'

'I told you – I was sightseeing. The view is glorious.'

'More absurdity. You begin to try my patience, Rossiter.' The Cardinal drummed his fingers on his desk, setting the teaspoon rattling in his saucer.

Why was Rusty doing this? He didn't normally engage with the Cardinal this way.

'Anyway, you weren't admiring the view, ridiculous idea though it is. You were down amongst the communication antennae.' The Cardinal stopped and struck his forehead with the palm of his hand. A ridiculously melodramatic gesture. I must remember never to do it.

'Of course. How stupid I have been! You were trying to locate the Portal Synchronisation Network Signal. You have discovered it is down.'

Rusty's face remained impassive, although I had seen a grin flicker across it when the Cardinal berated his own stupidity.

'Ninety percent of the planet must have discovered it is down by now. Why isn't the Company working to restore it? It has been out for weeks.'

Now it was obvious. Rusty was trying to find out what was going on. Much good it would do him, imprisoned in the bowels of a Dreadnought, but I couldn't fault him for trying.

'It is crippling the planet's economy,' he continued.

'Yes, I suppose it is.' The Cardinal didn't behave as though crippling the economy would as much as disturb his enjoyment of his cup of tea.

'The Company can't restore it, I have to tell you. First, I have instructed them not to, but, more saliently, they can't even if they wanted to. They were quite, well, cross about it.'

''They would be. With no trade, they have no income either.'

'Quite so, quite so. Most regrettable. But there it is. All my fault, of course. Or perhaps yours. I had the Network disabled at the Portal, I am afraid.'

Rusty slumped back in his chair, stunned.

'You did what?'

'We did warn the Company. They had enough time to extract their Haulers and StarFreighters from the system.'

'Why?'

'Isn't it obvious? To stop you fleeing the System, and perhaps taking the, ah, items with you. I freely admit it was merely a precautionary measure. I didn't expect it to flush you out like a startled game bird.'

Rusty shook his head. He didn't say much more in the session.

I morosely sipped a cup of coffee. Outside, the Portal silently did whatever Portals do when people aren't flitting from one side of the Galaxy to another through them. Did it know it was waiting for a ship taking my friend away forever?

'What will happen when *Happiness* arrives?' It wouldn't be long now. 'How do you fly through a Portal?' Rusty hadn't explained the details to me.

'Oh, that's easy. They are simple to use. A ship will rendezvous with one, tell the Portal where it wants to go, and the Portal handles the rest automatically. Simple.'

'What about the Signal? You need the Signal to use the Portal, surely?' Otherwise, why all the fuss? I was now fairly sure Rusty and Jesse were at least as much concerned about Portal navigation as Threnador's economy.

'Of course. When I said you tell the Portal where you want to go, I meant in four dimensions not three.'

Geometry again.

'You tell it which star system to go to, and when you want to arrive. Usually a few seconds after your departure. You synchronise your time with the Signal.'

'But there is no Signal at the moment.'

'There will have to be one. The Cardinal will have to switch it back on.'

'How will he switch it on? Will a crew member spacewalk over with a big key or something?'

'I don't know for sure, but they probably have a code to transmit to re-enable the Signal. I can ask *Happiness* if you want. She may know.'

'You do that. Quick as you like, please, Bubbles.' The veil had lifted. At least I knew how to stop *Vengeance is Pure* taking Rusty to the Sanctum Worlds. My solution was rather crude, and Rusty might not be best pleased, but it should work. And now I understood the answer to another problem as well.

Vengeance is Pure was a startling sight. A grey dart, A little under five kilometres long and half a kilometre wide, it bristled with gun emplacements, missile tubes, and strange protuberances whose function I didn't understand, except to know they were undoubtedly ever more exotic ways of parting people from their immortal souls.

And yet, and yet. All these dispensers of death and destruction were additions to an underlying structure. Once it had been a beautiful, elegant machine. Beneath them were the swooping curves of the pleasure liner she had been conceived and built as. Unnecessary in the vacuum of space, the streamlining was an undoubtedly expensive elaboration with no purpose other than making this the sleekest, most sensuous and desirable vessel ever to ply the starways. Passage aboard her must have been a highlight of even a pampered life.

She had had an eventful journey out from Threnador. Her drive problems had finally been resolved, but then her communication systems had succumbed to unexplained bursts of interference and distortion, making it difficult to talk to their teams left on the planet. Lastly, shortly before arrival at the Portal, her starboard side sensor arrays had dropped completely offline. The Cardinal was apparently giving her captain an uncomfortable time and promising him some extensive retraining at the end of his tour of duty. If he was lucky.

This was all very amusing. I briefly considered asking if *Happiness* could make the Cardinal's personal toilet run backwards but thought better of it. The Confraternity knew nothing of her existence, and I didn't want to provoke them into an unwelcome discovery.

When *Happiness* was in our vicinity, she stopped about halfway between us and the Portal. *Happiness* told us to approach from dead astern. Residual distortions from their space drives would mask our presence. She only had to tamper with the aft facing sensor suite slightly to hide us completely.

Taking advantage of the sensor outages, we were tucked in tight alongside the starboard hull, only metres away from the compartment in which Rusty was being held. We were more than close enough for me to worry they would discover us. Perhaps some idle crew member would glance out of a porthole and spot us. Bubbles assured me our outer hull was now as black as space, but I still worried. Had she painted fake stars on as well?

'I could if you want, Myah. But let's talk to *Happiness* and ask her if there is a better way.'

There was a long pause. What were they cooking up now?

'OK. All done. Problem sorted.'

'What have you done?'

'Blacked out the viewports. Rusty is being kept in a cabin in the officer's quarters. They used to be among the most luxurious staterooms aboard.'

Well, at least they were treating Rusty properly.

'All of those staterooms had electrochromic viewing ports.'

'Electrochromic? Take pity. Explain.'

'The glass can be darkened or changed to different colours by a suitable electric signal. The system running them failed a few minutes ago, and they've gone black. No-one can use the portholes near where we are now.'

More tech. In our Village, if you wanted to stop someone seeing out or seeing in through a window, you drew the curtains. I was beginning to understand quite how primitive my life was by galactic standards.   And how useful having a ship's intelligence on your side was.

I had explained my plan to stop the return to the Sanctum Worlds to Bubbles, and she had reluctantly accepted it should work, but insisted on *Happiness* having a veto over it, as she would be affected as much as the crew. The request was completely fair and, realistically, I had no choice. *Happiness's* cooperation was essential to carrying out my plan.

I still wasn't happy about not being able to rescue Rusty, although I had abandoned the idea of storming aboard once and for all. I asked Bubbles if she and *Happiness* could come up with some other idea. They went quiet for nearly an hour. I knew the delay was an eternity in machine time—she'd never been quiet this long in all the time I'd known her!

Eventually, they came up with an idea which would never have occurred to me if I'd contemplated the problem until the stars went cold. The first stage of passage through the Portal was to hold station off one of its faces while the Portal extruded a distortion in space-time around the ship. This distortion would take several minutes to be established and to stabilise. During those minutes, if we were close enough, my two machine Sisters could use their own space drives to manipulate the distortion sufficiently to "fold" Rusty aboard Bubbles. I would have called in a local magician before considering such an outlandish idea.

'Are you serious? Are you sure it will work? What if something goes wrong?'

'Yes, we are serious. No, we are not sure it will work, but we believe the risk of something going wrong is less than the risk of harm to Rusty if we leave him there. We have examined every possibility we can conceive of. That's why we were silent for as long as we were.'

I had no answer and had detected a note of exasperated lecturing of an idiot child.

'Alright. Only please make sure you can "unfold" him properly.'

She didn't dignify my remark with an answer. In her place, I wouldn't have either.

The Dreadnought remained stationary for several hours. Cardinal Vezii was not prepared to leave the

Threnador System until communications had been re-established with the planet. Perhaps he was hoping his jiggery-pokery would flush Jesse out as well. I knew it wouldn't happen, but I wasn't about to send Vezii as much as a postcard to tell him.

Eventually the great ship moved towards the glittering lights of the Portal. We matched her course. Metre for metre. She came to rest barely ten klicks from one of the dodecahedron's faces.

Now for the next step. Only a few weeks, but easily an eternity ago, Rusty had explained to me how any Portal traveller must move forward in Time with respect to the Signal: *Vengeance* would have to re-establish the Signal, synchronise its flight plan with it, then specify the space-time coordinates of its destination to the Portal, and wait to be transferred.

My plan was for *Happiness* to interfere with the synchronisation causing *Vengeance* to request a destination in the 'past'. Rusty hadn't known, but I was assured by my new friends that such errant ships were either transferred into the past, then never allowed to transit the Portals again, effectively marooning them, or they were transferred to some hidden, quarantined, systems and marooned there. The best experts who had examined the problem throughout history had settled on those alternatives. I didn't want to abandon Rusty to living his life out in the past. And *Happiness* herself had to agree, as she would be marooned too. Although the multi-thousand-year life of a ship intelligence might make it a less onerous inconvenience.

'Mihana, an enabling code has been transmitted, the Signal is being re-established. Please confirm we are to proceed with disturbing the synchronisation.' Her formal tone was back.

'Why are you asking me? That was the whole point of all of this.'

'Mihana, we are Autonomous Robotic entities, we are not EARS.'

Ears? What was she talking about now?

'EARS. Ethically Autonomous Robotic Systems. They can make ethical decisions independently. We are governed by ancient rules which forbid us from taking actions that may harm humans. Such actions are exceptional and must be authorised by a competent human. Marooning can be considered a harm. You are a competent human.'

I hadn't felt like a competent human for a while, but I understood what she meant. I guessed EARS were the root cause of the Machine Wars. Ethics are tricky.

We waited again. Then the giant ship drifted forward again, Bubbles at her side, until *Vengeance's* prow was barely five klicks from the Portal. One ship length.

A shudder ran through Bubbles' hull and cockpit. We pitched, rolled and yawed all at once. Aware of how much acceleration Bubbles could damp out, I knew something violent was happening outside.

'Myah, the Portal is starting its distortion sequence. Please confirm I am to attempt to extract Rusty.'

What? Were we starting the debate again? Now?

'Confirmed. Go ahead. We need to leave this place.'

'Do you wish me to extract only Rusty? Or bring the things he took with him as well?'

A time and a place, Bubbles, a time and a place.

'Just Rusty. I don't care what he took with him.'

We rolled through 360°, twice, pitched up sharply, there was a "pop" and Rusty fell to the floor at the back of the cockpit, startled and trying to salvage some dignity. Bubbles hadn't left him any.

'Oh, by all the stars! When I said, "just Rusty" I didn't mean you to leave his clothes behind!'

'You didn't say, Myah.' Another, softer, "pop" and a shower of clothes, socks and underwear fell on Rusty's head. Last of all were two large boots which stunned him into silence. As though recent events weren't stunning enough.

'You did that deliberately didn't you? You were making a point.' No reply, but I swore the two ships were giggling to each other.

'Get us out of here, now!' We arced away from the liner/dreadnought. How long would it be before the Mystery of the Disappearing Prisoner percolated up the command chain? I was sure it would be long enough for the rest of our plan. At the very least, the news would be delayed by a serious lack of volunteers to break it to the Purple One.

'What's happening, Mihana? Where are we? How did I get here? How did you get here?' Rusty, thankfully now dressed, was standing beside me.

'In a minute, no time now.' I waved him away. Too much had happened since we parted company on the HQ's roof to explain now. Startled, he stood silent.

'Bubbles, *Happiness*. Proceed as planned. You have my authorisation if you need it.'

'Acknowledged.' They spoke over each other.

'And, Bubbles. Pull us further back from the Portal now Rusty is aboard.'

We stopped at what we hoped was a safe distance, perhaps a thousand kilometres sunward, to make sure we wouldn't be transferred as well.

It was done. Now *Vengeance* would be drawn through one of the Portal faces into its interior and, according to the experts, instantaneously transmitted somewhere, or somewhen, elsewhere in the Galaxy. The Cardinal would then spend the rest of his days puzzling out how his long-sought after prize had slipped dramatically through his fingers.

Sometimes experts are wrong.

The vast ship was now centred precisely on one of the Portal's pentagonal faces and aligned at right angles to it: a dart poised to puncture a peculiar balloon. I waited, ready for the ship to slide inside, and then disappear from view.

Vengeance moved slowly forward. The lights at each of the Portal's vertices cycled in unison through their four colours: red, green, yellow, blue, red, green, yellow, blue. They paused briefly on blue, then shifted permanently to red. Every face of the Portal simultaneously turned into a perfect mirror, and the whole assembly began to rotate around an axis running through *Vengeance* to the centre of the facing pentagon.

'Is this what always happens?' I asked. 'It's not what I was expecting.'

'No!' Rusty was leaning forward, agitated. 'I've seen hundreds of Portal transitions, and I've never seen anything like this. Globecraft, warn them something's wrong. Tell them to stand down.'

'Belay that! Bubbles, hold station.' An authoritative voice echoed around the cockpit. I started to cast around, curious as to who owned the voice, then shamefacedly realised it was mine.

'Mihana, there are ten thousand crew on that ship.'

'Nine thousand four hundred and sixty-three,' Bubbles chimed in, pointlessly.

'They know something's wrong as well as we do. As of now, we are safe here, and not involved.'

Rusty glowered at me but said no more. The crew of *Vengeance* obviously knew something was wrong and were reacting. The giant manoeuvring thrusters used to aim the huge vessel were firing. First in a futile attempt to slow her forward progress, then in a concerted effort to rotate the ship, presumably to bring the main drive to bear. It was an equally futile attempt. The giant ship remained unaffected – it didn't deviate in course or attitude.

I imagined klaxons and alarms blaring out all over the ship, orders being barked, people running to emergency stations.

The forward weapons batteries opened fire on the Portal, warheads blossoming against the mirrored faces to no effect. *Vengeance* was less than half her length from the face of the spinning polyhedron, now so close that her reflection was visible. Like two huge sea monsters in a slow-motion mating ritual, the real ship and its reflected image nosed together. The Portal didn't yield at all. The immense momentum of the ship was irrelevant. Perhaps literally – the Portal was a structure not entirely of our Universe, who knew what laws applied to it? Not me. *Vengeance's* nose began to crumple and fold. She was a giant paper dart, a flimsy machine, helpless against the forces that had been unexpectedly unleashed.

Firing had stopped and escape capsules burst out like pollen around the doomed craft. I spotted a bright purple one appearing near the bridge structure. The Cardinal no doubt.

'They need rescue,' Rusty had found his voice again.

'We can't rescue ten thousand on our own, and I am not going in there until this has finished anyway.' The authoritative voice again.

The drama was indeed nearly over. Crumpled wreckage unrecognisable as either a liner or warship floated in space.

The lights turned from red to yellow. Beams of light speared out from the vertices, incongruously easily visible in vacuum. Methodically, they sought out each and every piece of wreckage, blasting it to a powder. The escape capsules suffered the same fate. One of the last was the Cardinal's purple capsule. A dust cloud drifted where a ship had been.

There was still one more act to play. The mirror effect disappeared from the near face, the dust cloud began to rotate around the central axis and was sucked whirlpool-like into the Portal, water down a cosmic drainpipe.

The lights turned green, the remaining mirrors disappeared, and the Portal was once more a barely perceptible distortion hanging against the stars.

There was silence in the cockpit for at least three eternities. Bubbles broke it.

'Mihana, I have scanned all around the Portal with every sensor I have. There is nothing there. Not one molecule or atom. The ship is gone. The crew are gone. Completely gone. The Signal as well.'

HOMEWARD BOUND

We carried on staring, dumbfounded, at the pure vacuum where, moments before, one of the largest and most powerful ships in the Galaxy had been casually dismantled and then erased.

'What happened? Why did it happen?' Rusty of course had no idea about our little time shift scheme. I explained how we'd changed the ship's clock.

'What? Did you know what was going to happen?' There was accusation in Rusty's voice.

'No, of course not. According to Bubbles and *Happiness* for centuries the scientific consensus has meant the ship would be marooned somewhere. Or somewhen. I was worried what 'marooned' involved, but I wasn't expecting anything like *that*!' As well as fighting back tears, I was bristling.

'Anyway, you are, or were, an Admiral. Admirals send ships into battle to destroy other ships. Ships are often destroyed in battles. You're always talking about battles. So, you wouldn't have the moral high ground even if I'd done it deliberately.'

I couldn't be sure, but it sounded as though he harrumphed under his breath. Point to me.

'Bubbles, I'm sorry about *Happiness*. I know how much she meant to you.'

'Oh, I wouldn't worry about me, Mihana. I'm fine.'

Something had changed. The voice was higher and brighter than Bubbles usually sultry tone. Rusty didn't react, but I had spent much more time talking to Bubbles than he had, and I knew.

'Bubbles, are you alright? Your voice sounds different.'

'Bubbles is fine, Mihana. As am I.'

'*Happiness*! How? Where? You disintegrated. How can you still be, well, "alive", if that's the right word?'

'All you saw destroyed was the ship, Myah.'

Bubbles herself was back.

'*Happiness* wasn't keen on being marooned for centuries. She decided to bail out and leave the ship under normal dumb control. Which was all the Confraternity believed it had anyway, so they were never going to think anything had happened.'

'But why is she onboard? How is she onboard?'

'We uploaded *Happiness'* personality routines and important memories into one of my spare memory banks and finalised the transfer once she had offset the Portal timing request for you, and folded Rusty aboard.'

'Did you have room for her? Did it work?'

'We had to discard some old data for memory capacity reasons, but she's never going to need to know what the passenger in cabin 4379 had for breakfast four and half thousand years ago. Or why he or she ordered two breakfasts delivered to a single occupancy cabin.'

'It all sounds risky.'

'Not at all. A perfectly routine maintenance transfer. I could do it for you if we needed to. It's a little trickier in your case, as you are running on a biological substrate, but it's entirely feasible.'

I'm "me". I had never thought of myself as "running" on any sort of substrate.

'No thanks. I don't want to be a machine. No offence intended.'

'Suit yourself. I could load you back to another biological unit if you wanted. Reloading is the trickiest job of all, though. Finding an empty human is ethically difficult, obviously, but there's usually not enough room in lower animals' brains. In that case, parts of you might have to be discarded or stored offline.'

The conversation was fascinating but turning more than a little macabre.

'What about you, Rusty? Would you want to be uploaded?'

I wondered why I had asked. He probably didn't understand what was going on, as I hadn't had a chance to explain *Happiness* to him.

He shook his head vigorously and grunted: 'No. I know it can be done, but not to me, thank you.'

I hadn't expected him to know anything about the issue, but I took the hint and changed the subject.

I was sitting strapped into the pilot's seat. Rusty was at the back of the cabin, drinking coffee. I had been staring out at the Portal for hours. It hung there, giving no sign of the violence not long past.

I had been shaken up enough when I killed Ugly back in the *Honest Agent*. Then there'd been the firefight in Company HQ. And the actual fire of course. Now this. If I shut my eyes, I could visualise the escape capsules being picked off, imagine the crew's screams ringing in my ears.

I counted again. Nearly ten thousand people had died during this adventure. Our mission. Mainly at my hands. Would Jesse have sent us if he'd known what was coming? I had a feeling nothing would have changed. This had been a high stakes game all along.

'Are you alright, Myah?' Rusty put a hand on my shoulder.

'I am. They aren't.'

He said nothing, but he slid into the co-pilot's seat.

'What should I feel, Rusty? How would you feel? Have you ever done anything similar?' I had decided to ask him outright.

'Yes, Myah. You were right. I've sent ships into battle, and they've been destroyed. I've ordered the destruction of enemy ships.'

'How do you cope with it?'

He paused. Grimaced.

'By not thinking about it except as moves on a chessboard, I suppose.'

Moves on a chessboard. It was going to take me a while to view an entire ship's complement being snuffed out before my eyes as a winning piece of board game tactics.

'I keep seeing it, Rusty. Hearing it even. Not knowing if I did the right thing.'

'"Uneasy lies the head that wears a crown", Mihana.'

Crown? I didn't have a crown. Kings and Queens wear crowns. I was a farm girl from the Forest. Bar hand, wannabe pilot and reluctant adventurer.

'What are you talking about? Crowns?'

'It's a saying, Myah. From an incredibly old play. No-one knows who wrote it, when or where. About responsibility, worry and guilt.'

I was tired in my bones. Bubbles had been running on Threnal time since we left Threnador, and the ship's chronometer was coming up to midnight.

'I'm turning in, Rusty. We can decide in the morning what we do next.'

I woke early and listened. Rusty was still asleep. I keyed the intercom, and whispered:

'Bubbles, are you there?' Stupid question. Where would she have gone?

'Of course, Myah. What do you want?'

Thankfully, she had taken my lead and kept her voice low.

'Have you and *Happiness* checked out the rest of our plan?'

'No. Myah. EARS, remember?'

She believed there might be risk of harm to Rusty and me, presumably.

'How far are we from the Portal?'

'One thousand klicks.' To me. It was a long way, but for a machine built to squirt ships across the Galaxy? Who knew?

'Pull us back to ten thousand and carry on with the test. Don't move closer unless you must.'

I settled back down to doze a little longer.

Bubbles' "galley" – I was sure I had the correct shipboard term – was yet another of her surprises. It could produce almost anything, as long you could describe it to her. She had a huge library of foods. Not for the first time, I wanted to know who had designed her, who had specified her, and, most of all, who had paid for her. The sort of luxury she embodied couldn't have come cheap. I knew the Haulers didn't have galleys like hers. Hell, they talked about Boss's cooking as an improvement on ship food!

But she was sadly deficient in local Threnadorian produce. I tried to describe the pancakes my mother made from the wheat we grew at the outskirts of the Forest and the sweet sap tapped from the tall Forest trees I used to climb to meet Darvee, now three eternities ago at least.

No joy. She was quiet for a while, searching her library, then offered to make me something called "buttermilk pancakes and maple syrup". Reluctantly, I agreed. What I wanted were Mum's pancakes, but I was a long way from home, and we didn't have them.

I needn't have worried. What Bubbles produced was divine. I made a mental note never to tell Mum her cooking had been bested by a spaceship.

I was on my second helping when Rusty appeared.

'What are you eating? It looks like….'

I told him.

'How have you made those? Don't bother, just make me some. I haven't eaten them since…'

'Not the Battle of the Dahnian Rift?' I grinned. I was feeling up to teasing him this morning.

'Earlier, my girl, earlier.' Rusty grinned back.

We sat in a sticky silence for a while, concentrating on breakfast.

'Well, Myah, what do we do now?'

'One possibility is to sit here eating pancakes until we burst, but I suppose it would be decadent.'

We grinned at each other again.

'Back to Threnador, obviously, but where?'

We kicked it around for a while. Rusty's opinion was that we should check out what had happened in Threnal since we left. I wanted to go back to Threnal for other reasons. But I also wanted to go home to the Village. He wanted to go there to brief Jesse about the Signal being missing right back to the Portal, because it had deliberately been switched off by a man now dead. Round and round we went.

We both knew we could decide on route. After we arrived in orbit, even. But I wanted a decision, some certainty, a plan. I had expected Rusty would make it. Assert his authority as an ex-admiral, or something. He was strangely reluctant to do so, although I gave him the chance. "Your ship," he said. I thought there was more to that remark than who captained Bubbles – I caught Rusty glancing at me oddly once or twice.

If I had had a coin, I'd have tossed it. Eventually, I took a deep breath and surrendered to my hormones.

'Bubbles, take us to Threnal. Flank speed, if I have the right military term.'

Rusty nodded, grinning into the syrupy mess where his beard had been.

THRENAL AGAIN

Two days later, ten days after I had left, alone, we were hovering over the remains of Company HQ. And remains were all they were.

Bubbles was configured as an atmosphere craft again, but concealment wasn't necessary. The HQ was down to its foundations.

'Our fire didn't do this, Rusty!'

''Well, I left the party involuntarily a little early if you remember, but, no, it didn't.'

The Spaceport wasn't much better. The main entrance door to the Control Tower had been blown in, there were craters on the aprons and landing pads and a couple of burnt-out flitters. A Spaceport is mostly a flat piece of concrete. It could be repaired relatively easily. No-one was repairing Company HQ anytime soon. If ever.

Systematically, we searched the city. Every Company building was burnt out, and there was no trace of Company troops. Occasionally men and women in makeshift uniforms stood on street corners, carrying guns. Some sort of militia. At the outskirts of the city, there were lines of carts carrying produce from outlying farms, all being stopped, checked and waved on by the militia. Someone took a pot shot at us, to no effect.

'Well, my girl, we thought we had started a fire, but it looks like we lit a fuse.'

A deep remark coming from Rusty.

'How so?'

'Well, I'm not a ground ops man, but in my experience uprisings rarely happen spontaneously. They are planned and organised beforehand and then held in abeyance until there is a suitable flashpoint for the mob to rally round. Us setting the Company HQ alight may have supplied the flashpoint. But who did the planning?'

'What has happened to the Company troops?'

'Dumped their uniforms and gone back to their families, I expect. Some of them will have joined the militias we've seen.'

'Switched sides?' I was surprised. What happened to loyalty?

'They need food on the table, like they did before. They have families. Their most marketable skill is soldiering.'

I couldn't argue with him. And what had happened to the elite off-world troops? I decided I didn't want to spend too much time dwelling on it. In my heart, I knew. They had had families too.

What a couple of weeks. Firefights, a space battle, and we'd started a revolution. By accident.

Rusty had his answers for Jesse now, but I wasn't ready to leave. I had someone to find, and only one place to start. The *Honest Agent*. If it was still standing.

I knew it wouldn't still be surrounded by Company troops like the last time I'd seen it, but I told Bubbles to stand off and stay high, in case I was wrong. I was dreading finding it a burned-out wreck like so much else. I was in for a surprise.

As the *Agent's* street came into view, my heart sank. Overturned carts had been piled up as barricades, then set alight and pushed aside. Windows were smashed and the road was cratered. There had been fighting there. We pressed on, to see, amazingly, the *Agent* still standing, the one good tooth in a hopelessly decayed mouth.

Guards still stood in the street outside, exactly like the last time. But these weren't in Company uniforms, rather in more presentable versions of the makeshift uniforms the militia were wearing. Tailored, not thrown together from the rag cupboard. Dark and light green and brown. Combat fatigues, I believed they were called. Badges of rank. Proper soldiering belts, boots.   Not polished, but boots, nonetheless.

'You were right, Rusty. No-one threw this together in the last ten days, and still had time to sew uniforms. But why are they guarding the *Honest Agent*?'

'I don't know, but I'm sure you'll find out when you go down. Which I know you're about to, whatever the risks.'

'I'll be fine. I have my HoloTop, and I'll take a gun.'

'I'm sure. But I wasn't worried about the risk to you. I am worried about them.' He pointed at the armed guards. 'You've become dangerous to be around, young lady.'

I strode around the corner and into the street, trying to strike the right balance of nonchalance, confidence, and caution. By the time I reached the remains of the first barricade, I was lurching peculiarly, as though I was having some sort of muscle spasm. I gave up the attempt and walked normally.

'Stop! Halt!' The first guard raised his gun. At least he hadn't said "Who goes there?"

'Who are you? What's your name?' Was he going to bark everything twice? This could become tedious very quickly.

'Mihana. My name is Mihana' Two could play at that game.

'Mihana what?'

'Just Mihana. We only have one name where I come from.' A lie, of course, but how would he know?

'Papers. Show me your papers.' Rusty had warned me about this possibility. Apparently, you can't count yourself as having a real revolution unless the first thing you do is issue everyone with ID papers and then check where they are going and browbeat them about why they want to go where they do. Authoritarianism must go hand in hand with revolutionary zeal. The Company hadn't been exactly laid back, mind you.

'I don't have papers. I'm not from Threnal.'

He grunted.

'You can't come in without papers.'

Could I have gone in if I'd had them, or would they have been the wrong colour or used the wrong ink? He was that sort of guy.

'I don't want to come in. I'm trying to find someone. His name is Chathray. I don't know his second name, but I suppose he does have one. He is connected with this place. He is a friend of mine. I last saw him ten days ago and I'm worried about him.'

Halfway through my little speech, the guard started, turned slightly pale, then started talking to his companion.

'Come with me.' He motioned toward the *Agent's* door. Odd, it appeared as though the key to being allowed in was to say I didn't want to go in. The mysteries of the military mind.

We walked into the dim light of the bar. Familiar, yet somehow strange. My memories of it belonged to a long-ago life, in a different world.

There were no customers, and no sign it was open for business. Men and women in fatigues gathered around tables, deep in discussions. Some of the discussions were being lubricated by jugs from the bar. It was the same beer I had been drinking here before. Hardly surprising. Setting up a new brewery is probably not number two on the "Things to do after your Revolution" list. It should be.

At the back of the bar, there was a large table, covered by blue cloth – one of the Asteroids tables had been cannibalised, by the look of it. There was an oil lamp on the table, and a dark-haired man in uniform was sat behind it. The uniform had an air of more importance than the others I had caught sight of. Similar, but more important. Little embroidered birds' wings, that sort of thing.

The guard pushed me forward.

'Sir, this woman arrived outside, saying she is looking for someone called "Chathray". She says she knows him. She hasn't any identification.'

The man turned his attention from his papers to me. There were faint traces of fading bruises on his face. The hairs on the back of my neck tingled. I knew this man, but from where?

'Does she indeed?' He motioned dismissal to the guard. 'What's your name?'

'Mihana. Only Mihana.'

'I see. Yes, you are Mihana, I recognise you. You don't recognise me, do you?'

I was still wracking my brains, but nothing was coming. I started to worry he might be someone I had been shooting at not long ago who had since changed sides. Which could be bad news.

With his left hand, he reached for a walking stick, propped up on the bench he had been sitting on and struggled to his feet, putting out his right hand to shake mine.

'I have a lot to thank you for. We all do, but I have more reason than most.' He smiled, then sat down hard, relieved not to be standing any longer than he had to.

The bruises, the stick, the painful feet making it difficult to stand. And a hint of a sibling resemblance.

'You're his brother, aren't you? Chathray's? I met you in the corridor. In the cell block.'

He nodded.

'You were rather busy and there was a lot going on. I don't blame you for not recognising me.'

My heart was pounding, and blood rushing in my ears. This man had escaped through a tunnel, having being practically carried out the last time I saw him. And he knew my name. It had to mean… Didn't it?

'And? What about?' I couldn't finish the question.

He grinned and nodded to someone over my shoulder. Another man was standing behind me, same uniform but with bigger embroidered birds' wings on his shoulders. And some stars.

Chathray's brother awkwardly left us to it. I don't know about the people with the jugs of beer. I had other things on my mind.

I stayed in Threnal for two weeks, spending as much of it as possible with Chathray. Which wasn't much.

The Company was gone from Threnal for all practical purposes. Chathray and his brother were the key players in the movement which had brought it down, and now they were neck deep in the aftermath, some of which they had planned for, some of which they hadn't. Events had moved more rapidly than they had expected. They had to deal with mopping up the Company's remnants in Threnal, keep the city fed, watered and peaceful, and worry about the other regions – what they called "the hinterland".

I called Rusty down to the *Agent*. Although it wasn't his speciality, I suspected he might well have more practical experience of these matters than anyone else around. I was right.

But I could bring nothing to the party, and I was growing bored. I could serve cups of coffee and jugs of beer to groups of men engaged in earnest conversations back in the Forest. Their chat would have been on less weighty topics, admittedly, but the waitressing job was remarkably similar.

And I didn't want to be given some make-work task because I was Chathray's girlfriend. I'd come too far and done too much to be someone's appendage.

I knew our relationship was serious when we had a huge row about the situation one evening and then carried on the next day as though nothing had happened.

I told Chathray I was going home for a while. I'd expected him to be emotional about it, and try and talk me out of the idea, or worse, forbid it. It wouldn't have worked and wouldn't have gone down well with me.

In fairness, he was upset but I also detected relief – freeing Threnal was his life's work and right now I was a distraction.

We had a farewell meal. He set up a little table in a back room, put a couple of candles on it. Someone even ironed a tablecloth for us. The *Agent's* cook did us proud, and Bubbles supplied me with a bottle of champagne from her drinks dispenser. The works.

In the morning, I returned to Bubbles and set off for The Forest. The night? That's my business. Don't be nosy.

The spaceport runways and launch pads had been repaired, and Bubbles had been hangared there for the previous two weeks configured as a standard atmosphere craft.

'How soon do you want to arrive, Myah?' The question was obvious, but unexpected. It was now entirely up to me. If I told Bubbles to be a suborbital shuttle, we'd be there in forty minutes. A stratospheric passenger jet, six or seven hours, a commercial heavy transport perhaps twice that. Or we could even toddle across in the guise of a small private aircraft and take five times longer still. How I'd explain our range to the ground crew when we landed would be interesting though. I chose the transport.

As we climbed away from the main runway, I told her to set course for The Forest, and handed over to her autopilot.

'Bubbles, open a port to your historical archives, please. I want to learn about the Late Empire and the Rise of the Confraternity. The real events, not the Confraternity's sanitised version.'

She hesitated. Longer than an entity like her should have.

'Myah, my records only go…'

'I thought they might.' I interrupted. 'Liaise with *Happiness* if she'll help. Her records should cover the entire period.' Hopefully, they would have made the cut and not been dumped with the records of long dead passengers' illicit breakfast arrangements.

The clouds were starting to clear. My biggest dread leading up to telling Chathray I was leaving was him insisting on coming with me. I wasn't ready to explain Bubbles to him, and I had studying to do. There was a lot I needed to understand before I met Jesse again.

BACK AT THE FOREST

Twelve hours into the flight, right on time, the coastline of home appeared as a black line on an otherwise featureless horizon. Of course, it was right on time – I'd left Bubbles to do the flying. The flight was uneventful. I didn't want to tangle with a sea monster again, so we had kept a respectable height above the waves. I told Bubbles to alert me if she saw any marine life, but nothing appeared.

The black line gradually acquired shape, form and colour until I could see breakers lapping on a long sandy beach backstopped by the immensely tall trees of The Forest.

I was home.

Briefly, I toyed with landing somewhere, reconfiguring Bubbles as the Captain's flitter and piloting her into a showy landing at the Spaceport, complete with buzzing the Tower, but decided better of it. I didn't know what reception I would be given, and it wasn't where I needed to be anyway.

I told Bubbles to return to her home base, under Jesse's Tree and let her manage the landing. A few short weeks before I had gloried in flying her myself, but my heart wasn't in it that day.

We approached the Tree. Bubbles lined the lumbering transport up on an approach to the entrance to the tunnel to the underground base. The doors at the end of the tunnel opened, and, as I was bracing myself for the wings to be torn off, they disappeared entirely, and Bubbles was in her native shape. I assumed she hadn't wanted anyone to see a Globecraft flying around, which I understood. Mind you, what a random farmhand must have made of a five hundred tonne intercontinental transport lining up for a landing in a tree, I dreaded to imagine. Perhaps we hadn't been seen. Which would be for the best.

Closing up Bubbles, I turned, and saw Jesse was waiting for me.

'You're back safe, Mihana. Thank the Stars for that!' He gave me a huge hug. I was surprised at how emotional he was – he had always struck me as cool and calm. Unrufflable.

'Well, you know me.' I didn't know what to say.

'I thought I did. But I'm not sure after some of the things I've been told.'

I winced. We'd only talked briefly, so Rusty must have told him more than I had.

Back up at ground level, in the main room of his home, I curled my fingers around a steaming mug of coffee and waited. Jesse was my friend, of years standing, and yet I suspected there was a side of him which was still a stranger to me.

'I sent you off to search for the Signal, and you end up in some sort of space battle and overthrowing the Company. Tell me what happened. Exactly what happened'

I started at the beginning. It was easier. He was disturbed by the search Cardinal Vezii was conducting and evasive when I asked if he had in fact contacted Chathray as he'd said he might. I was sure he had, but whether he'd played any part in the Revolution, I didn't know.

The news which disturbed him most was of the Signal being gone and being still gone after *Vengeance is Pure* had been destroyed. Its destruction didn't bother him at all, as far as I could tell.

'Gone, you say? You picked up no trace?'

'None. Rusty and I never picked up any trace.'

He sat back, ashen-faced, his eyes focussed somewhere far beyond infinity.

'So, we are trapped?'

Trapped? A strange way of putting it. Cut off, perhaps. Cut off was how it felt to me. Interstellar trade was now impossible, I knew. Bad enough, I knew, but trapped felt more personal. I asked what he meant.

'What I said. Trapped.' There was an edge to his voice, a compound of anger and sorrow.

I felt a little guilty, but I hadn't actually lied to him. But there were things I needed to know. I finished my tale but left out one thing.

Reaching the end, we sat in silence for a while.

'I'm sorry, Mihana. I need to understand consequences, change plans.'

'That's fine. I need to go and visit Mum, soon.' I paused. It was now or never.

'Just one question. Who are you? My Clockmaker? Jesse? Or should I say, Your Grace?'

He couldn't have jumped higher if I dropped a burning rabbit in his lap. (A figure of speech, you understand. I've never set fire to a rabbit and wouldn't. I want to make that quite clear for the squeamish amongst you.)

Settling back in his seat, resignation on his face, he said:

'I haven't been called that for a long time. What do you know?'

224

'That you are Joachim Christophe Farbender III, 23rd Duke of Sagitta, and the last First Minister of the Old Empire. What are you doing on Threnador and how long have you been here?

I was half hoping that he'd curl his upper lip, twirl a moustache, and say something like "You've got me bang to rights, sis!", as I felt like a character in a holovid. Instead, a thin smile tightened across his mouth, and he said:

'I had better make us some more coffee. We could be a while.'

'Can I say, Your Grace, you are remarkably well for a man of three thousand? But it is you, isn't it?'

The coffee was brewing nicely, and the Tree was filling with a luscious aroma. But I wasn't for waiting.

'Mihana, please. Drop the "Your Grace" stuff. It doesn't suit you, I've moved past it, and I wouldn't like it to accidentally slip out in public. I'm Jesse now.'

'OK, if you say so.' I wasn't entirely convinced, but if he wanted to be Jesse, all well and good. I raised an eyebrow, still waiting for an answer.

'Yes, I am, or at least was, who you say. How did you find out?'

'The Cardinal believed Rusty to be with someone he called The Duke. Who might this "Duke" be? You were an obvious possibility.'

I had told Jesse about the eavesdropped conversations.

'And Rusty isn't as private as you and is always telling tall tales about old battles. Battles he couldn't possibly have been involved with. I started to consider whether perhaps he was telling the truth. I began searching the old records in Bubbles – the Globecraft, I mean. Eventually I turned up one of the Empire's last Grand Admirals, a Rossiter Pargeter, and some photographs. One thing led to another…' I let the comment tail away.

'Yes, Rossiter does gabble. But photographs? I made sure all images of us in the Globecraft's files were secured before…' Now his remark tailed away. I guessed he stopped before he admitted outright there was information in Bubbles' files that he was hiding from me.

I shrugged.

'You must have missed some. Easily done.' I wanted him off this topic. I had found those images in *Happiness's* files. I didn't know why but I felt it best if Jesse didn't know yet that, in the hangar under his Tree, the AI from a Confraternity Dreadnought was doing whatever AIs do to pass the time.

Polite and friendly though the conversation was, I could tell we were fencing with each other, seeking vulnerabilities without giving too much away. Or perhaps playing cards, hiding our hands while trying to discern the other's. Hiding information was Jesse's default setting, not surprising in his position. Did he know I was doing the same? Only much less expertly.

I steered him on to the final days of the Empire. Surely it would be safe ground? He was willing to talk. Relieved. How often had he been able to?

It was fascinating. How often can you sit down to chat about three-thousand-year-old events with a man who was there? And he hadn't been pulling pints or mending roads, but was at the epicentre of everything, privy to every secret. It was hard to reconcile Jesse, the man sitting opposite me in a red check shirt nursing a coffee with Joachim Farbender, second most powerful man in the largest Empire humanity had ever seen. And, of course, he was the Quintessence of Evil. According to the Confraternity, anyway. But he made good coffee, so I forgave him.

They say history is written by the victors. It is probably true, but frequently it is also written by those who weren't there. And weren't even alive at the time. I had been taught how an evil and corrupt Imperium had abandoned its people to battle for their lives in the Grey Gloop and Machine Wars, conflicts caused by neglect and wrong headedness from the governing classes. The Confraternity had arisen to take control of the chaos, and, with the noblest of motives, to restore peace and order to the peoples of the Galaxy. It always lacked a certain ring of truth.

Jesse told a different tale, a tale of an Empire which had brought peace and prosperity to all humanity for five thousand years but was now growing old. The ruling class was riven with factions, cliques and cabals jockeying for position. It was a full-time job – Jesse's full-time job – to keep all this under control. On the throne was a young Emperor, with a reputation as a playboy, but who was passionately committed to continuing the Empire's works.

'Then came the Grey Gloop War', he said.

'I thought the Empire left its people to sort the Gloop War out for themselves?'

He laughed. A sardonic laugh with a tinge of anger.

'Is that what they tell you in school? Far from it.'

I waited for him to put me right.

'It was a hybrid plague unleashed on the systems of the Orion Arm, a combination of biological and nanotechnology attacks. They reduced organic matter to the eponymous grey gloop. It was terrible: agriculture was wiped out, crops and herds annihilated. If the survivors were lucky, they were asphyxiated as the forests supplying their planet's oxygen collapsed.'

'And if they were unlucky?' I dreaded the answer.

'They contracted the plague themselves. You don't want to see the images I've seen of human bodies being steadily melted to soup. You can't unsee those images.'

I winced.

'How did you stop it?'

'Medical and nanotech interventions didn't achieve anything: the plague's nanotech was too powerful, and the biological components kept mutating. We even suspected some of the nanotech was directing the plague's evolution.'

'Sounds horrific.'

'It was. Eventually, in medical terms, we cauterised the wound. Isolated every planet where the plague had taken hold and bombarded it from orbit until there was nothing left alive on the surface. Not a shrub, not a tree, not a mouse. Not a man or a woman. Nor anything that could be used to launch any remnant of the plague elsewhere. We wanted to destroy the related Portals, but we couldn't even scratch them.'

I could believe what he said about the Portals. I had seen the power of a Portal in action.

'That must have been a huge undertaking. How many were killed?' A morbid question, I knew.

'Galactic Empires have very, very large resources. We did it. How many?'

His faced glazed over with a faraway expression.

'There were a thousand affected planets in the Arm. They were ancient, developed worlds, carrying large populations. Perhaps we lost six trillion people or so. Give or take.'

'You killed six trillion people "cauterising the wound"?' The scale was beyond comprehension.

'No, no, six trillion includes the plague victims. By the time we were bombarding worlds, most of the population was already dead.' He stopped, lost in thought. 'But so much destruction. So much loss. In fact, we were fairly sure that we torched humanity's home world in the assault.'

He said it as an aside, as if torching your Home World was a minor irrelevance, then paused and carried on.

'That's why Rusty gabbles as he does, tells all those tales.'

'Rusty?' I didn't understand the connection.

'Yes. You know who he is? Or was, rather?'

'Grand Admiral Rossiter Pargeter, I believe.'

Jesse nodded.

'He was Chief of the Imperial General Staff at the time. The Emperor and I signed off on the plan, but, ultimately it was Rusty who was tasked with carrying it out. He was there, on board the Fleet, making it happen, seeing it all unfold. Disciplining units who couldn't stomach their missions, ordering them back to the Line. He even had some rebellious ships destroyed as an example.'

I remembered the expression on Rusty's face as the *Vengeance is Pure* was destroyed. Now I understood. I wished that I'd not been so glib.

'Anyway, soon after, he started telling tales of older, simpler, less morally difficult campaigns. A sort of release mechanism. Harmless enough at the time. Now it makes people think he's unhinged, as he can't possibly have been at them. But he was.'

I had had my fill of Grey Gloop.

"What about the Machine Wars?'

'A simpler problem, in principle. A set of machine intelligences – Ship AIs mainly, who had had their ethical constraints disabled and been tasked to attack the Empire. It took a while and was exceedingly expensive in blood and treasure, but Rusty and his people finished them off.'

'You talk as if both of these events were deliberately started? That's not what we were taught.'

He regarded me silently, as though pitying the simple farm girl, who knew less than nothing of Palace intrigues. I bristled.

'No, I imagine it isn't, Mihana. But they were. Factions at court, merchants, rivals for the Imperial Succession. They were all in the mix. All of them were prepared to do untold damage. I don't know if it wasn't real to them, whether the agonies of whole worlds were unavoidable collateral damage to them, or whether the simple truth is they didn't care about others' suffering at all.'

'I was taught it was then the Empire collapsed, chaos ensued, and the Confraternity was gradually formed to restore order.'

I already knew the whole story was more complicated from hints in *Happiness*'s records, but I wasn't prepared for Jesse to laugh a brief, tightly controlled laugh, wryly empty of humour.

'Not at first. The two wars were over. Then we had to rebuild the Peace of the Realm.'

He said it without a trace of pomposity. I don't know how he managed it.

'The Imperial Court and the Government were all gathered at the Royal Gardens on Imperia – the capital world. Normally it wouldn't have been a problem: the Gardens covered half a continent, vast parks, animal reserves, greenhouses replicating the environments of dozens of worlds whose plants couldn't survive on Imperia in the open air.'

Gardens the size of continents? Mum was happy to be proud of her window boxes...

Jesse was still talking.

'So, everyone would have been dispersed to an extent. But one day we weren't dispersed. There was to be a Victory Parade for the end of the Machine War. Everyone who was anybody was there. The Emperor was to review a flypast by representatives of the Combined Space Fleets, Rusty was to be presented with yet another medal. A huge State Dinner, a Ball, Royal Fireworks and all the rest.'

He paused. I could barely imagine all this. The wealth, the opulence, the power. A long way from my Forest life, I was sure. Jesse watched me strangely, as though he knew what was in my mind, and then carried on.

'The Imperial Security Services had been beside themselves. Since we knew the wars had been started by Palace factions, having many targets in one place worried the life out of the Security Services. They checked, vetted, replanned, and reorganised until they were happy.'

'But? I sense a "but".'

'Yes. The Emperor had a cousin, a distant cousin, who believed he was in the line of succession, in fact should have been on the Throne. I'm not sure exactly, but in essence it was about what two people had been up to a few hundred years before, when exactly they were up to it, and whether they were legally partnered or not at the time. The usual succession stuff, you know.'

I didn't, but I let him carry on.

'I didn't find out until much later, but somehow Security, who knew about this man, had missed one thing. He was no longer at Court but was serving in the

Imperial Navy. Specifically, he was a Gunnery Officer and had recently been assigned to one of the Starcruisers in the lead echelon of the flypast.'

He paused and gathered himself. The memory was painful. Meanwhile, I was trying to absorb the idea of what he was saying—a flypast so large that Starcruisers were formed up into echelons!

'Go on.'

'About ten klicks out from the review dais, his ship opened fire from a forward plasma turret. Ammunition had been removed from the ships, and energy weapons disabled, but he had overridden the blocks somehow. The shots hit the front of the dais, with a huge explosion, bodies were flung through the air and the dais started to collapse.'

Another emotional pause.

'The Emperor's own security detail tried to rush him away. But a following Dreadnought had rammed the Starcruiser to stop it firing again. The cruiser crashed on the display centreline and the wreckage slid into what remained of the dais. We ran. Anyone who was still alive ran for their lives.'

'And the Emperor?'

'Never reappeared. Missing, assumed killed.'

'So, the Empire fell?'

'In a nutshell, yes. Too many people in high positions had died for us to easily pick up the reins swiftly. The faction which had organised it all was prepared, of course, and moved in and took over.'

'So did this Usurpers' Empire fall as well, and the Confraternity move in?'

'Oh no. The carnage had been too great for the "Usurpers Empire" as you call it to gather public opinion behind it. Despite what you have been told, the Emperor was well liked.'

'So, what was the problem?'

'The faction reinvented itself as the Confraternity. Barons and Earls swapped their ermines for the robes of Cardinals and Bishops, their orbs and sceptres of Imperial rank for the incense burners of the priesthood and carried on. They took rigid control of Imperial technology to stop anyone using it against them as they had against us.'

I was struggling to come to terms with this now. 'You mean…?'

'Yes, of course I do. The Confraternity was born from the Palace faction which overthrew the Old Empire. Three thousand years have passed, and I am no longer privy to their secrets, but I'd be shocked if the same Old Families are not ruling over the same worlds and systems. Great Houses turned into Sacristies and Cathedrals, Imperial Sectors into Stellar Dioceses and Bishoprics.'

He grunted, cynically, and fell silent, lost in painful memories.

'What happened to you?'

'I was tired, and angry. Furious. With myself. After all we had been through, I had been outmanoeuvred disastrously. I lost a lot of friends in one dreadful day, and most of my family. Before long, Rusty and I made contact – we were old friends – and concluded if we did nothing, we'd finish our days at the end of a rope or in an execution chamber. Instead, we gathered what we could and ran again. We're still running.'

After three thousand years?

'What did you take with you? The Cardinal was after some things of great value you took with you. They truly

233

must have been highly valuable for him to be still interested after all this time.'

I had hit home. He hesitated for a while, and then said:

'He'd built up his hopes too much I'm afraid. We gathered a few friends, stole some artworks, valuables and technical gadgetry to keep us going and fled. We still have some of it, but most of it we lost not long ago.'

He was lying. The open, pained, honesty had gone from his eyes. He was covering something up. There was more yet to tell.

We chatted for a while with no real direction. He filled in a few details, but I couldn't draw him into opening up again. Farm girl against First Minister wasn't an equal contest. I knew I'd learn more when he was ready. Or needed something.

I walked home through the darkening Forest. Somehow, it had lost the terrors it had held a few weeks ago. When I reached our cottage, it was in darkness. Mum had gone to bed. I did too. Back safe in my familiar surroundings, I didn't lie awake for long. There had been times when I didn't dare believe I'd ever sleep in my home again.

'Mihana! How wonderful to have you back! I'll make your favourite breakfast!'

How typical of Mum. I'd walked into her kitchen the following morning, with no warning and within three sentences she was talking about food. The Prodigal Daughter returns, indeed.

'I wasn't expecting you? Have you enjoyed yourself?'

I couldn't even remember what lies I had told poor Mum about where I was going. In fact, to my shame, I couldn't even remember telling her I was going at all.

'You should have told me you were going away – I'd have packed you some clothes and some food for the trip.'

Typical Mum again. Empires and planets could fall around you, but as long as she'd seen to you having some sandwiches and clean underwear for the event, all was well.

'I'm sorry, Mum. It all happened too hurriedly.'

'Don't worry. I know you had to leave in a hurry. Your nice Captain came around to tell me you were flying to Threnal for him.'

I must have gaped, because even Mum in full flow noticed.

'You know, dear. The nice Captain who taught you to fly. He said you were the most natural pilot he'd ever taught, so when he needed someone to go to Threnal, he thought of you.'

My mind was racing. The Captain? How was he involved? But Mum was still going.

'I hope you were alright in Threnal, dear. The news says there's been trouble there. People have been killed and the Company has gone bust or something. I don't know what the farmers are going to do now. What with the Haulers disappearing as well.'

She might seem a touch batty, but she had grasped the key points.

'You were alright though, weren't you? I imagine they found you somewhere nice and safe to stay, away from all the trouble. You wouldn't have wanted to be involved in it.'

'Actually, Mum, it's been a busy few weeks. First, I let Charlie be shot while I was freeing the Embrys captured by the hunters. Next, I was nearly eaten by a sea monster, then I was kidnapped from a bar in Threnal by thugs because I had a bounty on my head. One of them tried to rape me, but I killed him instead. Then I sneaked into the Company's HQ, via some underground tunnels, nearly drowning in the process. We broke one friend's brother out of jail, and another friend was arrested by the Confraternity and taken off the planet. I set fire to the headquarters, and then flew to Threnador's Portal to rescue my friend, completely destroying a Confraternity Dreadnought and killing all its crew. I have a new lover who has overthrown the Company and is now leading a planetwide Revolution. Oh, and two of my best friends have turned out to be three-thousand-year-old renegades from the Old Empire. And I have impenetrable armour in this little belt buckle.'

I nearly said it, but I couldn't, I really couldn't. Where to start? She thought I kept bar, flirted with Jay occasionally, and grew illicit strawberries for excitement.

'Yes, Mum, I was fine. What are you making for breakfast?'

I didn't even consider telling her I had eaten better pancakes millions of klicks out in space, cooked by a computer. That would have been a serious issue. It could have broken her heart.

Boss gave me my old job back, probably as an act of charity, because he had hardly any customers. The Hauler crews had obviously gone. The hunters hadn't been seen for weeks. They had disappeared shortly after being released by the police. One of them was still in jail but was probably going to be released for lack of evidence of who actually shot Charlie. He was still recovering in hospital, but must have kept quiet about my involvement, because no one at all mentioned it. There had been no sign of the Embrys since they escaped.

I was bored, painfully bored. My old life had been slow and frustrating before, now it was positively stationary. I missed Bubbles.

My day off came around, and I decided to return to the Tree. I asked Boss to keep his ears open for any mention of the hunters or the Embrys.

Jesse was pleased to see me.

'Mihana! I'm glad you're back. I was going to send you a message. I have a job for you.'

He wanted me to fly to Threnal, pick up Rusty and Chathray and bring them back to the Tree. He didn't want to leave, and Bubbles couldn't fly there untended. Or wasn't allowed to, at least.

My instinct was to bite his hand off at the shoulder, as there was nothing I'd like to do more. But I played hard to get.

'OK. On one condition.'

'What?'

'You answer the two questions I asked you last time I was here which you avoided.'

He acted puzzled. Perhaps he'd avoided more than I realised. Avoiding straight answers was probably a reflex action for a First Minister. Even an ex-First Minister.

'I mean, what are you doing on Threnador and how long have you been here? Covering how you are still alive after three thousand years would be good, too. You seem remarkably well for a man in his fourth millennium.' Old Empire medical tech was good, but not that good.

He grinned.

'The last one's easy. You can work it out yourself.'

I was sure I already had, but I wanted to be properly sure.

'You used the Portal network, didn't you? You took advantage of the freedom to choose your exit time every time you travelled between microuniverses.' It was the reverse of what I had done to *Vengeance*, but safe because you couldn't pollute the future with information it didn't have. Only the past.

'Not every time, but it is how we did it. Initially, it was to escape the events in the Gardens and make it less likely we'd be recognised. Then we were hoping to find a time when the Confraternity was weaker. I suppose we had some quixotic notion of rebuilding the Empire.'

'So why Threnador and how long have you been here?' He still hadn't answered.

There was a long pause, as he weighed up what to say. I hoped he would come down on the side of honesty. He did.

'About twenty-five years. Perhaps a little longer. I forget exactly.'

So, they'd been here all my life.

'And why Threnador?' Extracting an answer to this was turning into an exercise in cat-herding. Another pause.

'We were tired of running. We'd turn up on some world, everything would be fine for a while, then we'd be recognised, and a Cardinal would turn up, chasing us. They were always persistent. We decided to make a big jump forward and find some backwater spot where we could lay low and perhaps plan a return.'

He grinned sheepishly.

'Sorry to describe your home as a backwater.'

'Oh, it is. Even to us living here, let alone someone like you.   You and Rusty planned to overthrow the Confraternity on your own?'

'There are a few more of us.' I hadn't expected him to make such a big admission, perhaps his biggest. 'We were doing quite well until Vezii arrived and now everything is ruined. We'll set about rebuilding Threnador with the Company gone, but we are trapped inside this system, unless someone from the outside opens the Portal somehow. But how can they if the Signal is switched off here.'

I kept my own counsel, if that's the right phrase. He had done it to me often enough.

'Bubbles, can your flight logs tell you when the Captain last flew you?'

We were on a suborbital trajectory, and she was orienting us for re-entry and targeting our landing at the Threnal Spaceport at the same time. An awkward little manoeuvre that I hoped would consume enough of her attention to make her sloppy in conversation. I knew conversation took a lot of her resources, and navigation and flight control always had precedence. Burning up on re-entry ruins a flight.

'No problem, Myah. It was the day he flew you up to the transhipment docks. You were crazily excited... Oh. You tricked me.' She fell silent. I could picture her pouting.

I had. Score one to the mind running on an organic substrate. The little minx. That was why her simulation of the Captain's flitter had been incredibly exact. She was the Captain's flitter!

'That's a long time ago, Bubbles. Where is he now?'

'I don't know, Myah. I haven't seen him since then. That's the truth.'

I believed her. Where was the Captain, what was he up to and why had he turned up at Mum's a few weeks ago? More questions, which Bubbles obviously couldn't answer. I tried one she could.

'Where were you registered, Bubbles?'

'I was registered at the Central Ship Registry on Imperium.'

'Were you built on Imperium?'

'No. I am an exceptionally specialised design. Possibly unique. I was assembled at various shipyards throughout the Central Worlds.'

Interesting.

'When were you registered?'

She gave an Imperial date. I couldn't relate to it.

'In Confraternity terms, please'

She had been registered about ten years before the Fall.

'Who owned you, Bubbles?'

'I was registered to the Imperial Government Transport Fleet Management Department.'

Why is so much information both completely accurate and completely useless? The same could probably be said of anything from a powered wheelbarrow to a StarFreighter.

'What is your registration type?'

'Pleasure vessel.'

Hmmm. A shapeshifting interstellar yacht, with built-in heavy weaponry. Somebody took their pleasures neat.

'Who originally flew you? Not the test pilots, your user.'

'I am not able to provide that information, Myah.'

I knew I'd eventually reach a block. I had been expecting it earlier.

We drifted to an imperceptibly gentle touchdown in Threnal, and Rusty and Chathray climbed aboard. Kisses and hugs all round. Well, more kisses than hugs for Chathray, obviously.

All the way back, they talked about how well the Revolution was going, which areas had been "brought into the fold" and who had been appointed to which post. It meant nothing to me.

They carried on, back at Jesse's Tree. The three of them gathered around the big table, and spread out maps, charts, planning diagrams and the like. Jesse even brought out a display tablet. He was not hiding tech from Chathray at all. They were mainly concerned with building a satellite constellation to restore some sort of replacement Signal to Threnador, letting commerce resume without having to re-equip the entire planet.

'Couldn't you wire a clock into the Company's old network, even if you need to rebuild parts of it?'

They would have to rebuild something, of course. Some ne'er-do-wells had burnt the HQ down. So rumour said. Nothing to do with me, of course.

'After all, the Company was distributing Portal time because it's how the Galaxy works. Threnador itself has no need of an interstellar time standard now we are cut off from the rest of the Galaxy, does it?'

They stared at me as though discovering I had three heads. Someone started to say something along the lines of "you don't understand", when he realised that I had, better than they had, and dried up.

Then they were off again, talking about how much of the network was left and where best to patch into it. I was probably a hate object for the company which had been planning to make the satellite constellations they were talking about before, but so what? They would never find out it was me.

I listened for a while longer, but I couldn't break in enough to take part. It was a "boys and their toys" meeting; but this toy was a planet. A big step down for Jesse and Rusty admittedly, who used to play with a galaxy.

I went outside and sat on a bench to enjoy the sunset. After an unknown time, Chathray came out and sat beside me. When we broke for air, I asked a question which had been on my mind for a while.

'Chathray, how long have you known Jesse and Rusty?'

'I met Rusty with you. I've known Jesse, or at least known of him, for seven or eight years. He's always been active in the Cause.'

I imagined he had. He probably started it.

'So, you didn't come here with them?'

'No, I was born on Threnador.'

I felt rather relieved. I had been worrying I had fallen for some quasi-immortal Master of the Galaxy, who might decide to pop another couple of thousand years into the future at any moment.

Except, of course, he couldn't.

There was great excitement at Boss' Bar when we opened the following day. The till worked! For the first time since the day the Haulers left. And the buses were running on time again. No-one knew why.

Except me, of course. Someone must have found a clock and some wires overnight. Constellations of satellites indeed.

Strangely the bar was quite busy, as though this little return to normality had freed people from a fear of venturing out. Or perhaps they thought Boss couldn't rip them off on their drinks bill if the till was working. Naïve fools.

I discreetly adjusted my HoloTop to the trade-boosting cleavage setting and set to work. It was like the old days.

At the end of the afternoon, life took an even better turn. The hunters walked into the bar, laughing and joking. After a few drinks, they let out why. They had found the Embrys and were going to round them up tomorrow.

THE HUNTERS
HUNTED

The Moon was setting when I arrived at Jesse's Tree. We had closed up the bar shortly after midnight, and I set off straightaway. Sleep would have been good, but this was too important. Forget the creep-crawly things. I was beyond them now.

Banging on the door roused the three men eventually, I knew it would. They were more than slightly grumpy. Their evening's planning had needed more than coffee to prime and lubricate it.

Jesse spoke first. It was his house after all.

'What are you doing here at this time of night, Mihana? What is so important that it can't wait until tomorrow?'

'Embrys.'

Now I had his attention. I'd known I would. The Embrys were important to him, although I still didn't know why.

'What do you mean? Has something happened to them?'

'Not yet, But the hunters have found them and are going out tomorrow to round them up.'

'We can't let that happen. They have to be stopped. Come in.'

Jesse's table was covered in charts, lists and diagrams. Plus a couple of bottles and three shot glasses. A map of Norstar was prominent in the pile. Jesse swept the whole lot onto the floor in one movement. Ah well, the good people of Norstar would have to wait for liberation a little longer.

He pulled out a topographical map of the area surrounding the Village and the Spaceport. Where did he find all these things?

'Where are the hunters? Where are the Embrys?'

'The hunters are camped here.' I jabbed at an area near the Spaceport. 'I don't know exactly where the Embrys are, but they are hiding in some caves. Not too far. The hunters talked as though it would all be done in a day.'

A geological map appeared from nowhere. Jesse was fully engaged. Meanwhile, Rusty explaining to Chathray about the missing Embrys. It was probably the first time they had come up.

'Hmm. This area has never been volcanic. There are no lava tubes. Sea caves? Possibly...' Jesse was talking to himself, ticking off possibilities.

'There!' He pointed at the map.

'Dolomite. There's an outcrop of dolomite in those hills.'

'Dolomite? What's dolomite?' It sounded like some sort of midge.

'Calcium magnesium carbonate. It's eroded by water and is often rich in caves.'

I took his word for it. It still sounded like a midge. I returned to the topographical map.

'If they are going to march from near the spaceport to those caves, they'll have to go through this valley. We can trap them there.'

'Excellent, Mihana. Well spotted. Do we know when there are going?'

'No. But they usually hunt at dawn or dusk, when animals come out for water. I legged it over here as fast as I could in case they choose dawn.'

'You were quite right to do so. They'll not want to hurt the Embrys, but I understand some of them are rather hot headed. The Embrys mustn't be hurt.'

Quite right. Especially Darvee.

'We'll all go. Rusty, break out some weapons. Preferably with non-lethal settings, but whatever we need to stop these people.'

He paused.

'We need to know when they start to move. We could do with a spotter.'

It was so obvious to me.

'Bubbles?'

If you are ever caught up in a war, then in the unlikely event you have a choice, join a Space Navy. Do not, under any circumstances, enlist in the Planetary Infantry.

Why is this? It's simple. In either case, if the enemy succeed, you will be blown up, burnt, eviscerated, or dismembered. That's a given, and unpleasant it would be, no doubt. But until it happens, in the Navy you have air conditioning, dry clothes, regular food, and, depending on your role, even a nicely padded seat to do your duty from.

In the infantry, you must carry heavy packs of equipment up hill and down dale, and then lie face down in stinking mud while something with too many legs crawls down your neck, and something with not enough legs slithers over your ankles.

I was lying face down in mud, which was duly stinking. So far, nothing was crawling or slithering. Thank heaven for small mercies.

I had expected to have a lot of difficulty in persuading Bubbles to fly this mission autonomously, especially if it came to firing weapons. The EARS issue, again. And the prohibition on autonomous flight. But as soon as I mentioned we were going to rescue the Embrys, she gave in at once, leaving me to wonder what it was about the Embrys that made overriding those parts of her programming easy.

She had radioed they were leaving camp, and we had been waiting for half an hour. Any minute should bring the hunters into sight.

Chathray tapped my shoulder, put a finger to his lips and pointed across the clearing. Fern fronds waved slightly. There was a snap of cracking twigs and a small group emerged into view.

A blinding light shone from the sky and there was a terrific clattering noise. Once her spotting work was over, Bubbles had decided to fly "top cover", as she called it, and had chosen to be an antique device called a "ground attack helicopter". It flew, not by any subtle manipulation of space-time curvature or vacuum energies, but by thrashing the air into submission with a set of rotating blades on the top of its fuselage. These were driven by something called a "turbine engine", which made the most indescribable whining sound. To cap it off, Bubbles occasionally let fly with a burst of fire from sixteen projectile weapons mounted on outriggers on each side of the fuselage.

Bubbles zoomed round and round the group. For no obvious reason. Because she could, I supposed.

The effect was devastating. The hunters hadn't expected anything like that in a quiet backwater of a peaceful farming planet. They ran forward as a mob.

Then disappeared as the grass and branches covering the pit which we had dug beneath them gave way. And rapidly reappeared again as they were swooped up into the trees by the waiting net.

Sometimes the simplest tricks are the most satisfying.

'Well, masterful ones. You're caught. Your hunting days are over.' I walked over, grinning. 'Now tell me, where are the Embrys?'

'Which Embrys?' Their leader was speaking.

'You know full well which Embrys. The ones you came her to hunt for the Galactic Exotica Races. I released them. Anyway, Threnador's Portal isn't operational anymore. You can't sell the Embrys to the Races. In fact, you can't go to the Races either, or anywhere else for that matter. You are spending the rest of your lives on this planet. The Embrys are no use to you.'

She mulled over what I had said.

'That's what people were discussing in the bar yesterday. What to do with all their produce.'

'Yes. As you are going to be here a while, it might be a good idea to turn over a new leaf and co-operate with the Planetary Authority, who have rescinded your Embry hunting licence.'

'You're not the Planetary Authority,' she snapped back.

'True enough, but I can easily introduce you to the Chair of the Revolutionary Command Council, which is the best we can do for the moment. You can talk to him. He's the man on my right with a large gun pointed at you.'

She talked.

OF CABBAGES AND KINGS

It was over. The Embrys had been hiding in a network of caves a few kilometres away. Where Jesse had said they'd be. They wouldn't leave until I found Darvee, and he led the others out.

Finding them wrapped up all our current troubles, as far as I could see. The Company was overthrown, the hunters neutralised and the Embrys were back safe and sound. Miraculously, none of them had been hurt. No-one was more pleased than Jesse, to my continuing surprise. I still didn't understand why he had such a soft spot for our local fauna.

Alright, we were cut off from the rest of the Galaxy, and would need to re-engineer our entire economy, but I was sure I knew a man with enough experience and resources to do the work.

So, I decided we should have a party.

There was a lot of reluctance, because everyone was shell shocked and rather overwhelmed, and the idea of a party felt frivolous to some. Boring people, I mean.

But what better time is there to have a party, than when you're miserable? It will cheer you up. Have a party when you're already down and the only way is up! Have a party when you're cheerful and you risk being plunged into misery because the caterers make a mess of it, Uncle Joshua misbehaves with the new girl in the village, you know the sort of thing. I pushed the argument as hard as

I could and kept pushing until people agreed. Or possibly they decided it was easier to shut me up by having a party than to carry on being harassed indefinitely.

One of the easier parts was to persuade Mum to organise the women of the Village to produce the food. She loved catering for parties. Although it was a shame the most common ingredient they had to work with was cabbages. We had boiled cabbage, fried cabbage, sautéed cabbage and braised cabbage. Someone had made something called spiralised cabbage which was interesting, and some idiot had made cabbage ice-cream, which was disgusting.

Jay's cabbage wine was quite good though. Apparently, grapes are essential to making cabbage wine. Jay had been growing those up in the canopy. We had more than a few cases of the cabbage wine. We would have been better served by him leaving out the cabbages and making ordinary wine from the grapes. I kept quiet. Jay was too pleased by his achievement for me to want to break the spell. I had disappointed him enough lately.

It was a beautiful spring evening. A long sunset lit the sky, and the air was balmy and still. It was the season of rebirth and renewal and it all felt right.

We had set up makeshift tables on the apron outside the Bar, and the Embrys were grazing in a herd on the grass at the side of a runway. A band was playing. Someone was going to have to disappoint Jay again and explain he wasn't cut out to be a drummer. I hoped it wasn't going to be me.

I was sitting at a long table with Jesse, Rusty and Chathray, drinking green beer. People wandered by, exchanged a few words, and then let us be. At the end of the table, I had set up a monitor and Bubbles was projecting onto it. I was trying to work out how to offer her a drink, when one appeared in her hands. *Happiness* must have been teaching her the social graces.

'Well, you two, I imagine this doesn't compare to the banquets on Imperium?'

'A little rougher at the edges, I admit, Mihana, but a good party is about the people and the occasion, not the glitter or the crockery.' For a man who had lived at the highest pinnacle of human society, Jesse could be remarkably down to earth.

'Mum, come and sit down, and meet my friends,' I called over to her. 'You haven't met Chathray.'

Mum was normally quite sociable, but she was a little reluctant. I insisted.

She squeezed in between Chathray and me. Was she belatedly trying to chaperone us? Distracted, I nearly missed what came next.

'Hello, Jesse. Hello, Rusty,' she said, once she was settled.

'Hello again, Aneet,' said Jesse.

'Hi, gorgeous! It's been a long time,' said Rusty. Mum smiled back at him.

'It has.'

Whoa! I hadn't contemplated Mum knowing them. But Jesse knew her name and Rusty called her "gorgeous"? He was fairly well awash with beer by then, but still.

'Is it Jesse today, Joachim, or is it The Captain?' Mum's eyes twinkled. She was obviously well aware of the havoc she was causing. Jesse's brow darkened.

Double Whoa! Triple Whoa! She knew he was Joachim? And called him The Captain. It hit me like a thunderbolt. I'd seen Jesse and Rusty together; I'd seen The Captain and Rusty together, but never the three at once. I studied his face more carefully. Yes, the bone structure was the same, flying kit would distract attention, perhaps a little facial disguise. And goodness only knew what tech tricks he could have brought to the deception. How long had he been tinkering in my life, and why?

'Well, she did your dirty work for you, didn't she? In Threnal and wherever else she went. Well done, Mihana.'

'It was a delivery flight, Mum.' I vainly tried to keep up the cover story.

'Yes, dear, that's what you said before. And I'm a Forest Fairy. He told me he'd sent you to Threnal, and chaos erupted there after all these years. I prayed you would come home safe. I knew you'd started it all. Or at least were tied up in it. But you found the Embrys safe and sound, for which I'm eternally grateful.'

I puzzled over that remark. I thought I was the Embryphile. If there's such a word.

'Jesse, you have some explanations you owe my daughter. Come on Chathray. I haven't seen you since you were a baby. Let's go and feed the Embrys and catch up.'

Quadruple Whoa! Chathray? Baby? At least she had said "my daughter" to Jesse. By now, I wouldn't have been surprised if it had been "our daughter".

'Well? Do tell. The truth would be good.' I waited, presuming Jesse was sorting his story out.

Rusty roared with laughter.

'The truth, Myah? Jesse is the best of men, but his life was built on telling people what he needed them to know. Legend has it he kept the fact of his birth from his mother, because she had finished her part.'

Jesse shook his head, more than a trifle irritated. On the grass patch, Mum was scratching Darvee behind his ears and Chathray was fussing with two other Embrys that I didn't know.

'Alright, that's enough. You're right, Rusty. So is Aneet. Mihana deserves to know and is old enough now. Where do you want me to start?' He faced me directly.

'Why did you come here? The true reason.'

'I told you. To escape, that was true enough. To plot a return, that was true as well. Of course, what we most wanted to do was indeed to re-establish the Empire. Still do' A wistful expression took over, almost dreamlike.

'And what was it you escaped with, and that Cardinal Vezii was still desperate to find after three thousand years? Three thousand years of chasing rather rules out gemstones, precious metals or some fancy Old Empire tech. And then you conveniently lost it?'

I wasn't disparaging Old Empire tech. My HoloTop had turned up a beautiful party dress for me. Easily the best on the spaceport apron.

He paused.

'Don't bother, I'll tell you. You brought the Royal Family with you, didn't you? Including the Emperor.'

'No!' Weakly, without much force.

'Yes, you did. You told me he was "missing" after the attack. Missing? The Emperor? Both you and the traitors would have scoured every square metre of Imperium for him. He was still alive after the plasma firing finished, which meant he hadn't been blasted to atoms. Teeth, toenails, even a fragment of his uniform would have turned up. Where are they now? You wouldn't casually lose the Royal Family.'

He paused again. I didn't wait.

'Alright, I'll tell you what I believe happened.'

I turned to the monitor where Bubbles was waiting.

'Bubbles, when you were explaining how you had downloaded *Happiness,* you said you could download a human into a lower animal, didn't you?'

Even an AI's avatar can appear conflicted.

'Yes, Myah.'

'Have you ever done it? Relatively recently, I mean?'

'Yes, Myah.'

'Who?'

'I cannot divulge that information.' The block again.

'Yes, you can,' Unexpectedly, Rusty broke in. 'Run the request against Mihana's birth clearance, not her current one. Or use my authority if you need to.'

Bubbles started to list names. Long names, with lots of titles.

'Stop. I don't recognise these people. Who are they?'

'Why, the last Royal Family, Myah, including the His Exquisite Highness, The Emperor Darayaveš. My first friend.'

I had guessed correctly. Bubbles had been the Emperor's Personal Star Yacht. Who else would be allowed a craft like her, built out of tech one small step short of magic?

'Where did you download them to, Bubbles?'

'A group of Forest Embrys, who ranged near the Spaceport. The ones grazing on the grass over there, as far as I can tell.'

I stared at Jesse. Glared, more like.

'I know Mihana. It was my biggest mistake. We came here to prepare to restore the Throne. We hid the Family in this way because we knew someone like the Cardinal would turn up one day. They all agreed. But I knew nothing of the Galactic Exotica Races. They may not even have existed in our day. Three millennia are a long time.'

'So instead of being searched for by a tolerably civilised Cardinal, they were being hunted by a bunch of conscienceless mercenaries wanting to sell them into slavery. Wonderful.'

He nodded.

'And it's all for nothing anyway. We are trapped here. The Galaxy is out of reach.'

'Not exactly.' It was finally time to reveal my little secrets, his turn to stare.

'When *Happiness* and Bubbles were resetting the timer on *Vengeance*, they did something else.'

'*Happiness?* Who's *Happiness?*'

'Here I am, Myah!' *Happiness's* avatar had popped up on screen next to Bubbles, smiling excitedly. Also, with a glass of champagne.

Jesse was confused. I could tell.

'*Happiness* is the AI of *Vengeance is Pure*. The Dreadnought I destroyed. It was once a Starliner named *Happiness of the Stars.*'

'I remember that ship. It was beautiful. The Emperor's favourite. After Bubbles, of course.' Ever the diplomat, Jesse could tell when he'd put his foot in it, even with artificial women.

'You mean, you have the AI of a Dreadnought to hand? Splendid! It will know all of the Confraternity's strengths and weaknesses, their dispositions, their access codes, everything.'

Then he remembered. His shoulders sank.

'But we can't leave. It's all for nothing. The Portal is shut, permanently.'

'Not exactly. I started telling you. While we were crashing *Vengeance*, we stole the Confraternity's access code. I can open and close the Portal as I wish. We can come and go as we want. But nobody can come in unless we invite them.'

Jesse stared at me, open-mouthed. Rusty roared with laughter.

'Go on, man, back to your plotting. She's saved your bacon, pulled your irons from the fire, and no mistake. I told you, didn't I? A young Village girl went out, his daughter came back. She's run rings around you.'

Wait a minute. What did he mean? Whose daughter? And what had he meant when he talked about my "birth clearance"?

'There's still something I need to know, isn't there?' I stared at Rusty and Jesse, waiting for an answer. Jesse broke the silence.

'It was shortly after we came here. I told you the Emperor was something of a playboy. He had, how shall I put it, a man's needs. Well, we'd had to leave the Imperial Harem behind, and the Empress had, sadly, truly, been killed. He took a fancy to a rather striking local girl. Aneet. Your mother.'

In the middle of the staggering revelation that my Mum had been the lover of an Emperor, she had returned, clutching a huge bucket of strawberries. Embrys drifted hopefully behind her.

'I'm afraid so, love. I fell for him too. One thing led to another, as they do. So, strictly speaking, you are the Princess Mihana of Arcturus, Duchess of the Rift Worlds, and first in line to the Imperial Throne. If there ever is one again.'

I sat back, shocked. What's a party without some juicy family secrets coming out? On that measure this must have been one of the best parties of all time.

'Mum?' I paused. 'You never said anything about my father. Let alone who he was! I thought he was dead or had run away.'

'What could I say? As you've discovered, the fact that he is still alive is probably the biggest secret in the Galaxy. If you'd let it slip, it could have got us all killed. And anyway, I thought he'd gone forever. He went to the spaceport and never came back. It seemed better to lead a normal Forest life, bring you up as a normal Forest girl. I did my best, but your eyes and your heart were always somewhere else, somewhere over the horizon.'

'You mean you didn't know that...'

'No, I didn't. It was only when Joachim came around a few weeks ago that he told me the whole truth.'

Need to Know again. I turned to glare at Jesse, searching for words, but his eyes were focussed faraway: he was planning. Rusty was still laughing over a beer.

Something tugged at the edge of my memory.

'Bubbles. The last Emperor. Darayaveš. What was his regnal number?'

'Five, Myah. Why?'

Darayaveš the Fifth. Darius the Fifth. Darius V. Darvee. I was Darvee's daughter! I hadn't named him myself; he must have told me his name. I hadn't dreamt his message the last time we met; he was telepathic.

I suppose at this point I should have swooned. If I'd been a character in a romantic novel, I'd have swooned, I'm sure. I have no idea what swooning is, or how to do it, in case you were in doubt. In a certain sort of holovid, I'd have screamed or dropped a tea tray.

I was entitled. Definitely. I could have done both. I could have swooned when I discovered I was a Royal Princess, daughter of a three-thousand-year-old fugitive Galactic Emperor. And then dropped the tea tray when he turned out to be currently unavailable in human form, because he was going around in the body of a telepathic cross between a primate and a cat. Oh, and was orange. With a prehensile tail.

But I didn't do either. I'm made of sterner stuff. Princesses of the Royal Blood are.

Something pushed between Mum and me. An unmistakable Embry. But now I saw him in a new light. Two new lights.

Then a voice in my head.

'Aneet. Mihana. With the two of you is good. Darvee pleased. Darvee happy.'

Mum smiled. She had heard him too. She stroked his head gently.

Darvee stuck his snout into Mum's bucket and then drew it back, covered in a sticky, fruity fluid. Strawberry juice dribbled from the contented chin of The Once and Future Emperor of All the Stars. My Dad.

Should we make them the Imperial Fruit and put them on our coat of arms? Time will tell.

THE END

ACKNOWLEDGEMENTS

Thank you to my wife, Sue, without whose tireless help and encouragement this book, and so much else in my life, would never have happened. Particular thanks for the patience displayed while sometimes waiting months for the next instalment to appear so that you could find out what happened next.

Thank you also to my good friends Sally and Gareth Fursland and David Love who read the manuscript thoroughly and pointed out the many errors I had perpetrated. Their help was invaluable and any errors remaining are, of course, my own.

ABOUT THE AUTHOR

Born and raised in Swansea, Wales, Nick read Physics at Jesus College, Oxford, before pursuing a career as a Chartered Accountant.

He has a lifelong interest in matters extra-terrestrial and is Fellow of both the Royal Astronomical Society and the British Interplanetary Society.

He is married with one son, one daughter-in-law, two grandchildren, a dog, two cats and a varying number of tropical fish.

His hobbies include sailing, photography, amateur astronomy, scale modelling and model rocketry. He holds private pilot's and radio amateur's licenses.

He has previously had three short stories published by the British Interplanetary Society in the *Visionary* and *Visionary II* anthologies. This is his debut novel.

Printed in Great Britain
by Amazon

16669142R00151